SKIRTING THE ABYSS

Nuada and his people made their way upward in silence, each concentrating on footing and staying close to the outside tunnel wall. The only sounds were the shuffling of their feet; their labored breathing in the close, fetid air; and the thick, doomful gurgling of the poisoned stream flowing downward in its channel below them. The liquid's odor in the confined space of the tunnel was much worse, and became stronger as they progressed. The sense of being trapped and suffocated grew to a near-maddening, near-overwhelming height.

Somewhere ahead of Nuada, there was a sudden wild cry and a crackling sound as a portion of the rocky edge gave way, sliding into the stream, a human form following, toppling from the edge, plunging into the viscid fluid below. Others swiftly followed, yanked off balance in a chain of disaster, one, two, a third toppling over the edge, falling, splashing into the stream's deadly embrace.

Nuada only had a heartbeat to register all this before the young woman ahead of him was falling too. She'd released the hand of the hapless man before her but retained Nuada's, flailing out madly with her freed arm to save herself.

She failed. Her feet, too near the crumbled edge, slid out from beneath her. She dropped down, yanking Nuada down after her.

Also by Casey Flynn:
  The Gods of Ireland, Book One: *Most Ancient Song*

Be sure to ask your bookseller for other Bantam Spectra
Books you have missed:

By Raymond E. Feist
  The Riftwar Saga
> *Magician: Apprentice*
> *Magician: Master*
> *Silverthorn*
> *A Darkness at Sethanon*

  Daughter of the Empire, written with Janny Wurts

By Katharine Kerr
  The Bristling Wood
  The Dragon Revenant

By Dennis McKeirnan
  Dragondoom

By Margaret Weis and Tracy Hickman
  The Darksword Trilogy
> *Forging the Darksword*
> *Doom of the Darksword*
> *Triumph of the Darksword*

  Rose of the Prophet
> *The Will of the Wanderer*
> *The Paladin of the Night*
> *The Prophet of Akhran*

  The Death Gate Cycle
> *Dragon Wing*
> *Elven Star*

By Angus Wells
  The Books of the Kingdoms
> *Wrath of Ashar*
> *The Usurper*
> *The Way Beneath*

The Gods of Ireland
Book Two

The Enchanted Isles

CASEY FLYNN

BANTAM BOOKS
NEW YORK · TORONTO · LONDON · SYDNEY · AUCKLAND

THE ENCHANTED ISLES
A Bantam Spectra Book/July 1991

SPECTRA *and the portrayal of a boxed "s" are trademarks of Bantam Books,
a division of Bantam Doubleday Dell Publishing Group, Inc.*

ISBN 0-553-29151-3

Published simultaneously in the United States and Canada

Bantam Books are published by Bantam Books, a division of Bantam Doubleday Dell
Publishing Group, Inc. Its trademark, consisting of the words "Bantam Books"
and the portrayal of a rooster, is Registerd in U.S. Patent and Trademark Office and in
other countries. Marca Registrada. Bantam Books, 666 Fifth Avenue, New York, New
York 10103.

PRINTED IN THE UNITED STATES OF AMERICA

OPM   0 9 8 7 6 5 4 3 2 1

To the memory of my father,
Casey Senior.

Pronunciation Guide

Here is a hopefully useful reference to pronouncing some of the more difficult Celtic names:

Bobd Derg	Bov Dearg
Cuthach	Coo-ak
Diancecht	Dee-an-kekt
Goibniu	Gov-new
Mathgen	Matgen
Nuada	New-ada
Onairaich	On-ar-ak
Tarbh-chu	Tarv-koo
Tuirbe	Tewr-bay
Magh Mell	Ma Mell

Part One

The Gauntlet

Chapter 1
The Fog

The armored giant's single eyelid rasped shrilly as it slowly lifted.

The lid was more like a crescent-shaped visor for the otherwise blank, barrel-shaped metal helmet that formed the giant's head. As it opened to a slit, a brilliant ruby light came into view, forming a curved line, hairbreadth thin, but still of near-blinding intensity.

A narrow beam of the light then shot outward from the apex of the curve. It slanted downward from the head, widening slightly as it fell to play upon the body of the man.

A voice clanged out from within the massive helmet: "You failed me, Captain. Your life is therefore forfeit to me."

"Please, no, Commander!" the man in the beam gasped. He trembled violently from both fear and pain. Beads of sweat sprang into being across his brow. "I did everything I could!"

In response to his plea, the slit widened fractionally. The beam became more intense. The man stiffened, whimpering in his agony. Sweat soaked his clothes, ran in rivulets down his face. His exposed flesh grew ruddy as it began to broil.

"Don't destroy him, Commander."

This plea came from one of a line of men standing at rigid attention behind the stricken one. Like him they were clad in simple uniforms: tunic and trousers of a dull grey, their only embellishment the small triangles of silver metal on their left breasts.

"You defy me, Captain Eagal?" the ringing voice of the giant demanded.

The man addressed took a step forward. He looked up at the black metal-clad figure who towered above him. "I present reasons, my Commander, why his story should be heard," he bravely returned. "Captain Nadur is a fine officer. He is as brave as any of us. His loss would be a waste."

"Very well," said the giant. The metal eyelid screeched again as it slid down. The beam was cut off, and the one called Nadur breathed deeply in relief.

"Tell me then, Captain, exactly what you did," the voice ordered. "The entire truth."

"We did as you asked, Commander," the man said, his voice gasping as he breathed in cool air. "I led a party to where the ones called Sons of Nemed lived. Their fortress was abandoned. We tracked them across the island to the eastern shore. We found some ships in a bay there, but others had clearly sailed. I ordered Captain Eagal to take three ships to scour the sea to the east. I took three more ships and rounded the isle to search out into the western sea."

"And you discovered nothing, Captain Eagal?" the giant asked.

"No, Commander," that man hastily supplied. "Not a single vessel did we sight."

"But you, Captain Nadur, you *did* find a ship."

"Yes, Commander. A lone ship. From the shape and the type of sail, we're certain it was one of theirs. We pursued. We were closing . . ."

"And then it got away," the commander finished, hammering out each word.

"We didn't *let* it escape us," said Nadur. "Not exactly. It —it vanished. It entered the great barrier fog."

"And you didn't follow it in there?"

"What good would that have done?"

"What good?" the giant thundered. "Coward. You've lost my best chance to have them. I might have learned how they survived the plagues and poisons we used upon them and defeated a Fomor host five times their size. I might have wrung from them the names of those who helped them. Most important, I might have discovered from them where the Departed Ones are. Do you realize what such knowledge would do for us? To find *Them*. To gain their magic skills. It would make us a power in the world again!"

"I know, Commander," Nadur said miserably. "I understand. But what could I have done? Entering the fog would have been no help. We would only have vanished, as has every other vessel that has ventured into it."

"Legends say there is nothing beyond that barrier," put in Eagal. "It's the edge of creation. An abyss. Nothingness."

"Tales for children," the giant boomed. "The possible gain should have been worth any risk. I will not give up because of your failure. I want every ship out, searching the whole sea in every direction from that isle. More of these people's craft could still be out there. And I want a ship to probe that fog!"

"Do you mean mine, Commander?" Nadur asked.

"Not yours," the giant answered.

Its metal eyelid lifted, this time opening a wide crack. A thicker beam of crimson light shot down to bathe the captain.

Nadur's head was thrown back as his body went rigid, spasming in pain. His mouth opened to vent a gasping cry of agony. His grey uniform burst into flame. The flash of blazing energy enveloped him, consumed him. In an instant Nadur had become a pillar of fire, filling the room with a red, lurid glare, starkly revealing the panicked faces of the others who flinched back.

The beam shut off with a metal clang as the eyelid slid down again, covering the incandescent ruby eye that had projected it. The last flames flickered out. A small black pile of smoldering ash, was all that remained of Nadur's body.

The metallic voice echoed out once more, tolling the words ominously: "Captain Eagal, as Captain Nadur's friend, I am certain you will want to take on this task for him. And if you think to disobey me, please remember his rather fiery end."

It was soon afterward that sleek ships of grey metal were

gliding out between vast, open doors set into a sheer wall of rock.

Above the rock rose a spectacular pinnacle, like a tower of ice whose smoothly polished sides reflected sharply the bright stars in the clear night skies. The massive structure stretched some thirty stories above the dark sea and the fleet emerging at its base. There was a score of ships now, turning to move off in all directions from the rocky islet on which the tower sat, drawing lines of fluorescent wake behind them as they slid away across the black surface.

High above, within the tower, the black giant stood alone at an immense window, looking down at them.

"Someday, we will find them," the metallic voice rumbled from within the helmet. "Someday our most ancient enemies will face Balor again."

And down below, at the same time, Captain Eagal was standing on the stern deck of his ship, staring back at the tower as it receded into the night.

"Look well at our Tower of Glass," he said to a young seaman beside him. "It's likely the last time you'll ever see it."

"You don't think there's a chance we'll return from the barrier fog, Captain?" the seaman asked.

"No. Thanks to Commander Balor, we're almost surely as doomed as those poor fools who went into it before us."

He turned and looked past the ship's bow, toward the dark, unknown skies to the west.

"I wonder where they are now," he said musingly. "That is, if they're even still alive."

The wooden ship drifted silently, wraithlike, through the fog. The thick, billowing grey-whiteness surrounded it, hiding all but the tiny patch of ocean that was close about its hull.

It was a seagoing vessel of the simplest kind. Small, wide, and shallow-drafted, it had a single mast with a sail now hanging limply in a breeze so faint that it barely fluttered in the heavy cloak of fog.

All about upon its deck were scattered human figures, lying huddled or sprawled, apparently asleep. Only at the stern tiller was one man awake, steering the vessel before what wind there was and keeping up a vigil.

He was a young man of massive form, wide, tall, and extremely muscular. His wiry, long hair was braided loosely at his back. His head was a rectangular block, with thrusting jaw, jutting brows, and broad nose that made his mouth and eyes seem small.

It was he alone who saw the peculiar light.

It popped quite suddenly into view some distance off of the ship's port side—a faint, silvery glow bobbing in the fog.

"Finally," he murmured. "Something. After all these days!"

He did not hesitate in turning the ship's bow toward it, his face brightening with hope. As he did, the faint breeze strengthened slightly, puffing out the square of sail. The craft began to glide slowly forward, heading for the light.

But the light drew no closer. It seemed to have some power of movement of its own, staying always the exact same distance ahead, bobbing on through the fog.

The young man stubbornly kept his ship's bow pointed after it.

"Oh, strange light," he murmured as if addressing it, "we are out of water and food now. We're getting near our end. You are our only hope. If you're not just some creation of my weary mind, I pray to you to please lead us *somewhere.*"

For a long while it seemed his plea had gone unheard. He played a game of tag with the moving light, still never coming any nearer to reaching it.

Then, abruptly, the ship burst free of the fog. It tore out through a sheer high wall of the grey-white, drawing out streamers of cloud that clung like shredded cloth for a few moments before fluttering away.

In an instant's transition the vessel was gliding across a smooth and blue sea under a clear daylit sky. Those sleeping upon the deck began to stir, lifting up, opening eyes, blinking around them at the wondrous, bright scene.

There, not far ahead, lay a shoreline of gleaming gold sand and shimmering green hills. A glistening fortress sat perched upon the brow of one rounded hill like a jeweled crown.

But the most amazing sight lay closer to the ship and the startled gazes of its passengers. The young man at the tiller, especially, stared in wonder at the thing whose glow he had so long followed, its true nature now strikingly revealed.

It was no ship or natural creature of the sea that moved along only a spear's throw before the prow. It was a huge and horse-drawn chariot of war, riding over the wavetops as if it were on dry land!

Chapter 2

Lir

The chariot rolled forward across the waves, its silver-rimmed wheels cutting fleeting furrows through the smooth crests of the ocean swells.

The chariot's miraculous ability was fittingly complemented by its appearance and by the team that pulled it. The vehicle's car was shaped like a magnificent swan, neck arched high at the front, wings sweeping back to form the sides, all worked in bright silver with such fine detail that its glowing feathers seemed to flutter with the sea breeze.

To the chariot's pole were harnessed a pair of proud, powerfully muscled steeds of gleaming gold-yellow hide and flying crimson mane. They pranced along as if on a hard-packed road, drawing the large conveyance with ease.

The most ordinary aspect of the whole assemblage was its driver. He was a tall, rather gawkily constructed man of long face, large but pleasant features, and a mass of thickly curling golden hair. His lanky form was clad in a simple tunic of white edged in gold and an emerald-green cloak fastened about his shoulders by a large gold pin fashioned as two twining serpents.

On either side of his vehicle, as if in escort, a sleek dolphin swam and leaped. Several more of the creatures es-

corted the vessel that followed along behind him. Its single
sail was now furled. Instead, a dozen long oars projecting at
either side were being used with great enthusiasm by the
vessel's crew to propel the ship along in the chariot's wake.

In the bow of the ship stood two figures. One was a
slender but muscular young man of long, dark blond hair,
clean and striking looks, and inquisitive blue-grey eyes. Beside him stood a much taller, much leaner man of greater
years, his brown hair beginning to grey, his grave face showing lines of wear.

Both were gazing fixedly at the shoreline, which was
now very close ahead.

The small island they approached glowed with a crystal
clarity, a brilliant, gemlike quality resembling a rare spring
dawn. A beach of white-gold sands sloped back and upward
from the shore to meet the shimmering green of hills above.
Atop the highest, central hill—a symmetrical, smooth-
domed knoll—sat a large structure gleaming with the soft
tone of burnished bronze. About it, encircling the hill's
brow, was a wall that seemed to be made of polished white
stone.

The chariot's driver steered the vehicle straight in toward the beach. Without a break in stride, the team of
horses trotted from water to sand, drawing the chariot clear
of the lapping waves. There the driver pulled them up.

The ship was run in right beside him, its prow grounding
in the shallows. Immediately the massively formed young
man who had held the tiller jumped over the side and waded
in.

"Throw me the line, Nuada!" he called to the young
man in the bow.

Nuada acted swiftly, casting a thick hawser out. The big
man took it, the muscles of his arms and legs springing to
sharp definition as he strained to draw the vessel ahead.

In an amazing display of strength, he alone dragged the
vessel up half its length onto the sands. He threw down the
hawser and beamed in delight at his accomplishment.

People began to clamber out over the sides of the ship at
once. There were altogether some thirty of them—a dozen
women, the rest men. Most were of a similarly youthful age,
generally of tall, lean, and vigorous physique, light of color-

ing, clad in simple garb of long, woven tunics, the men trousered as well.

Most also seemed similarly grateful to be upon dry land, voicing sounds of relief and gratitude, stretching, even kneeling to pat the clean, firm sands beneath them.

Some few among them were striking in their individuality. One was a shorter, wiry man of a curiously scorched-looking complexion and energetic movements. Another was an odd, eerie figure, gaunt and sinewy, of wild, blue-black hair and ice-blue eyes, clad in animal skins. A third was a man of thinning dark hair drawn back from a wide brow and a disquieting light of cunning in his always-probing, always-shifting dark eyes.

The man in the chariot leaped down and moved to join the others, amused at their goggling, openmouthed amazement.

"So, you do like the place, eh?" he said amiably. "It *is* quite a sight. Though its shine can be almost blinding on a really sunny day."

"Thank you for guiding us here," said the young man called Nuada. "We'd been days wandering on the sea, lost in the strangest bank of mist."

"I know," the other said. "That's why I rescued you, of course. You might well have been lost in there forever. To pass through is to enter another realm, a place set off from the world you know. The barrier of fog surrounds it, conceals it. It sends anyone who enters it off course and wandering. 'Astray' we call it here. It's meant to protect us from those of the outside."

"Meant?" echoed the older man, clearly fascinated. "You mean it's something you've . . . created?"

"Some simple sorcery," their savior casually replied. "Weather magic is among the most elementary."

"And what about that?" asked the huge young man, pointing to the wave-skimming chariot. "How's that done?"

"Just more magic," the man replied with a dismissing wave. "Look here, I'm certain you've many questions, but you must be thirsty, hungry, and very tired from your ordeal. Why don't you come with me? We'll see to your needs, and then we can talk."

"We have to get our weapons from the ship," said Nuada.

"Oh, you don't need them," the green-cloaked man assured them. "It's quite safe. Or don't you trust me?"

Nuada eyed him, then looked around to his fellows uncertainly. It was the older man who answered for them.

"You saved us when you might easily have left us to die," he said simply. "It would be both ungrateful and illogical for us not to trust you now."

"The healer is right," seconded Nuada. "We'll leave our weapons here."

"Fine," the green-cloaked man said cheerfully. "Then just follow along, will you?"

And with that he turned and started up the sloping beach toward the fortified hill.

The newcomers, drawn by both need and curiosity, joined him, crossing the sand to a pathway that wound up the grassy hillside.

"I am called Diancecht," the older man said to their guide as they moved along. "As Nuada just mentioned, I function as the healer for our company."

"And I'm Goibniu," the wiry little man of the blackened skin announced in a brisk tone. "The smith for this lot, I am. Make anything you want of metal, I will. Sparks and soot and white-hot iron—that's my life!"

"Somehow I had guessed that," the lanky man said, grinning. He glanced around toward the massive young man clomping along behind them. "And who is the large one?"

"He is Dagda, our strongest fighting man," Nuada supplied.

"Something else I might have guessed. Well, you can call me Lir."

"Lir?" said the shifty-eyed one in surprise.

That man looked sharply around to him. "Yes. Why?"

"Oh . . . oh, nothing," the other said hastily. "It just seemed a . . . a familiar name, somehow."

"Did it? And may I ask just who you are?"

"I am Mathgen," the other replied with a note of pride. "Son to a great shaman of the Eastern Clans."

"Are you now?" Lir responded, sounding unimpressed. "How wonderful for you."

"You do in some way seem familiar, Lir," the healer put in thoughtfully. "There is no possibility that we have ever met before?"

"I speak no lie to tell you that you have never made the acquaintance of *this* Lir," the man breezily assured him.

"Of course," Diancecht accepted. But both he and Mathgen continued to cast scrutinizing looks at their guide.

They were by this time approaching the hilltop. As they drew near, the new arrivals could see that the wall they approached was formed of purest white marble cut in enormous sheets, joined by nearly invisible lines, and polished to an almost glasslike sheen.

Its single opening had a pair of gold, intricately filigreed gates, but they stood thrown completely back. No guards showed at the gateway or upon the walls.

"The defenses aren't really needed," Lir explained. "I've no enemies here. They're simply . . . well, for the look of the thing, I suppose. 'Tradition' you could say. Some ancient need for things to look secure."

He led them in through the gates. Beyond was a courtyard paved with flags of more polished marble, this of a pale pink shot through with threads of gold.

"All the finest stone," Lir announced. "Very nice. Hard to keep clean though."

Ahead, at the exact center of the court, rose the single building encircled by the wall. It was an octagonal structure, each of the flat sides rising up over two stories in height. From the top of each, a wedge of roof slanted up and in, joining with the others in a cone, its peak some five stories above the ground. All the surfaces seemed to be of lustrous, gold-brown bronze.

"By all the gods my fathers swear by!" Goibniu said in open awe.

"I thought it might appeal especially to you, good smith," Lir said with a smile. "Several lifetimes of work for you there, eh? Well, shall we go in?"

Each of the building's sides had four large windows with shutters, also of bronze, thrown back. The side facing them had in addition a central doorway, again wide open. With Lir still in the lead, they passed through it.

They found the structure's interior to be one vast space.

In the center was a firepit a dozen paces across, enclosed by a hearth of more marble—silver-grey this time. Just outside it, a ring of slender roof pillars soared up to support each section of the eight-faceted roof. They were fashioned in the shape of several serpents intertwined as a single, sinuous column, heads fanning out at the top to form arching rafters.

These rafters, like all the interior walls and ceiling, appeared to be of copper, more reddish of hue and more softly burnished than the walls outside. As a result, the fire blazing in the pit, reflecting from all the surfaces, imparted a ruddy, warm, and pleasant glow to the whole interior.

Several tables and benches were set up around the pit. They were laid out with plates, pitchers, and goblets of silver.

"Already prepared for a meal," Diancecht commented. He quickly counted the plates. "And just the number for our company. Were you expecting us, Lir?"

"Certainly," he said airily. "Now, all of you take seats. We'll see you fed at once."

They moved in, circling fire, treading on gold-brown rugs of a soft, thick, and furlike texture. They sat on the benches while Lir sat on a separate armed chair in their midst.

Suddenly, and as if out of nowhere, a flood of young people came into the room from all about them. They were a most comely people, both girls and boys of willowy form, fine features, and pale coloring. Flowing hair was largely white-gold to silver; eyes were of the brightest greens and blues; skins were of a smooth, unblemished, creamy white. All wore similar knee-length tunics of pastel hues and soft clinging fabric.

Some of the group bore trays heaped with foods that they passed out to the guests. Others moved around the room playing upon smooth horns and bow-shaped harps to fill the air with a sweet and soothing tune.

When all were served, the tray-bearing youths melted away as swiftly as they had come, leaving only the musicians to entertain.

"Now please eat," Lir invited, calling the attention of his bedazzled company to the plentious food before them.

The famished guests readily turned their interest to the more practical, pressing matter of their insides. For some time the sounds of enthusiastic eating all but drowned out the music.

At last, when enough food had been consumed to quiet the hunger pangs of a company twice as large, Lir spoke again: "If you feel sufficiently refreshed, perhaps you can tell me the tale of how you came to be lost out there."

The one named Nuada looked to the sober-faced healer. "Diancecht, you are our eldest now, and wisest of us. Would you be our voice?"

"Very well," the man accepted. For several moments he considered. Then, in a slow, careful, and precise way, he began to speak: "We are of territories far to the east. They are harsh lands, filled with warring chieftains who take power by force and kill or enslave all who defy them. Some few clans of us, mostly craftsmen and herders and farmers, banded together under a man called Nemed and set out seeking a new place where we might live peacefully. We settled on what we thought was the last island on the western rim of the great world. We called it the 'Blessed Land.' "

"Blessed Land," Mathgen sneered. "Cursed was more like it."

"Quiet!" the one called Dagda barked at him. "It's the healer who's telling this!"

Mathgen instantly subsided, though giving the big man a sidelong glare. The healer, unruffled by this interruption, continued: "It *was*, to some extent, cursed to us. We came for peace and freedom. Instead we soon came afoul of a race of pirates known as the Fomor. Do you know of them?"

"I have heard vague tales," said Lir. "Most grotesque fellows, aren't they?"

"They are indeed beings of terrible aspect," the healer agreed, "with the heads of beasts, most lacking a hand or a foot, cruel and rapacious of nature. They tried to force a terrible tribute from us—two thirds of our corn and milk and of all children born during the year."

"You didn't submit, of course," said Lir.

"Certainly not. We rebelled and defeated the creatures."

"Very brave of you to go against such formidable opponents alone," the host commented. "Or . . . had you other help?"

"We had," Diancecht admitted, "from a man of some knowledge, even some magic. Liam he was called. A somewhat . . . peculiar man."

"Peculiar?"

"Yes. A ragged wanderer of mysterious and most eccentric character."

"Eccentric?" Lir echoed. "Still, no doubt a noble and courageous fellow."

"Oh, assuredly so. In the end he sacrificed himself in our aide. With his help we stormed the Fomor stronghold and chased them out to sea. But I'm afraid we went too far." Here he looked to Nuada. "I think you should tell him this part," he said to the young man. "You were part of the chase."

"All right," said Nuada, taking up the tale. "Well, the Fomor ran before us, making for a thing far out to sea—a huge, gleaming pinnacle, like a tower of ice. As our ships chased theirs closer to the tower, we saw a figure appear upon its top. It was shaped as a man, but one of giant size, all clad in black. From its head there shot a most terrible beam of crimson light that destroyed many of our people."

"Made whole ships just vanish in a great *whoosh* of fire!" put in Dagda, still clearly awed at the force he'd witnessed.

"Now who's giving interruption?" Mathgen snidely remarked.

But Lir seemed intrigued by the big man's description. "Did it really do so?" he asked. "And do you know who the giant being of this tower was?"

"No," said Diancecht, "except that it was in league with the Fomor. And its great power was the finish for us. The result of this last devastation, following earlier Fomor atrocities, was to leave our people decimated. Of the few survivors, most chose to return eastward to our old homelands." He waved around him. "This handful, the more daring"— he gave a little smile—"or perhaps the more foolhardy, chose to go on into the unknown seas of the west, seeking whatever might lie here."

"Most daring, *and* most foolhearty," said Lir. "Without my finding you, you'd quite likely have perished."

"We thank you again," the healer said. "But you've heard our tale. Can you now tell us just where we have been brought to, and just who you are?"

"Ah, well, you might say I'm a guardian. A sort of watcher upon this tiny outpost."

"Outpost?" Nuada repeated quizzically. "Of what?"

"Of this realm within the mists. There are three times fifty islands that lie scattered out in the sea to the west of us. They've many names, but the Isles of Promise is the favorite one to me. Each is a place of its own wonders. Each is as fascinating as the others."

"Most intriguing indeed," said Diancecht.

"Yes," said Nuada. "It sounds like the place we have been seeking. So many islands. So many chances to explore, to discover new things, to find a place for ourselves."

"I'm afraid that might be rather difficult," said Lir. "You are not even supposed to be here, you know."

"We're not?"

"Oh, no. You see, I broke a rule in helping you to penetrate the barrier fog, and another by feeding you."

"But we know there is nothing behind us. There is nowhere left to go," Diancecht pointed out. "Why couldn't there be someplace for us here?"

"If it were up to me, you'd be welcome to seek as you wish," Lir answered. "But it's not. It's for Danu to decide if you can stay."

"Danu?" repeated Diancecht. "Who is that?"

"The queen who rules over these islands. She lives to the west of here, on an isle in the very center of all the rest. Magh Mell, the Pleasant Plain, is what it's called."

"We certainly don't mean to defy this queen or to be seen as invaders of her realm," said Diancecht.

"The answer to that is simple," Nuada said brightly. He looked around at the rest of his people. "What do you say, my friends?" he asked. "Do we go back? Or do we seek out this queen and ask her leave to stay?"

Clear, hardy voices in favor of this last choice were raised by all the others. But Lir shook his head, his look most doubtful.

"It will not be so easy," he told them warningly. "You see, it's many hundreds of years that Danu has kept these isles safely hidden from the outer world. She'll not be pleased to have you petition her, or even to discover that you have entered our realm. She may well see you as a threat."

"But we are not," Diancecht told him. "We are simply a people seeking a place to live. Surely we can convince her of that."

"Perhaps," Lir conceded. "You are certainly a people of great courage and will. It may be you *can* appeal to her. If so, she might grant leave to stay, at least for a time. At best. At worst . . ." Here he hesitated.

"Yes?" prompted Diancecht. "What then?"

"At worst," Lir grimly went on, "with a wave of her hand she can make you all quite dead!"

Chapter 3
Setting Out

"Are you absolutely certain that you want to do this?" Lir asked the young man named Nuada.

"We're seekers, Lir," the other told him. "It's why we didn't return to our old homelands with the rest of our people."

They stood on the beach below the marble wall of Lir's fortress. Around them were gathered the rest of Nuada's company, preparing their vessel for its new voyage. A swarm of Lir's youthful servants was flitting up and down the hillside from the fort's gateway, bringing food for the visitors to store away on the ship.

"But I want you to understand," Lir went on more emphatically. "This journey will not be an easy one."

These words caught the attention of Diancecht, who moved closer. "How do you mean?" he asked.

"That you aren't the first outsiders to penetrate the barrier of mist. Over the many years there have been a few others who, without my help, have still found a way through. But none of them survived."

"Danu?" asked Nuada.

Lir shook his head. "Not she. None made it so far.

These are islands of wonder, but also of many strange and terrible forces."

"It's of no matter," Nuada assured him. "We've already faced many risks and many terrors searching for a place in the world. We can't simply sail away from the possibilities of these marvelous new lands."

"I thought as much," Lir said, adding regretfully, "and I'm sorry I can't go with you. I'm afraid you're very much on your own from here on out. Danu would have the living skin off me surely if she thought I'd led you to her. Bad enough if she finds out I even pointed the way."

"She won't," assured the healer. "We understand and we appreciate the risk you have taken for us. This is our choice alone. We'll find our way."

"I will be lookout from the masthead," said a low and rasping voice.

They looked around to see a being of wild, raven-black hair and gaunt, leather-clad form. It had moved up to them quite silently; and after its one terse statement, it slipped as silently away.

"Those are the first words she's spoken since we started our voyage here," said Nuada, watching the figure climb into the ship and clamber up the mast to the crosstree with the speed and nimbleness of a squirrel.

"'She,' is it?" said Lir. "I wasn't certain. Just who is she?"

"Morrigan she calls herself now," said Nuada. "The raven-woman. The Fomor made her so. They poisoned her and caused her to give birth to most gruesome monsters. The horror of it did something to her mind. She cast off her old self and became a creature of the wild, living like the birds and beasts of prey. It gave her senses more acute than any man's. It also gave her a taste for blood."

"Blood?" echoed Lir, grimacing in disgust. "Then they made her into something terrible indeed."

"Yet she was once a most beautiful, most loving woman," said a sorrowful voice.

It came from the one called Dagda who stood nearby. He looked after the woman fixedly for a moment, then turned abruptly and moved away to hide the tears that had sprung to being in his eyes.

"He seems deeply moved," Lir said, looking after the big man.

"He has a right to be," Nuada told him somberly. "She —or what she used to be—was his wife."

The smith called Goibniu bustled up to them.

"Ready to go," he said briskly. "I've checked over every plank and shroud of the ship. We've crammed every bit of food onto her that we can. A dozen days worth for us at least. And plenty of water too."

"Then let's make the most of the daylight," Nuada said. "Tell everyone to prepare for sailing."

As Goibniu hurried away to pass the word, Lir looked to Nuada and Diancecht.

"Go with my hopes for success, my friends," he told them earnestly. "Take care. It is all your strengths and skills and even your beliefs that will be tested now. Always remember one of the other names our realm is known by: the Isles of Enchantment. Beware of everything. Trust in nothing but yourselves."

"That we will do," Nuada assured him, clasping the man's hand in a parting gesture.

"But tell me one last thing," Diancecht said, also clasping hands with the man. "I'm curious—why is it that you took this risk to save us? We are only more outsiders."

"That you are not," Lir answered him. "I sense in you a spirit that I've felt in no others. We have been too long shut away here, feeding on ourselves. It seemed to me time for a gust of new air, a surge of new blood from the great world." He grinned. "You might just give things here the good waking up they need."

"We'll do our best to oblige you," Nuada said.

Others made their own farewells to their genial host. All but Dagda and a half dozen of the sturdiest men then boarded the ship. These last few shoved the vessel clear of the sand and clambered aboard as well. Soon the oars were swinging out rhythmically at each side, pushing the ship away from the jewellike little isle.

Lir could be seen standing alone on the beach below his fortress, a bright flock of his young people behind him, all watching after those departing, growing smaller as the ship drew away. But the explorers had not gone far across the waves before there came a sharp cry from the masthead.

"Look there!" cawed Morrigan, shooting an arm out to point back at the isle.

The whole company looked. Before their startled gazes, the man, his colorful attendants, and the glowing palace were fading. Like traceries of frost swept by a blast of heat, the figures seemed to swiftly evaporate, their forms and colors thinning to vague wisps that finally fluttered away.

In only moments there was nothing left but a bare island.

"By all my father's gods!" cried Nuada. He looked to the healer. "Diancecht, where has it all gone?"

Diancecht, staring in fascination, shook his head. " 'Trust nothing,' he told us," the man said musingly. "Clearly this is an enchanted place indeed."

The rowers pulled on until the island had dwindled away behind and fresh sea breezes gusting up from the southeast caught them.

They drew in their oars then and raised the single sail, letting the wind sweep them on into the unknown west.

The sea here was calm, a rippling surface of deep blue stretching away beneath a clear, bright canopy of sky. Yet there was much to occupy the attention of the travelers.

They caught glimpses of vast flocks of unknown birds soaring at great distances and heard the fine, high trilling notes of their strange songs. They saw schools of huge, white-bellied salmon that swam and leaped about the ship on every side, so thick and furious in their swimming that they churned the water to a silver froth.

Behind them sleek, black, gleaming seals swept through the waters, frolicking in the shimmering, rolling wash from the ship's stern. And beyond the seals could be seen the greater black humps of some much larger creatures, thrusting up from the sea like rounded islands, propelled by broad and steadily thrashing tails.

"What are those things?" Nuada asked Diancecht. For he and most of the others were especially watching after the huge creatures with looks of great interest mixed with a bit of dread.

" 'Whales' is what I believe they are called, from the descriptions I've heard sailors give. They're not often seen but by those who venture far out in the great sea."

"They're certainly large enough to sink us easily, if they attacked," put in Dagda.

"They're said to be gentle creatures," the healer told him, "not harmful to men. And they seem to be keeping their distance, only curious about us as we are about them. I say they, at least, are not something to fear."

Thus assured by their learned man, the company lost fear and watched the whales and the other life about them with nothing but delight as their ship hove on toward the western curve where sea touched sky.

They had sailed on half a day when the untiring and vigilant Morrigan hailed the crew from the masthead to say another island had come into view ahead. All rushed to the ship's sides to see it.

It was small and low and featureless—little more than a dry patch barely thrusting above the waves. But there was something peculiar about its surface.

"Why is it that the ground there seems to move?" asked Dagda, peering out from the bow with Nuada and Diancecht.

It was indeed a restlessly shifting kaleidoscope of many bright colors.

"Could it be a field of flowers ruffled by the wind?" suggested Nuada.

"No," said the healer. "I believe it's birds."

In moments they had swept in close enough for all to see that Diancecht was right. The moving field *was* birds, many hundreds of birds crowded so densely that they all but blanketed the isle. The confused cacophony of squawks from their many throats filled the air, and separate birds could be seen flapping up or gliding back down into the assembly.

"What do you think, Nuada?" said Dagda. "Should we land?"

"We've come to seek out new places," the other replied. "I don't think we can afford to pass anything by."

"I agree," said the healer. "My feeling is strong that if

we're to survive in this place, we must discover all that we can about it."

The rest of the crew agreed. And so the bold explorers sailed in and grounded their ship on a thin strip of beach that surrounded a higher plain where the fowls were perched. They climbed out and moved up to more closely examine this rookery.

The birds certainly warranted their attention. They were of a most remarkable kind. Built somewhat like cranes, they had round bodies and flexible necks—both covered by soft pink feathers—and spindly legs. But they also sported flaring crests of a brilliant green and flowing tails of lush purple and gold plumage: very striking in total effect, if a bit garish.

"I've never seen the like," said Nuada, looking around at the uncountable, seething mass of birds now keeping a wary distance from the interlopers.

"They *have* no like," Morrigan rattled in her clipped and harsh-toned voice.

They looked to her in surprise.

"There are no birds of their kind left anywhere but here," she went on. "For their bright plumage they were hunted to near extinction by men many, many years ago. These found a last refuge in this hidden place."

"How do you know?" Nuada demanded.

She shrugged. "They tell me," she said tersely. "They have been singing out their story since we arrived, fearing we will harm them. I understand their speech."

"Nonsense," Mathgen said in a haughty, belittling way. "You put any words to their squawking that you wish so as to impress us with your supposed skill. They are only birds."

"Still," said Nuada, "we've no wish to disturb them without need. Let's make a quick search of their isle and be away."

They moved forward through the flock that hastily opened a way for them, advancing toward the center of the island. Here they found a small, clear pool, surrounded by many scores of sitting birds.

But these rose up with sharp alarm at the invaders' approach, lifting in flight or loping awkwardly away on their long legs. Their movement revealed the nests upon which they had sat—hollows in the sandy ground thickly lined with their own feathers.

Nuada looked around him. "Well, there are no signs of human life here at all. Nothing but the birds."

Mathgen peered into one of the nests. "This one seems to have been sitting on two eggs," he said.

"And this one," said Dagda, looking into another.

A swift survey revealed that each of the nests seemed to have a pair of eggs within its cozy confines, all abandoned by their alarmed incubators.

Mathgen lifted one of the eggs out to examine it. It was of colorful aspect, being of deep blue spotted with pure crimson.

"You should put that back," Dagda warned.

"Yes," said Diancecht. "And we should leave here. We should not keep these birds from their nests too long. The eggs might die."

"What difference?" Mathgen said carelessly, keeping hold of the egg.

Morrigan stepped toward him, her look sharp, her voice crackling with roused ire. "What difference! Only whether these birds survive or not. Deaf man! Can't you hear the sounds of pleading in their cries?"

"That I cannot!" he said stubbornly, challengingly meeting her gaze. "They're mindless birds. They've hundreds of eggs. And I have had no taste of a fresh one in too many days."

Before anyone could stop him, he jammed a finger through one end of the egg, cracking a hole in the shell. With a laugh of victory he lifted the egg and sucked the golden contents into his mouth.

"Ah! There!" he said with satisfaction, smacking his lips and casting the drained shell away to smash against the ground. He looked around at the others. "You see? Good eating for the taking. I say why don't we all . . ."

He stopped suddenly, jerking up taut. His body shuddered. Then he began to scratch furiously at himself.

"My . . . my skin!" he said in an agonized voice. "It's on fire!"

From out of the neck of his tunic, long pink feathers suddenly sprouted. More sprang into view from his sleeves.

And out through his hair, like spring buds bursting from the ground, the bright green fingers of a comb thrust upward, swelling rapidly.

His face convulsed in sudden, excruciating pain at the hundreds of eruptions through his skin. He shrieked his agony and thrashed wildly in panic, flailing at himself.

"To the pond!" Morrigan snapped. "Quickly. Get him in! While there is time!"

Without hesitation, Dagda obeyed her. The huge young man seized the frantically squirming Mathgen, jerked him from the ground, and hurled him bodily toward the pond.

Mathgen soared out and crashed down into its water. It was quite shallow, and he landed sitting, the water up only to his waist. The pink feathers continued to sprout, the green comb to grow. His tunic now bulged outward from the many feathers sprouting beneath. His face was growing fuzzy and pink from its own growth. His nose was swelling rapidly, dragging his mouth and chin along to form a great curved beak; and his neck was stretching grotesquely upward, thinning as it went. He gurgled and screeched in a tortured, strangled way.

"Wash him down," the dark woman ordered. "Wet him all over!"

Nuada and Goibniu waded in, grabbed the stricken man, and began to wash him. None too gently they scrubbed him all over, splashing water onto him, dunking him beneath the surface to thoroughly soak him down.

The treatment worked. The wet feathers began to dissolve, melting away like spiderwebs washed by rain. The skin of his face reemerged; the crest shriveled to nothing. Neck and nose shrank back to normal size.

"That's stopped it," Goibniu declared.

They released him and stepped out of the pond, leaving him to sit spitting water and gasping for breath.

"How did you know that would work?" Diancecht asked Morrigan.

"Again, it was the birds told me," she answered. "It wasn't a plea for us not to eat their eggs they were making, but a warning of the danger if we did. They are protected by this Queen Danu's magic. Only wetting the skin can break the spell, if done in time. A moment longer and the change would not have been reversed."

"Mathgen would have replaced the life of the bird he took," said Nuada. "That seems fair enough. And without Morrigan's ability to understand the birds, we would not have known how to save him."

Dagda looked to the soaked man who was now climbing to his feet. "It seems that someone should give apology for doubting her skills," he said pointedly.

"I apologize," Mathgen said, but harshly, and with resentment at his so-public shaming quite evident in his tone.

"It also seems that these simple fowl are of more humane nature than some of us so-called humans," added Diancecht. "Especially in choosing to save one so callous." With a rare grin of amusement, he asked, "Do you want any more eggs, Mathgen?"

"I may well never eat an egg again," the man shot back, wringing water from his sodden tunic.

"Then," said the healer, "I suggest we depart this isle at once and leave these creatures in peace."

They made no delay in returning to their ship, and set off once again through the peaceful seas.

The sun was beginning its last slide toward the western horizon when another island came into their view.

This one was larger—a wide sand beach running up to green, gently sloping hills topped with lush and inviting groves. There seemed no sign of other life, either bird, beast, or human.

Again, the travelers decided that they should stop to investigate. Once more they brought their vessel in to land, grounding it on the fine sands of the beach.

They climbed out and looked around them. It seemed a quiet, pleasant, and most normal place.

"As it's so near sunset, perhaps we should stay the night here," Nuada suggested. "We can rest well on firm, dry land; and we'll not run the risk of missing some other place in the night."

The others agreed.

"That grove above seems a better place to camp," said

Dagda, pointing to a stand of deep green trees on a hilltop not too far above them. "We can gather wood for fires and have our food hot."

"A good idea," said Nuada, "but for safety, I think this time we should protect ourselves. Lir warned us there might be dangers anywhere."

So men and women both took arms from the ship. Wood-hilted swords in bronze-banded leather scabbards were belted around waists. Throwing spears of slender but sturdy yew bole and barbed, keen-tipped point were taken up; and round shields of hammered black iron were slipped onto arms. Thus all prepared, the party of adventurers started up the grassy slope.

Morrigan, as scout, moved some little way ahead, quartering the ground. The rest followed, moving at a good pace up the gentle, thickly grassed incline.

But halfway up to the grove, one of the young men stumbled suddenly, falling to one knee.

"What is it?" Dagda asked him, halting with the others.

"Ah, it's just some rock," the youth said irritably, giving the large, rounded, grey-white object he'd stumbled upon a hard kick.

It rolled over, and the group found themselves looking at the black eyeholes and grinning teeth of a huge, weathered human skull.

Chapter 4

Challenges

"By the gods!" exclaimed Nuada. "Look at that!"

Dagda knelt and took hold of the skull, lifting it from the ground. He held it up in both hands so all might examine it.

"Its owner was surely a giant," Goibniu said in awe.

It was indeed massive, dwarfing even the huge Dagda's impressive head. Aside from the size, it was essentially of human structure, save that the forehead was low and sloping, the eye ridges were sharply jutting, and the jaw was very pronounced.

"There's another bit," said a young man, pouncing on a spot. He lifted a long bone knobbed at either end.

The others searched about them. They soon found and gathered many bones half buried in the sod, hidden by the tall grasses. Two more huge skulls were among them, along with enough pieces to make up the skeletons of three immense bodies.

Diancecht took up another long bone and looked it over closely.

"Most definitely an upper leg bone," he declared, then matched it against his own upper leg. In both length and thickness the comparison was almost ludicrous.

"These beings were of at least twice our own size, I'd estimate," he said. "Most formidable."

"Armed too," said Nuada. With an effort he lifted from the grass a large stone chipped into a rough wedge shape and fitted to the rotted remnant of a thick wood handle, making a hefty ax.

"Crude, but still very effective," remarked the healer, looking it over. "Unlikely many ordinary men or weapons could stand up before a swing of that."

"That's certain," Dagda wholeheartedly agreed. "Makes you wonder what it was that could have killed these three."

"Quite a force, I'd say," put in Mathgen, indicating one skull whose rounded cap had been all but pulverized by what must have been a powerful blow.

At this, all in the party looked searchingly, warily about them. There was nothing but the same peaceful, pleasant landscape.

"Shall we go on?" asked Goibniu.

"I found no marks of man or animal about here," rasped Morrigan. "No danger seems close by."

"These lads have been dead for some while," said Nuada. "Could be they killed each other. I say go on."

The others agreed. They moved on upward, though now a bit more cautiously, still making for the inviting grove at the hill's top.

Not far below it, they crossed a low rise and found the ground beyond dropped away into a small valley that had been hidden to them before. They paused on its edge, looking down upon the newly revealed scene.

A rivulet of silvery water sparkled along the bottom of the gentle fold of ground. Lush-grassed slopes dotted with bright flowers rose up on either side. And along both the rivulet's banks were scattered several dozen fat, white objects. The explorers had encountered other living creatures at last.

"Sheep," said Nuada, examining them.

They were grazing placidly on the grass, moving slowly along the banks, apparently quite ordinary and quite harmless beasts. Nuada and his companions moved down the slope toward them.

On approach the company realized that the sheep were not quite completely ordinary after all.

"Why, the beasts are huge!" said one young man. "The size of ponies!"

"Are all the things here of giant size?" asked another.

"And look at their fleece!" said one of the women. "I've never seen finer, or purer! Almost silver-white it is."

The wool of the huge sheep was a thick billow about them, clean and glowing like bright puffs of cloud under a spring sun.

"Think of how much clothing could be made from the shearing of just one!" said Nuada.

"And of what quality it would be," added another of the young women.

They looked around at their own clothing—woven tunics, shifts, and trousers—all grey and threadbare from much hard wear.

Diancecht saw their looks and frowned in disapproval.

"I know what you're likely thinking," he said, "but I say we touch none of these beasts. Remember that last island. Remember Lir's words. We must beware of everything!"

"Ah, you're right," said Nuada. "It's only that we're . . ."

He cut off as a sudden sharp bleat sounded from not far away. They had drawn near to the outskirts of the flock, and one of the animals had taken note of their approach, giving voice to its alarm.

The whole flock reacted instantly, bunching and trotting away, filling the air with a confused chorus of frightened *baaaas.*

"Now we've panicked the lot of them," said Diancecht irritably. "We should not have come so close. I've been a fool not to stop us earlier!"

"But we mean them no harm," said Nuada reasonably. "We'll give them a wide berth and go on past."

"No!" said the healer sharply. "Better to go back. I have a disquieting feeling about this."

"I have as well," put in somber Morrigan. "I scent danger."

A louder, deeper, more strident bleat sounded from above, echoing along the valley. They all looked up toward its source: the grove atop the opposite slope. Objects were moving out from behind the cover of its trees into view, heading down the valley's side toward them.

"Too late!" said Diancecht unhappily. "I should have guessed."

The approaching objects were rams, a dozen of them. They were thicker, darker, scruffier in look than the fluffy sheep. They were also much larger.

"Look at them, will you?" cried Dagda. "As big as cows they are!"

"And see their horns?" said Goibniu.

Each ram had not a pair, but four, five, even six horns growing out side by side across their wide foreheads, curling back into tight spirals as if they were giant fists thrusting forward, ready to strike a blow.

The beasts trotted halfway down the slope and stopped in a compact mass. Then from their midst moved one to stand alone before the rest. This one was the largest, with the bulk and the brawn of a full-grown bull. On its broad wedge of a head nine horns were ranged. Their huge, bony curls, set tight together, formed a single mass of a sharply glinting silver-grey, as if fashioned of a forged and polished iron.

"Now *that's* a head strong enough to smash down a fortress's doors," commented Dagda in open appreciation of such raw strength.

"There stands a battering ram in truth!" added Goibniu with no hint of amusement in his tone.

"Well," said Nuada, "at least we know what killed those fellows down below."

"What should we do?" asked Mathgen with a rising note of panic. "Should we run?"

With a loud snort of rage, the animal charged toward them.

"No chance for that!" said Dagda. "Here it comes!"

The creature was picking up speed rapidly on the downhill run, soon descending upon them with the ferocity of an avalanche.

"Form a line! Shields up!" Nuada commanded. "Make a barrier!"

They swiftly formed up in an open wedge, the round

shields out and interlocked before them, creating a solid wall.

The animal hit the stream, splashing through its shallow water without missing a stride, hurtling on toward them with speed unslowed.

All in the company braced themselves. But if they believed their barrier of shields would stop the beast or turn it aside, they were wrong.

The ram smashed straight on into the midst of them, a hard-cast projectile of solid iron slamming through a wall of twigs, shattering the line, sending the defenders reeling, flying, hurled aside, knocked down, trampled beneath.

In a nightmare instant, four lay writhing or unconscious from being trod upon. A dozen more lay stretched out all around, stunned by the impact. The rest were staggering away, scattered by the force that had blasted through them.

The beast went on, not even slowed by its penetration of the obstacle. It ran up the slope beyond a little way, then began a wide curve that would bring it around for another assault.

Diancecht, unhurt himself, ignored the new threat and moved at once to examine the trampled ones. The others, dispersed and disoriented by the violence of the first onslaught, looked about them helplessly. None had a chance of making a defense against the creature descending like some god of fury upon them once again.

None but one.

Dagda, shield and spear lost in the first impact, moved bare-handed yet boldly into the charging animal's path.

He set himself, crouching, hands up before him, muscles of his massive arms and legs bulging as he tensed for the collision. A grin drew up his mouth and lit his face with real pleasure at this chance for single combat. His eyes glowed with a battle light.

"Come on then, my fine lad!" he called in a challenging voice. "Come try all you have on me!"

It drove in right at him, head down, horns ready to strike. In the instant before it hit, Dagda made a lightning move, shooting both arms out to grip either end of the row of horns.

Planted as he was and leaning forward, the ram first

pushed him before it, his set legs actually plowing into the soft top-sod before the power of the beast's run. Then the big man was forced backward, off his feet. Still hanging on to the horns, Dagda was now dragged, his own legs pulled under its driving hooves.

This lasted only a moment. Realizing Dagda was keeping his tight grip, the ram gave an enraged bellow and tossed its head up with great violence, seeking to cast him off.

Dagda was swung out and upward, body arcing, legs flying up over the beast's head. But as he rose, he agilely twisted around in midair, coming down with a jolt astride the ram's broad back.

Dagda's powerful legs instantly clamped tight about his opponent's body, heels sinking deeply into its sides just behind the still-pumping front legs.

His grip on the horns was cross-armed now, and he took advantage of it, using his strength to begin twisting the beast's head around. His chest swelled with the effort, neck musles stood out like strained hawsers, and sinews popped out in stark ridges from tautly flexed arms.

The ram began to jerk about furiously, its own powerful neck straining as it fought to counter Dagda's hold, its body bucking wildly as it fought to cast him free.

But he hung doggedly on, his leg muscles knotted like corded tree trunks as their vise grew yet tighter.

On the slope below, grim-faced Morrigan hefted her spear and started toward the embattled pair. But Nuada raised a staying hand.

"No," he told her firmly. "Stay back."

"He needs help," she rasped out.

"He wants none," Nuada replied. "You know that. He'd never forgive our interfering."

She nodded, reluctantly holding back.

The others stood motionless, watching, enthralled by amazement. The other rams also only watched, seeming content to let their own champion decide this contest alone.

For a time that contest seemed even. The two beings of such incredible power remained locked together in their duel of strength. Then, at first barely perceptibly, Dagda began to win.

The ram's head—slowly, steadily—was being twisted

over. Driven to frenzy by desperation, the animal began to wheel around. This was a mistake. As its head came around to a downslope position, forced into its awkward posture, the ram lost balance. It began to topple, rolling down onto its side.

Dagda yanked his leg clear of the crushing weight as the beast slammed to the earth. He leaped forward, across its horns.

Quickly he again shifted his hold on the ram's head before it could recover, now throwing his whole weight into keeping the pressure on, twisting the neck farther around, rolling the beast onto its back.

It gave a long, shrill bleat, a sound of pain and fright. Its eyes were bulging in terror. It fought to writhe free. He held on to the head, giving it a sharper twist. The neck came farther around, throwing a massive strain onto the ram's spine. Dagda gave a grim smile of victory.

Diancecht, looking up from his tending of the injured, saw Dagda, saw the battle fire glowing in his face, saw the animal's head strained round, neck close to snapping. One more savage jerk by the big man would do it.

"Dagda! No!" he shouted. "Don't kill it!"

Dagda looked to him in astonishment.

"What? But after all it's done . . ."

"We brought on this challenge," the healer called. "The animal's not at fault. It's merely defending its home. Release it! Let it go!"

"And what am I supposed to do with it then?" Dagda shouted back, keeping the pressure on.

"Think of the isle of birds!" Diancecht said pleadingly. "We're the invaders here. Don't cause any harm!"

The young champion considered this, then nodded in agreement. "If you ask it, I'll try it," he said. "But I hope you're right!"

With that he released his grip on the ram, backing swiftly away and setting himself for a possible new attack.

Instead, the animal merely shook its head, clambered to its feet, and stood motionless. After exchanging a long stare with Dagda, it gave a final snort, turned, and trotted away, back up to its fellows.

They gathered close around it, standing with heads to-

gether for a time as if in a conference. Then, in a body, they
started away. They moved along the valley to where the
flock of sheep waited, herding the other animals ahead, on
down the little stream and out of sight.

Dagda and his company looked after them, somewhat
nonplussed by their abrupt departure.

"So, they're leaving us alone," said Goibniu.

"Convinced, I think, that we mean them no harm," said
Diancecht. "It would seem that the creatures of these islands want nothing more than to live without disturbance."

"We *are* learning about how this land works then, as you
hoped," said Nuada.

"It is learning about us too, I think," the healer said in a
thoughtful way. Then the plight of the trampled ones re-
called him. "Well, that's of no matter now," he said briskly.
"We must do what we can for our companions."

"Back to the ship?" asked Nuada.

"I think not right away. The rams have given us leave to
stay, and these people are badly hurt. The grove is close.
They'll rest more comfortably there. Once I've seen what
can be done for them, we can decide on our next move."

At his direction, the four damaged travelers were gently
raised by their fellows and carried up the last stretch of
slope to the grove.

They found it to be a place of great delights. Bright-
leaved trees arched their branches to form a sparkling canopy above them. The air was sweet and filled with a soft
music of the breezes playing in the treetops.

There were apple trees there, limbs heavy with red fruit;
and venerable, broad-leaved oak trees; and hazels glowing a
rich yellow with their bounty of ripe nuts. The ground below them was as soft as piled furs from its thick blanket of
deep green moss.

They lay the hurt upon the bed of moss and Diancecht
examined them in more detail.

"How are they?" Nuada asked.

The healer shook his head. "Broken bones mostly. Arms
and legs. Some ribs. And I think two are hurt badly inside.
Young Rudrach is coughing blood. The bones I can bind.
The rest . . ." He shook his head again, his expression
grim.

"Do what you can," said Nuada. "We'll stay at least the night." He looked to the others. "We'll gather some wood. We'll build a fire. And why don't some of you collect fruit and nuts?"

"Is that a good idea?" asked Dagda. He looked to Diancecht. "You said not to cause harm."

"I have a feeling that it will be all right," the healer replied. "Try gathering a few to try. But *just* a few."

So they made a camp in the pleasant grove. Diancecht treated the injured with the skills he had. The others built fires, cooked some of their own food, and collected a sampling of the hazelnuts and apples.

No ill came upon those who did the gathering. The curious explorers—only a few of them and only very cautiously at first—tried the foods. They found them both savory and quite invigorating.

Soon the rest were sampling as well.

"It gives me a most definite sense of renewed energy," said Nuada, taking another bite from his plump, rosy-cheeked apple. "Like a warm wave surging through my body."

"Yes!" said a surprised Dagda, munching a handful of hazelnuts. "And it feels as if my weariness and soreness from the fight are being washed away."

"My bruises as well!" said one young woman who had been knocked down in the ram's attack.

Others with minor injuries examined their own marks. Scrapes and bruises were fading away with miraculous speed, taking all pain with them. Soon expressions of good cheer and high spirits filled the camp.

"As I hoped," said the healer, watching his companions and carefully tasting the foods himself. "I had a most strong feeling that our finding such rich harvest here was to be seen as a reward. It's as if our making the right choice won us the freedom to come here, to reap these wondrous foods safely, to suffer no ill effect from our trial. Bring more to me. The others must be fed."

Fruit and nuts were brought to those sorely hurt. The nourishment worked as magically upon them. In moments bones were knitting, wounds were closing, and healthy color was returning to the four. Even the pain-racked Rudrach was soon sitting up and laughing with the rest.

"Most useful medicines," an impressed Nuada said, examining the effects. "It would certainly seem prudent to take a supply of them along." He looked to the healer. "Oh . . . meaning nothing against your own fine healer's skills, Diancecht," he said apologetically. "But . . ."

Diancecht raised a staying hand. "Say nothing more. I understand. Still, I'm not certain taking them is a good idea."

"We've already used them safely," Nuada reasoned. "It must be all right."

"Very well," the healer conceded. "If you wish, why not?" He shrugged. "I'm not certain it matters very much in any case. I will be curious to see."

They stayed a peaceful night through in the grove, soothed to sleep by the lullaby of the gentle winds strumming the treetops. Bright sunlight flickering down through the leaves awoke them, all refreshed.

In exultant mood they strolled back to their ship, carrying food sacks brimming with apples and nuts. When they reached the shore, they noted the flock of sheep with its protecting rams had appeared on the slope above. But the beasts kept their distance, seemingly having only come to watch the visitors depart.

The company climbed aboard the ship, cast off, and once more headed out to sea. Behind them, the sheep stayed visible until they and their island had shrunken out of sight.

"At least *they're* real!" said Dagda. "Not some kind of magic."

"Not these, though," said Nuada, overturning one of the sacks they had filled with apples and hazelnuts.

Only a fine, sandlike powder spilled out to be caught and whisked away by the breeze.

"All that's left of the fruit and nuts," he said with chagrin. "In an instant they just shriveled away to dust before my eyes." He looked to Diancecht. "Obviously we weren't meant to take them away with us after all."

"Fascinating," said the healer, looking at the few remains. "And if my notions are right, I'm afraid it means there is yet more danger ahead for us."

Chapter 5

Storm

"I say that we give over the idea of stopping to explore each new isle we pass," Nuada suggested as the isle of rams was left behind them.

"Why would you say that?" asked Goibniu. "Each one's been wondrous."

"And a fine challenge," added Dagda.

"And we might be missing something of great power or some vast treasure if we don't search every one," added Mathgen.

"But each time we do, we may well be putting ourselves in the way of new risk," Nuada pointed out, mindful of Diancecht's warning. "Unless the place seems to have human habitation, or is large enough to be this Magh Mell of Queen Danu, I say we pass on by. Otherwise we could well take eternity to find our goal."

Before this practical viewpoint, the other young people had no choice but to bow agreement. And the ever-cautious healer also readily assented.

"It may be of little matter anyway," he said rather cryptically.

"You have made that remark before," a puzzled Nuada

commented. "Would you like to explain just what you mean by it?"

"I'm afraid I can't—at least, not entirely," was the reply. "It's only a feeling, and you know I dislike making judgments without fact. Still, I've a strong notion that if we're meant to stop somewhere, events will see to it, no matter what we will."

"No one can control *our* will!" Dagda put in most emphatically.

"Maybe not," Diancecht replied. "But can we be sure of anything else except that it will do us no good to go back?"

At this unsettling question, Dagda and Nuada exchanged a wondering glance.

Yet neither seemed inclined to pursue the idea any further. After all, there seemed little cause at the moment to take the dour man's concerns too seriously. Throughout that day they sailed on across a calm and azure sea that sent them gliding smoothly ahead with its caressing breezes and let them laze and bask under its warm sun. The voyage seemed ever less one of high adventure and ever more one of leisure.

They passed by other isles, each time sailing in close enough to investigate with their eyes. Each one was small, each one seemingly a home for its own, single, and very unique species of animal life.

One isle was occupied by creatures vaguely manlike, but small and covered with fur. They swung about amid the branches of the isle's thick covering of trees on long, lithe, curling tails, and filled the air with constant, shrill chattering. Their unsettlingly human little faces were cunning of expression, and they peered out at those on the slowly passing ship with curious eyes.

"They're most amusing," remarked a young woman, laughing in delight at their antics.

"They're grotesque," Mathgen said in revulsion.

"Something about them *is* bothersome," said Dagda, exchanging a long stare with one larger creature whose massive head, jutting jaw, and small eyes were not unlike his own. "I don't quite know what it is."

"Could they be some degenerated form of man?" Nuada asked Diancecht.

"Or a more advanced one," the healer said, looking at the active beings. "In any case, I think we'd find ourselves the victims of great mischief if we went among them to find out more."

No one argued this. They sailed on.

They passed another island, this one populated by lizardlike creatures of an enormous size. Their grey and smooth-skinned bodies were barrel-shaped, tapering to a pointed tail at one end and a serpentine neck and small head at the other.

Some few crawled on the crescent of gold sand that formed their isle. Here they moved slowly and awkwardly on short, broad, oar-shaped flippers. Most swam and dived in the large bay enclosed by the isle's curved ends. Here the sleek creatures were in their element, strikingly lithe and graceful in movement as they cavorted in the waves.

The creatures showed little interest in the passing ship, but they were easily large enough to sink it if roused to attack. The explorers were most content to stay well clear of them.

Late in that day they passed yet a third small isle. This one was a place of open rolling hills lushly covered with tall grass. Across the green slopes browsed a herd of some three score animals who were, once again, both unique and wonderful to the travelers.

They were horselike, of tall, sleek, lithe, and cleanly muscled body. All were white, with flowing manes and tails that streamed and glinted like streams of molten silver as the creatures moved. In this much, they were impressive-looking but still ordinary creatures. Their claim to uniqueness came from the single, long, tapering horn that protruded from the forehead of each.

In the adults, who were mostly grazing on the tall grass, this horn was longer than a man's forearm, formed in a slender spiral. In the dozen or so spindle-legged colts that gamboled about the elders in play, the horn was yet no more than a round-tipped bud.

"Have you ever seen the like!" said Goibniu.

"Actually, I think I have heard mention of such beasts in my own youth from a very ancient bard," Mathgen replied. "Fabulous creatures from some distant land that had long since died away."

"Except for here," added Dagda.

"Another form of life the wide world sees nothing of," Nuada commented musingly. "Living here, peacefully, safely on its own little piece of land. Diancecht, there can't be any chance to this."

"No," the healer agreed. "Someone has surely brought them here. All creatures of rare kind, I would say, all vanished from the lands we know. Driven from them, or hunted from existence perhaps. Given a sanctuary, a last domain here. And if it is this Queen Danu who brought them, then she is a person of great compassion indeed."

"I hope that it applies to us as well," Nuada said with feeling.

They had swept in closer to the isle as they spoke. Now the grazing animals took note of them. Instantly the strident neigh of a large stallion alerted all the rest.

They reacted swiftly and efficiently to form up a defense. The colts were prodded together by the adults who then made a square about them, shoulder to shoulder, facing out, creating a solid wall that bristled with the spikes of their keen-tipped horns.

"We've alarmed them," said Nuada.

"That would surely be a most deadly barrier to try passing," Dagda said admiringly.

"Very nicely organized," remarked the healer. "They must be quite intelligent."

"Well, we won't disturb them further," Nuada declared. "Let's turn the ship away."

They turned their vessel's bow out from shore, rounded the isle at a greater distance, then once more set their heading toward the west. Morrigan at the masthead and others on the deck kept keen gazes always searching the horizon ahead, hoping for the first sight of the larger land they sought.

But fortune now seemed to turn against them.

Two days more passed by without any sign of land. And on the third day the dawn sun showed a sky dark with grey-black clouds whose swollen bellies hung so low the mast's tip sliced a gash in them.

No more isles. No more sun. The adventurers sailed on through a sea growing rapidly more wild.

"Are we lost now?" Nuada asked. "What was the word that Lir used? 'Astray'? Have we somehow been set astray on some empty portion of this magic sea that has no boundaries?"

Sounds of growing alarm were heard among those of the crew. And the words of a near-panicked Mathgen incited them the more.

"This is why no outsiders survive here!" he cried in a voice grown shrill. "The sea destroys them. We're doomed if we go on!"

"We will not go back," Nuada said forcefully, taking control. "We know what is behind. There is nothing more for us but what's ahead."

They went on. But the winds lifted rapidly about them in hard, sharp voices like wraiths of death keening in their shrouds. A noise like the tramping of many thousands of feet rose up from the sea. Waves heaved up into sheer cliffs at either side, thrusting high in rough-peaked mountains impossible to climb, their steep slopes casting the ship down into the deep valleys between, looming above it, rolling over with foam crests threatening to crash atop it in an avalanche of white water.

A great fear came on the travelers then. The sense of certain doom to which Mathgen had given a voice seized them, wrung their minds and bodies tight.

But Nuada, refusing to let the terror win, spoke to them, shouting out across the screaming of the wind and the crashing of the waves so they could hear his rousing words: "Don't let yourselves be defeated now, my comrades. We've come too far together, meeting the eye of death. We must be brave again. Stand with me. Fight!"

His defiant words gave them new heart. They moved to the task, following his commands.

The sail, already much tattered by the winds, was drawn in and tied. The oars were thrust out, powerful Dagda leading the other rowers in rhythmic, powerful thrusts into the waves, slowly, slowly pulling the ship's stern around and into the snapping, keen teeth of the tempest. After that, they rode more easily, coasting on the mountain slopes of waves, running ahead of the blasting wind at an incredible speed.

Throughout that stormy day and a tumultuous, black night they labored to row, to bail, to keep the ship afloat and before the wind.

As a new dawn came, barely lighter than the night, it revealed only dimly a crew near to exhaustion. The darkness also hid from even Morrigan's piercing gaze the presence of another isle lying dead ahead until they were nearly upon it.

When her cry of warning did come, Nuada brought the tiller hard around while the rowers, regalvanized by the new danger, pulled frantically to turn their craft.

It was too late.

The driving wind cast them straight forward. Like a hurled javelin, they flew toward the stony shore, the wood hull splintering as it scraped up across the sharp rocks of the beach, and came jarring to a halt, run fully aground.

The violent jolt of its stopping cast all the travelers to their vessel's deck. Stunned by the impact, drained by their struggle, they lay there for some while, recovering wits and strength. Meanwhile the storm—as if its only intent had been to accomplish the task of grounding the ship—began swiftly and suddenly to die away.

The winds faded. The sea grew still. The heavy overcast remained, leaving the world suddenly one of a vast, ponderous stillness, where even the becalmed ocean seemed motionless.

The first sounds and signs of renewed movement came from the recovering travelers.

Dagda was first to regain his senses and his feet. The others soon followed, but rising slowly, stiffly, favoring their bruised bodies and aching muscles. They clambered from their vessel to inspect its damage and their new locale.

The ship was seriously disabled. In many points the heavy planks of its bottom were staved in by the jagged points of the stony shore.

"Can we fix it?" Nuada asked of Goibniu.

The little smith in turn looked to a lithe young man of angular feature. "Luchtine, you are the master carpenter," he said. "What do you say?"

"If we have proper lumber and some time," the other replied optimistically, "there's nothing that can't be done."

"Proper lumber," repeated Nuada. He and the rest looked around them. The shore upon which they'd grounded was a narrow and most barren strip of rock. Beyond it, grey cliffs rose in a sheer wall, stark and forbidding.

"It seems we'll have to go up there and have a look," Nuada said. "I hope the rest of this place isn't so barren as here."

"Wait!" rasped Morrigan, who had moved away from the rest to stare fixedly up the shore. "There's something else there." She lifted a lean arm to point. "Maybe a ship."

They peered through the greyness that still lay thickly upon the day to spy a vague form that certainly seemed shaped like a vessel's prow.

The group eagerly started toward it, but Nuada's words called them back: "Hold on. Let's not all rush there headlong. Remember, we've no idea what dangers could lurk here. We must take care."

He had them fetch their weapons from the ship. Half were assigned to keep watch about their own craft while he and the rest moved up the shore in a tight defensive ring.

As the investigating party drew near, the object, and its true nature became clear, their expectations dwindled rapidly away. Though it was indeed the bow section of a vessel, it was the only intact fragment of a shattered craft.

It had been a massive ship, judging by the arch of bow soaring up over twice their own height. The few remaining ribs and keel and stays of its long hull lay stretched out along the rocks like the bones of one of the largest of the whales they had seen.

"It's been here some years, I'd judge," said Diancecht, looking over the wreckage.

"Yes," said a chagrined Luchtine. "Too long for any of it to be of use to us. Not even this bow." He gave a light punch at the planking of the intact section. It crumbled away. "See there? Rotted to dust."

"I think there are others," said Morrigan, again pointing along the beach. "Up there."

They followed her farther, discovering quickly that she once more spoke the truth. The remains of what seemed to be several ships were scattered on the rocks. So old, so broken by the elements, so tangled were the skeletons of the wrecks that their exact numbers were impossible to determine.

"Lir spoke the truth when he said other outsiders had penetrated the barrier of fog," said Diancecht.

"Looks like they all ended up here," said Nuada, kicking at the decaying remnant of a broken mast. "I wonder what happened to their crews?"

"I've a feeling that, one way or another, we're going to find out," said Dagda.

They moved on, past yet more ship remains. Then, beyond a spur of rock, they came abruptly upon a craft that seemed intact.

They stopped as it moved into view, and stared in surprise. This vessel was a most unusual one in many ways.

Its long, slender, and sleek hull seemed made of metal, not of wood, striped irregularly with wide patches of grey and streamers of red-brown. It had an odd superstructure upon its deck near to the stern that was shaped like a stepsided pyramid. Other than that, the craft was featureless. It was also devoid of any visible means of propulsion. There were no signs of masts, no holes or locks for oars.

It lay among the rocks, its hull dented in places, but apparently intact. They approached it warily.

"Be very careful, everyone," Nuada warned. "We've seen a ship like this before. It belongs to no friend."

"No!" said Dagda. "It's like the one that we pursued toward that strange tower of ice. Its people are allies of the Fomor."

They reached its side. Luchtine, Goibniu, and Diancecht began a close inspection of the hull's structure. Nuada and the others made a tour around the craft. Lithe Morrigan, bolder than the rest, managed to leap high enough to grasp the bulwark's edge and haul herself effortlessly onto the deck.

"The hull's formed of large separate plates," said Goibniu, examining a joining in the metal. "Somehow they're forged together, fastened by these rivets." He touched a row of studs that lined the joint, then looked along the sweeping stretch of hull with awe. "What skills in metal the makers must have had!"

"It looks unholed," said Diancecht. "Could we use it?"

Goibniu shook his head. He took up a loose stone and slammed it into one of the red-brown spots. It cracked through, causing the surface to break into rough-edged chunks.

"Rusted away," he said sadly. "All those red streaks are metal as rotted as the wood on the other ships. Shift this hull and it'll break into tiny pieces. Too bad."

Meanwhile, having reached the rear of the ship, Nuada and his group were making a discovery of their own.

The curved stern of the ship was wedged high upon a vee of rocks, lifted clear of the shore and fully exposed. From its base thrust a round shaft of metal as thick as Dagda's wrist, and to its end a peculiar device was fixed.

"It's like the paddle ends of four metal oars all fixed to the single handle," Dagda suggested, examining the thing closely.

"Or like the shape of a clover with four leaves on its stem," a young woman suggested.

"Yes, but with the leaves each twisted a bit from the flat," added Nuada. "Still, I think Dagda's description comes closer to the purpose of the thing. Could it be what pushed the ship along, its four blades driving through the water?"

"How?" asked Dagda.

"By this shaft being spun."

"How?" the big man asked again.

"How would I know that?" the other said with some exasperation. "Maybe some crew within the ship's belly turned it. It might be useful to look there."

A sharp caw from above brought all their attentions upward. There, looking over the bulwark at the ship's stern, was wild-haired Morrigan.

"You must come up," she said brusquely. "Everyone stand back."

They stepped away from the stern as she lifted something high and tossed it over the bulwark. A coil of thick hawser fell, unrolling, snaking down the side. Nuada looked it over carefully. It was old and weathered but still strong enough to hold the weight of several men. Without hesitation he took a grip and began shinning upward. Next Dagda and then the rest began to follow him.

He climbed over a rail onto the ship's deck. Here it was no more than a narrow walkway just behind the odd pyramid. Morrigan waited for Dagda to reach the deck and then started briskly off, leaving the others to catch up.

She led the way around the structure to a narrow stairway at its front. This took them up to the second level of the pyramid, a platform with its own metal rail, now half-rusted away. Here they found the only feature to break the structure's smooth, bare sides: an oval opening to the black void of the ship's interior. The oval, metal door that was meant to seal it was thrown back on massive hinges.

"I found it closed," she rapped out in her harsh voice. "I managed to open it. Look inside."

Nuada stepped up to the doorway, peering into the dim interior, waiting for his eyesight to adjust. When it did, he recoiled in alarm, his hand going to his sword hilt.

A strange man stood in the darkness, grimacing at him.

Chapter 6

Cats

"Be easy," Morrigan said, moving up beside Nuada. "That one's long dead."

He realized then that she was right. The figure facing him was a mummy, skin dried and withered into a fine network of lines, jaw and cheekbones jutting sharply, clouded eyes bulging, lips drawn back from yellow teeth.

The man stood behind an immense wheel affixed to a post thrusting up from the deck. It was like a slender, spoked wagon wheel, but one made entirely of metal. In diameter it was nearly as large as a man's height, and Nuada saw that the dead man was erect only because he had been lashed there.

Nuada moved forward into the room. The air within the long-enclosed space was very cool and dry, but very stale. Even the open door could do little to alleviate the smell.

"I think being closed in here kept the body from decay," Morrigan said in her death rattle of a voice, most appropriate in the present situation.

She and Dagda moved in after Nuada, the immense warrior squeezing a bit to get through the narrow opening. They stepped close to examine the dead man.

He was clad in an outfit unusual to these travelers of

simple, homespun dress. He wore a form-fitting suit of trousers and tunic, both of a tightly woven fabric with a faintly silvery sheen. High boots and belt of glossy black completed the outfit.

He was strapped spreadeagled to the big wheel, his wrists tied with cord to the far outer rim at either side. His shriveled, bony hands still clutched the metal tightly. His forehead leaned forward against the wheel's upper curve. A deep dent across the skull there was clear evidence of what had brought his death.

"I'd say this thing steers the ship," Nuada said, touching the wheel. "They must have been caught in a great storm as we were. Likely this man was lashed here to keep him at his fight to control the course. He lost the fight. His ship was cast up here. The collision rammed his head against the rim with great force. Most probably he died at once."

"Then maybe he was a lucky one," Morrigan said.

A curious Dagda tugged tentatively at the wheel. It moved only slightly, but even that was too much for the mummy. The body, dried to fragile sticks, crumbled apart, falling to the deck in a broken jumble of bones and tissue held together loosely by the clothes, leaving behind the two hands still in a death clasp on the wheel.

Acrid dust puffed up from the form as it collapsed, causing the three invaders of the makeshift tomb to recoil, coughing, exclaiming in disgust.

They turned their attention to the room around them. Its walls were thickly mounted with an array of devices: round circles of metal and glass that seemed painted or etched with strange designs; ranks of shiny objects like large jewels of red, blue, white, and yellow; sticks and knobs and handles, many hinged or set in slots as if meant to move. But whether these things had a function or were only someone's idea of decoration, the investigators did not know.

"What is all this?" asked Dagda, awed by the bewildering display.

"Well, Diancecht could make better judgments than I," said Nuada. "But it's my own guess they have to do with making this vessel work, a thing we likely can't begin to understand."

Dagda, still acting like an inquisitive pup, put a hand out toward a row of knobs.

"Hold it!" Nuada said sharply. "Anything here could be very dangerous. I say we touch none of it."

Dagda looked disappointed, but nodded agreement. "I suppose you're right."

"There is a ladder," said Morrigan. "Back there."

They looked into a back corner. A round hole in the deck revealed a metal ladder leading down. It descended only a few rungs before vanishing into complete blackness. An odd, strong, cloying smell wafted up from the depths below.

"It'd be foolish to blunder around down there in the dark," Nuada declared. "Let's get back out into the light."

His companions made no argument, and they hastened to leave the confines of the room for the relative cheeriness of the overcast day outside.

The others of their party waited there, and together they searched the rest of the vessel's deck thoroughly, finding nothing more of interest. They left the ship, sliding back down the cable to the rocky beach. Here they found Diancecht deep in conversation with Goibniu and Luchtine.

"Anything?" the healer asked.

"One long-dead man," Nuada reported. "And a great many unknown things that might once have made this vessel sail. But I don't think even your knowledge could reveal their workings to us."

"It doesn't matter," said Goibniu. "This ship will never move again. We've been all about its hull. It's half-rusted away."

"Somehow I'm not surprised," said Nuada. He looked up the cliff face looming above the shore. "That leaves us only what's up there. Hopefully we'll find some trees that we can use for repairs. Maybe even human life."

"Yes," said Goibniu. "No judging from here what might be atop there. Why, this could even be that Queen Danu's island itself!"

"It might be," said Diancecht very guardedly, "but I've a definite feeling that it is not."

Dagda heaved the grappling hook upward with all the power of his massive arm.

The huge metal claw had been fashioned from an intact section of the metal ship's rail reshaped by Goibniu's skilled hands. Both strong and light, it soared toward the crest of the cliff as if it were no more than a cast pebble. It drew behind it a length of line also scavenged from the rusting ship.

The hook shot up past the clifftop, arched, then dropped back, landing out of sight beyond the ragged edge. Dagda gave a soft tug on the line, and then a harder one. The hook stayed caught somewhere above.

"I'll go first then," said Morrigan. "I'm lightest. I'll see that the hook's well set."

She slung her round shield over her shoulder, grasped the line, then climbed swiftly and agilely upward.

She vanished over the top and was out of sight for a few moments before her bushy-haired head popped back into view and a lean arm waved down to them that all was well.

Dagda went next. As he hauled his great form up the line, Nuada turned to address the others gathered about.

"You all should stay close to our ship," he advised. "Keep up a careful watch. We still don't know just what might happen here."

"And you be careful as well," Diancecht admonished him. "I'm certain now that nothing that happens to us here is by chance. Remember Lir's words. Think about everything you do."

"I always try to do that," Nuada assured him. "Goodbye, my friends. We'll return as soon as we can."

Dagda had by this time reached the top, and Nuada followed, shinning briskly up the line. He came over the edge to find Dagda and Morrigan crouching defensively, shields up, swords out, guarding their toehold on the clifftop as they waited for him.

He unslung his shield, drew his own sword, and joined them in a scrutiny of the new territory ahead.

A narrow rim of open, rocky ground ran right along the edge of the cliff. Beyond it rose a forest that had clearly been a place of majestic trees once—a mix of great oaks, out-spreading yews, soaring pines—but now had something most strange about its look.

Many of the standing trees were completely dead, thrusting bared limbs starkly up toward the overcast sky. Some others had fallen, leaving gaps in what had been a densely populated wood. Even those trees still alive were stricken. The leaves of oaks and yews were sparse, greyish-yellow. The fir trees' bristles were no longer evergreen but a dry, brittle-looking brown.

"This forest," said Dagda, "it seems . . . ill."

His attempt to give a word to his impression was accepted readily by Nuada: "Yes. In this season it should be lush, the foliage abundant. Instead, it's blighted. As if the frosty touch of autumn were upon it."

"Worse," croaked Morrigan. "The ice hand of winter's death."

"Not the paradise of this Queen Danu, I'd say," said Dagda, disappointed.

"Likely not," said Nuada. "Still, there's nothing for us to do but make a search of it. Maybe one of those trees is yet healthy enough to give us the strong wood Luchtine needs."

He turned back to the cliff edge and waved down to those below. Goibniu at once tied their casting spears onto the line and Nuada hauled it up.

Each sheathed sword and took a spear. Dagda detached the grapple, coiled its line, and threw the coil over one arm in case it should be needed. Thus prepared, they left the cliff edge and moved boldly into the trees.

They made their way forward slowly, blazing their path through a maze created by the many dead trees fallen this way and that. As they went, they became aware of another factor contributing to the eerie atmosphere of the place: its unusual stillness.

Dagda made mention of it first.

"Strange it is," he said. "This place should be full of life. But I've heard no bird calls from the trees or seen the sign of a single creature in the underbrush."

"How is that possible?" asked Nuada.

"I know," said Morrigan, she of the beast's and the hunter's keen senses. "Look here." With a spear tip she pointed out the decayed and almost invisible remains of a small furry animal lying beneath a bush. "And there." She moved the tip to indicate the bones of a bird at a tree's base not far away.

"I've been seeing the dead since we entered the forest," she said grimly. "Hundreds . . . thousands there must be, scattered everywhere. No natural predator it was who killed so many and just left them to rot. No. Something has wiped out all the creatures here."

"Pestilence?" asked Nuada. "Drought?"

"Or poison," she added most darkly.

"I like the feel of this place less and less," said Dagda, looking around him uneasily.

"Let's find our tree and be away from here as soon as we can," said Nuada.

They picked up their pace through the woods, scanning around them for proper trees as they went. At last they came into a large clearing where a vast, ancient oak towered upward, lifting still lush and green foliage to the sky.

"Well, here's one tree at least that should give us good, healthy lumber," said Nuada.

"It also seems the only tree still winning the battle to keep its life," Morrigan pointed out. "A fine tree. A proud tree. A tree of many ages' growth."

"We have no choice," Nuada said.

"This is not our land!" she returned with force. "We've no right to violate any of its life."

"I know what you feel," he returned. "I've no liking for this either. But if we don't take this tree, we may find ourselves trapped forever in this dying place."

"Then let us *be* trapped," she said adamantly. "How dare we claim our lives to be more valuable than this oak's? If the tree has to fight to survive, then so should we."

"There is a sense to what she says," Dagda put in. "Nuada, you know that she, more than any of us, understands how valuable life is. For us to needlessly cause damage, pain, death . . ."

"I know," said Nuada. "I understand. I feel a sympathy too. But we can't make this decision ourselves. To stay here for the sake of a single tree might be condemning everyone!"

"He's right too," Dagda said to the raven-haired woman, clearly perplexed, his big face drawn into a frown.

"We must go back to the others," Nuada said reasoningly. "We have to tell them what we found, discuss the . . ."

He broke off as a roaring sound came to them. They looked toward it. But then, from other points around them, there came answering roars—two, three, several, joining to roll through the forest in a single thunder.

"Well," said Dagda, "so there is *something* else alive out there."

"Many somethings," corrected Morrigan. "We are surrounded."

Forms moved suddenly into view amid the trees on all sides. They rushed in, converging on the oak in the clearing. The three caught first fleeting glimpses of the beings as they flickered between the trunks: beasts like cats, but much larger than men, rushing forward with long, lithe strides.

There was no open avenue for escape. At least none but one.

"Up!" cried Nuada. "Up the tree!"

They sprang for tree branches arching just above, and hauled themselves up quickly. Clambering higher, well clear of the ground, they then set themselves on three sides of the tree, lifting spears and shields in defense.

The cats came bounding into the clearing and surrounded the trunk. But they made no move to climb it. Instead, they turned and for a time prowled about it in an evenly spaced circle, snarling and growling. Then they stopped, sat back on their haunches, and lifted heads to stare up into the tree.

The three above got a close look at them. There were fifteen of the beasts. They were short-haired, tawny-coated felines with massive heads, bright green eyes, and long tearing fangs curving down from their upper jaws. The teeth said clearly: carnivore.

"You can't escape us," said a low, growly, but still quite clear voice.

It came from the largest of the beasts, an animal sporting a great, shaggy mane.

The three exchanged wondering looks.

"You speak?" asked Nuada.

"Certainly we do," the beast replied. "And you are trapped."

"You are only fifteen," said Dagda. "We could fight our way through you."

"You would lose," the cat replied with certainty. "We are most ferocious beings and most desperate ones. Hunger has made us so."

Their appearance gave testimony to that. All were painfully gaunt, ribs clearly visible, bellies drawn tight.

"If you mean to make an attack on us, you will not find it easy," said Nuada, hefting his spear meaningfully.

"If we want to kill you, we do not have to attack," the cat told him. "We have only to wait here. Soon enough your wasted forms will drop from the tree, fluttering down to us like dried fall leaves."

"Surely there'll be little meat left upon our bones by that time," Nuada said. "Too little food to make your long wait worthwhile."

"That is true," the cat agreed. "No gain for any of us. But let's make an arrangement between us, then. Isn't it a fat food sack that's slung about each one of you? Give what you have to us, and we'll promise to let you go."

"We do have victuals," Nuada admitted. "Three days supply apiece. Though, it'd be little more than a mouthful for each one of you."

"More than we're likely to get from you any other way," said the cat. "Give it, and go away from here in peace."

Nuada looked to his friends. "Can they be trusted?"

"Once they have our food, they'll gain little staying about to see us starve," Dagda said.

"I get no sense of their natures," said Morrigan. "They are most strange animals. Still, what have we to lose?"

Nuada agreed. The three opened their packs and dropped their food—hard loaves of bread, salted meats, and dried fruits—onto the ground below.

The beasts moved in carefully, lifted the pieces in their jaws, and moved away. The three watched warily for any hostile signs from them, weapons ready to strike. But the cats took the food off to the very edge of the clearing and gathered there to eat, dividing the food evenly among themselves under the big cat's direction.

Seeing the animals absorbed in this, the three climbed cautiously from the tree. The beasts glanced around to see them, but made no approach.

"You've nothing to fear," the big cat said to them after swallowing down the last of a haunch of pork. "Our word is good. We really had no wish to threaten you at all. But times, as you no doubt see, are very hard. Once, the game would have been most abundant for our needs. Then we would have let men pass unchallenged."

"What happened?" asked Morrigan. "What changed the forest to this?"

A second of the cats spoke up for the first time, this one in a voice that was also gruff, but lighter, gentler than that of the big cat.

"The giants it was who did this. They, like others, were driven here by a storm, even their vast ship vanquished by its fierceness, smashed to pieces, the fragments thrown up on the rocks."

"We saw the ship," said Nuada.

"Most crews are lost in such shipwrecks, but the giants were very strong. Three of the crew survived."

"All of *our* crew was saved," Dagda put in with a note of pride. "Thirty men and women. And our ship was *not* destroyed."

"Indeed," put in a third cat of shaggy, greying mane and rumbling voice. "Then you are people of great good fortune indeed."

"Good fortune, and courage, and strength, and just a bit of skill," Nuada said modestly. "But what did these giants do?"

"They searched inland, like you," the softer-voiced cat explained with great sorrow coming into its tone. "They explored. They found a metal, a most precious one to them. Their years of gathering it have ravaged the whole isle."

"The metal must be dug out of the earth," the biggest cat put in. "It must be melted, worked, refined to a pure form. The process blackens the sky, poisons the land and water. Slowly but steadily all the life has died away. Now only some few strongest trees and ourselves still survive. We are the last. But even we will die soon. And you'll die too if you stay."

"Can't you fight?" asked Dagda. "Can't you stop this ravaging?"

The big cat shook its head. "That we cannot do. They are too strong. So, take my warning: If your ship survived, leave this doomed place. Sail away from it as quickly as you can."

"We have some repairs to make," Nuada said. "But once that's done, we could take you away with us as well."

"We will not leave," the cat returned. "This is our isle. Its life is our own. We will stay here and die with it. Goodbye to you. Escape while you still can."

With that, the cats rose and slipped away swiftly, silently, vanishing in an instant into the trees.

For a moment the three stood looking after them. Then Dagda turned to look at his two friends.

"Are you two thinking what I am?" he asked.

Morrigan nodded.

"Time for some foolhardiness again," Nuada said.

Chapter 7

Wasteland

"And so I say that we can't simply sail away and let these creatures die," argued Nuada in conclusion.

He addressed the others of his group. They were gathered around a large bonfire on the beach beside their ship. It had been past nightfall when the three explorers returned to find their comrades at supper. After joining them in a restoring meal, the three spun out their tale.

The rest had listened raptly, without interruption. But now Diancecht spoke.

"You are so certain that these . . . these catlike beings are going to perish?"

"Judging by what we saw, I am surprised these last few have survived so long," Nuada replied. "They must be at the very end of their resources."

"They will die," added Morrigan in her ominous, rasping voice. "Not long after them the last of the trees will die. Then this isle will be a wholly dead and ugly place."

"It's not a great beauty to see now," said Goibniu, gazing around at the wreckage-strewn rocks and brooding cliffs, then up to an overcast sky where lightning flicked fitfully to reveal the thick, black rolls of clouds.

"I say it's total folly to risk ourselves for these beasts," said Mathgen vehemently. "We've got the means to fix the ship. Let's make use of them. Patch it up and sail away!"

"These are not just beasts," Nuada said. "They spoke. They must be very intelligent and very rare as well."

"True enough," the healer agreed. "It would be a great shame to let them just die."

"That is not our concern!" Mathgen shot back. "Look, they're content to stay and die here, aren't they? They refused to let you save them, didn't they? So why should we take a chance that we might be destroyed? Nuada, you said yourself that we shouldn't take more risks. You said we should sail on, find Danu's isle."

"He's speaking some truth there," said one of the other men.

"I know what I said," retorted Nuada sharply. "But I meant taking risks for no reason. We're here now, by no choosing of our own, and we've been given a reason."

"Have we?" challenged one of the women. "Is it truly a good enough one? I thought we'd come seeking a new home."

"We also came to find new challenges," Dagda told her. "How can we turn away from this one? To let these giants destroy an entire isle just for the sake of some precious metal."

"Precious metal?" Mathgen said, his ire replaced by a new interest. "You didn't tell us it was something valuable they mined."

"I say we can turn away from this quite easily, if it can destroy us," said another of the men. "Maybe Mathgen's right, that saving these animals is less our concern than saving ourselves."

"Now, wait. Wait," Mathgen said quickly, an avaricious light awakened in his eyes. "Let's not be hasty. There is something to be said for helping our fellow beings and stopping these rapacious brutes. Uh . . . assuming the risk isn't too considerable, that is."

"Just three giants?" said Dagda, giving a contemptuous snort. "Against thirty good warriors such as ourselves? Why, I'd welcome a chance to take on one alone!"

"It's still not an easy choice, Nuada," said Luchtine

more reasonably, trying to intercede between the disputing groups. "It's hard to know what to do."

"*I* know," said Morrigan.

She rose, casting a coldly glittering black gaze around her at the group. Her sharp and strident voice jabbed out at them: "I know what it is to see what you love poisoned, perverted into some monstrous thing, destroyed! And all of you should know what it is to see a blight lay waste, as the Fomor plague did to so many of our people in the Blessed Isle. Didn't the sight of your families dying in pain sear your eyes? How can you let some other foulness, some other evil, wipe away more life—any life—for its own selfish gain? Well, whether or not you go, I mean to stay. But *if* you go, you deserve no Land of Promise, no better fate than these poor creatures you'll abandon here!"

The massive form of Dagda rose and moved up beside that of the slender woman.

"I stay as well," the big warrior announced. "My heart is one with my wi—with Morrigan. These beings need champions."

"Of course," said Mathgen. "Our great fighting bull would go blindly into battle against any odds." He looked around him at the rest. "Personally, I'd like just a bit more assurance of victory first. Can we so casually challenge a force whose powers or defenses we know nothing about? We could well have no chance."

"We'll not go against them blindly," said Nuada. "We'll spy them out and find some way to deal with them. We've dealt with greater challenges before."

"Yes, and usually lost hundreds of our people in doing so," Mathgen said nastily. "I'd feel much better if I knew our weapons would have an effect on them."

"Then perhaps *this* could be of help," said Diancecht, lifting a long, blanket-wrapped object from the ground beside him. "If I can discover exactly how it works."

He unwrapped the object and held it up. Nuada and the rest examined it curiously. It was a slender, spearlike thing, its haft of a smooth, dull grey metal and as thick as a man's wrist. In a socket at one end was set what seemed to be a large, faceted jewel shaped in a teardrop. It glowed with a soft, blue-white light as if illuminated from within.

"Where did you get it?" Nuada asked.

"In the bowels of that metal ship," the healer explained. "Goibniu and I went down into it with torches to explore."

Nuada shook his head. "Dangerous. Very dangerous." Then he smiled. "But I should have known that that insatiable curiosity of yours would draw you to do it. What was it like there?"

"Filled with vast, hulking things it was," put in Goibniu with great gusto. "Very sinister-looking to me, but very interesting. The healer and I think they were some kind of means for moving the ship. We found other dead men too."

"Yes," said Diancecht. "Half a dozen more, scattered about the interior. Apparently also killed in the wreck and preserved as the first one was. Quite fascinating. One chamber was a storage room with some little of its contents left. Some pieces of those strange clothes the crew wore . . ."

"I've one bit of that!" proclaimed the smith, lifting arms to display the smooth-textured, grey tunic he now wore. "My own top wasn't much more'n rags."

". . . a few helmets . . ." the healer continued.

"Got one of those too!" said the smith, holding up a rounded helmet of a black metal with a long, flared back piece to protect the wearer's neck. "Well made, practical, very light and yet very, very strong. I'd give my hammer arm to know what metal it's made from."

". . . and four of these," the healer finally concluded, patting the spearlike object across his lap.

"A greater wonder yet," said Goibniu. "That jewel thing has gone dark in all the others. But this one still had a glow to it."

The blue-white luminescence from the faceted teardrop was indeed intriguing to all. Dagda stepped forward, especially taken, like a babe with a bright toy.

"It clearly has some kind of energy within," said Diancecht. "You see these devices?" he asked, pointing to a row of marks and bumps on a slightly raised band about the center of the long shaft. "I think these might control it."

"What is it?" asked Dagda, putting out a finger to the glowing tip.

"Don't!" cried the healer, moving to jerk the thing away. Too late.

The finger touched. There was a flash like a small lightning bolt as power leaped from the jewel, shot up Dagda's arm in a crackling snake of light, and exploded into a network of fine lines, enveloping him in a flaring, blue-white net.

The burst of energy lifted his huge form and flung it backward for a half-dozen paces. He crashed down upon his back. The web of light played over him an instant longer, then flickered out.

He lay for a moment with clothes smoking and scorched, stunned but still alive. Then he sat up, shaking his head, and stared about him in bewilderment.

Diancecht stepped up and looked down at him, exasperation tightening his usually emotionless face.

"It's a weapon!" he said tersely to the big man.

"Are you all right?" asked Nuada with greater concern as he and Morrigan moved to help their friend up.

"Seared at the edges," Dagda replied, slapping at a still-smoldering spot on his sleeve.

"Dagda, sometimes you do let that body of yours act without its brain," the healer said with uncharacteristic heat. "It's only lucky that you're ox-sized and that the power this thing contained was nearly gone." He looked at the jewel, turned to a lightless, dark grey stone. "Ah, well, it's *all* gone now, curse the luck. We'll never know *what* it might have done." He tossed the useless object down.

"How about some sympathy for me?" asked Dagda, taking up a waterskin to sluice down a smoking shirt hem.

"For being a fool?" the still-vexed healer shot back. "For destroying something that might have been useful? Just you be grateful it didn't blast you to a smoking lump, as it was likely meant to do."

"I'm sorry," Dagda said contritely. "You know I didn't mean harm."

Diancecht relented, his usual logic and his basic fondness for the man taking charge again. "Yes, yes, I know. And I'm sorry you were hurt. I should have given more warning. But let it be a lesson—to all of us. Assume that anything we find here can be most dangerous."

"Well, miraculous weapons or not," said Nuada, recalling them to the central matter at hand, "I say we must go and see if anything can be done to stop these giants." He looked around him at the rest. "But I'll make no demands on any of you. Anyone who wishes can stay behind."

The others appealed to Diancecht. "What do you think?" Luchtine asked him.

"I've said before that I think some power or some fate has had a hand in what's happened to us," he slowly, thoughtfully replied. "I say we've been brought here. I feel this opportunity to give help has been purposely offered to us. It's my belief—though based on no real facts—that we cannot ignore it."

There were general noises of agreement from those in the gathering at this assessment.

"I'll go," said one, raising a hand. "And I," said another, and then the rest swiftly began to volunteer.

Mathgen, the last holdout, looked around him, then lifted his own hand.

"I'll not be left alone here," he said. "I'll go too. After all, there is precious met . . . I mean, precious life to consider."

"Grand!" said Nuada with pleasure and pride. "I knew you'd choose to help. We go at dawn!"

In fact, before the overcast sun had risen far enough to illuminate the dying forest, the adventurers were already entering the clearing surrounding the ancient oak tree.

They drew up about the massive trunk in a defensive ring, searching about warily, weapons ready. Nothing could be seen moving in the tangled shadows of the dying forest stretching away on all sides. No sound broke the vast and heavy stillness save their own tense breathing.

"No sign of the cats," said Nuada. "We'll need them to guide us."

"I'll bring them," said Morrigan.

She dropped back her head and gave voice to a loud, throaty roar, in exact mimicry of the cry the cats had given the day before. It echoed away through the silence.

They waited, listening. In moments a roar came in return, quickly joined by a chorus of others. Soon afterward the sinewy shapes of the big cats could be seen approaching through the trees.

The creatures pulled up at the edge of the clearing, forming a tight bunch, staring keenly, guardedly across to the human band.

"Why did you come again in such a force?" the big cat growled. "What do you mean to do?"

"Only to help," Nuada assured them. "To stop the ones who are destroying your isle."

"What, the few of you?" The cat gave a derisive snort. "They are too strong for you."

"That doesn't sound promising," Mathgen observed.

"We have much greater strength than you might think," Dagda told the being. "We wish at least to see if we can help."

"Yes," said Morrigan. "Show us where these giants are."

"Why should you do this?" the cat asked, still suspicious. "I told you that you did not need to risk yourselves."

"We understand that," Nuada said. "We still wish to do it. We have all decided."

"Indeed?" said the cat, great surprise evident in its gruff tone. It turned to the others and they conferred together for a few moments in low growls. Then the big cat turned back to them.

"We are most amazed by your willingness to help. We would question this seeming unselfishness from such as yourselves, but you can well see that there's nothing to be lost by us in letting you make the attempt. We will lead you to where the giants live. But the way is very deadly, and the task you face is great. It's quite likely that none of you will survive."

"That we will see," said Nuada. "We have made our choice. We have vowed to help. You'll find we are a people who do not go back on our vows easily. Please, lead on."

So, with the pride of catlike beings moving ahead of them, the party of would-be saviors traveled inland.

The woods about them grew ever more grotesque as they went. The numbers of dying trees increased from some to most to nearly all. The numbers of dead trees increased as well, more and more fallen, or canted over in death throes, or thrusting up starkly, skeletally against the sullen sky.

And that sky, too, became ever more unpleasant in appearance as they progressed. From a general, boiling sea of overcast, it changed to even thicker, rolling masses, like distinct, consecutive, and definitely curving ridges of grey-black waves.

They entered an area where only sparsely scattered trees still struggled for a grim, yellow-grey semblance of life. Here each footfall raised a puff of pale grey dust that hung in the still air. As one of the company brushed by the branches of a dead evergreen, a massive cloud of the same dust billowed up from its dried bristles.

On noting that, Dagda swatted at a nearby bush. More of the dust arose from the surfaces of its dead leaves, wafting into his face and up his nose. He snorted and then gave a tremendous sneeze.

Startled by the noise, the cats looked around.

"Careful," the big cat warned. "Don't stir up more of that than you must. It comes from the giants. It's created by their work. It settles down and covers all in its thick coat. It slowly smothers and finally it kills. Breathe in too much of it, and you'll die too."

"Then just how *do* we breathe?" asked Mathgen.

"As little as possible," said the cat. "That's what we've learned to do. And it will get worse. I said the way was dangerous. Do you wish to go on?"

"Dust won't turn us back," said Nuada. He looked to the others. "Tear strips from your clothes," he said. "Tie them across your mouths and noses. That should keep it out."

"A most sound idea," Diancecht endorsed.

The adventurers followed his advice, and soon the masked band was again moving on in the cats' wake.

Once more the nature of the forest changed. They had finally reached a territory where no living thing survived. Ahead of them now were only the remains of trees long dead. Their sorry corpses had been stripped of all leaves and needles and bark, and even of branches. Worse, the tops of most of them had been roughly whittled down as if ravaged by fire or eaten by rot.

On entering this section, the cats stopped, turning to those who followed.

"From this point I cannot let the others of my clan go on," the big cat told the humans. "I will not risk them in the more deadly things ahead. But if you still wish to continue, then I will still lead you."

"We're ready," Nuada told him doggedly.

"*You're* ready, you mean!" Mathgen muttered to himself. "I'm not at all sure how much *I* want to go on with this."

The other cats drew up in a line as the humans moved past, following their leader. They sat watching as the adventurers trudged determinedly ahead.

As the band plunged yet deeper into the forest of death, Nuada and his companions found it growing darker with each step. The clouds above were growing thicker, lower, until the company walked in a twilight gloom. The coating of dust was turning from grey to a black, blanketing everything like a death shroud. Even the skin and clothes of the explorers were becoming coated with it, leaving only the red-rimmed whites of their eyes to stand out strikingly, eerily, like the eyes of some night wraith.

They came upon the banks of a small stream. Its bed may have carried clear, sparkling water once, but now it was a channel for a thick, grey-green sludge adding its acrid stench to the already befouled air.

The curious Dagda leaned down over it, stretching out a finger toward its viscous, oozing surface.

"Don't touch it," warned the cat. It kicked the decayed remnant of a log over the bank. The piece fell upon the surface and began to smoke instantly. Its remaining wood crumbled away and sank into the stuff.

"Very deadly," the creature explained. "It comes down from the lake where the giants live, carrying away their venom to defile all other streams, ponds, springs. We have only to follow it now and it will lead us to its source . . . and thus to them."

They moved along the bank. The sky ceased to become any darker, but the landscape continued to become more bizarre. The remains of the dead trees surrounding them were growing constantly shorter, more eaten or burned away, until some were down to little more than stubs.

A fat drop of liquid plopped into the dust, sending up a

small squirt of black cloud. Far away another fell. And another. Then more.

"Rain?" said someone, noting the last strike.

Several of them looked up.

"Ah!" cried Luchtine, slapping a hand to his forehead. "A drop struck me. By the gods . . . it burns!"

"The poison rain!" growled the cat. "The only chance now is to reach the cliffs. Everyone, run!"

The creature took off, and they instantly, unquestioningly followed.

The volume of rain grew swiftly. The drops—thumb-sized globules of an oily yellow-red—grew tighter in their spread. There were more cries of pain as drops struck exposed arms or legs or heads.

"Hold the shields above you," the lion roared back to the others. "Keep off the rain. For your lives!"

All lifted the broad, flat circles of iron to hold over them as they ran. Drops splashed and exploded against the thick metal, sizzling there like hot fat on a heated pan.

In moments the drizzle had become a shower, growing on rapidly toward a full-fledged rain. The company pelted ahead at their best speed, zigzagging their way through a treacherous nightmare landscape thickly dotted with the nubs of what had been countless trees.

Ahead a high wall of rock came into view, already hazy through the thickening screen of rainfall.

"See the opening!" the cat told them. "The cave! Make for the cave!"

The hole was just visible—a large black spot shaped like an open mouth right at the base of the high wall. The stream they had been paralleling seemed to be issuing from there.

They rushed toward it at their best speed. The rain was turning the dusty ground to caustic muck, steaming on the soles of their leather boots. Diancecht, eldest and least physical of the band, stumbled badly, nearly falling headlong into the awful stuff. Dagda seized him up and, as if carrying a grain sack, tossed him over a shoulder. Sheltering both of them beneath his own huge shield, he went on unslowed.

The cat rushed into the shelter of the large opening's stony lip. The first of the adventurers followed in seconds, passing into the darkness beyond. Nuada, one of the first, pulled up just within the mouth, turning back to see his people past into safety.

The rain had by this time increased to near downpour. Still, it seemed that it would be only moments more before everyone would safely reach shelter.

Then one of those near the back of the company slipped.

He staggered, falling sideways. Two more—a young man and woman—stumbled over him. The man went down at once, toppling face forward. The woman made it past a few staggering steps, but then dropped onto her knees.

All three of their shields had fallen, giving no more shelter. The rain, now in torrents, poured over them, soaking them down.

Smoke rose from their skin.

And they began to scream.

Chapter 8

Hazards

The smoke rose up in trickles from places all over their bodies. These grew swiftly into streams, combining, forming a screen of greasy yellow-grey that enveloped each of them. The liquid burned into their eyes, filled up their mouths and nostrils, ate at their flesh. In seconds they were left blinded, helpless, thrashing wildly with the intense pain.

At first unaware of their plight, their comrades had run on, each one intent only on reaching the shelter. It was Nuada, standing at the cave's mouth and looking back, who had first seen them go down. Instantly he had lifted his shield and started back for them.

But a huge form had come into his way, blocking the opening. It was the cat.

"You can't go," it had growled. "You'd have no chance in that."

The screams from outside had by this time drawn everyone's attention back to the stricken three. There were cries of horror and alarm.

"We can't just leave them," someone shouted, and all—save a reluctant Mathgen—surged forward as if to force a way past the huge beast.

"You can't save them," it said with force. "It's too late already. Look!"

The two men who had fallen at full length had now ceased to move, and lay stretched in the soft muck. The woman, still upon her knees, had thrown her head back in a last, gurgling cry, only to freeze that way in a death spasm, upturned face dissolving away.

The rain boiled in the sockets that had held her eyes. It turned her brow, her nose, her cheeks, her lips to soft clay, sending them streaming down to expose jutting bones and teeth of the skull beneath.

Her body went limp, toppling to join the others. Their flesh, too, was swiftly melting away, fully soaked by the downpour, liquefying, sloughing off to join the acidic mire, stripping the bones bare.

Many of the watchers turned away in revulsion at the sight. One retched violently. Some sobbed. Others stared on in grotesque fascination.

The haze of smoke boiling up from the three fully involved forms obscured a clear view of them for some moments. Then it faded, its last streamers dissipating in the rain to reveal what was left. In a few score seconds three living beings had been reduced to skeletons thrusting starkly up from the grey-black mud. Three familiar faces had become three grimacing skulls.

"By all the gods," muttered Diancecht.

"Now I'm sure," said Mathgen. "I *don't* want to go on with this!"

As if somehow placated by the three deaths, the storm immediately began to let up. In moments more the rain died away, leaving a last few fat droplets to plop onto the sodden ground. The tree stubs and the stark bones continued to give off a faint steam from the caustic rain still clinging to them.

The stunned adventurers stood unspeaking, lost in grief, huddling together to give each other comfort. It was the big cat who spoke first, its rumbling voice brisk and contrastingly unemotional.

"Over quickly, as I thought," it said, gazing toward the leaden sky.

"How can you be so uncaring, so unmoved by what we've seen?" Dagda asked.

The animal looked around to him. It rolled its muscled shoulders in a shrug. "Because I've seen it so much before. All the creatures of this island died that way. But you are lucky. These rains come far apart. Even allowing time for the ground to dry enough for safe walking, we should be able to return before another storm begins."

"Return?" echoed Nuada in a puzzled way.

"Yes. Go back. To your ship. I thought that now you would truly believe how hazardous your quest is. It will not get easier. Surely you'll wish to go back."

Nuada looked to Diancecht. "Healer, what do you say?"

"I'll make no more judgments that might sway the others," he said. "They must decide themselves."

"I say that we've more reason to go on than before," one said.

"Yes," another said fiercely. "It's ourselves now that the poison of these giants has harmed. Our own dead to be avenged."

"Those dead may include more of you before we're through," the cat said ominously. "Even all."

"We understand the risk well enough," said Goibniu. He looked about at his companions. "Do any here vote not to go on?"

Mathgen began to lift one arm, but realized he would be the sole dissenter. He subsided, muttering, "Idiots. Idiots!" to himself.

"Very well," said the cat, clearly surprised once more by the humans' tenacity. "Then we go up." It lifted a paw to point back into the darkness. "This opening is a tunnel. It slants upward, a conduit for the stream."

They looked down at the flow of sludge, dimly seen in the shadows. Here it narrowed and ran along a channel grooving the center of the tunnel floor. Only a stride's length separated the dropoff from the tunnel walls on either side.

"This is all overflow from a lake on the plateau atop the cliffs," the cat went on. "It is there we will find the giants' lair."

"Is it a long way?" asked Nuada.

"No, but it is very dark. My eyes can see through it, but yours cannot. I must lead. One of you must hold my tail and the others hold hands with that one in a line. You must not get out of line or release hands. The space between the stream and the tunnel wall is even narrower above. Any deviation from my path could mean the end. Do you all understand?"

They nodded.

"Nuada," said Dagda, nodding back toward the three skeletons, "what about them?"

"You cannot touch them now," the cat said brusquely. "Too dangerous. It doesn't matter anyway. A few more rains, and it will be as if they never were. Now, are you ready to start?"

"Yes," said Nuada. "Morrigan, you take the lead. Your senses will serve better there. Diancecht, then Dagda, then the rest. I'll bring up the rear myself. All right, my friends, let's go."

The lion led the way, Morrigan keeping a grip on its tail's tip, the rest strung out behind.

The tunnel ran straight inward a short way, then began a steep climb. The outside light faded away behind them. Without it, they could see that there was light from another source: the stream itself gave off a faint, hazy, greenish glow. Not enough to see more than some vague shadows, but enough to reveal that the channel was cut much more deeply into the slope. The turgid flow of deadly liquid was now over two yards below the edge.

The party made its way upward in silence, each concentrating on footing and staying close to the outside tunnel wall. The only sounds were their shuffling feet; their labored breathing in the close, fetid air; and the thick, doomful gurgling sound of the poisoned stream flowing downward in its channel so near beside them.

The liquid's odor in the confined space of the tunnel was much worse, and became stronger as they progressed. The sense of being enclosed, trapped, suffocated grew to a near-maddening, near-overwhelming height.

Somewhere ahead of Nuada in the dark a voice spoke out in sudden panic: "The edge . . . is . . ."

The rest was swallowed by a wild cry and a crackling sound as a portion of the rocky edge gave way, sliding into the stream, a human form following, toppling from the edge, plunging into the viscid flood.

Others swiftly followed it, yanked off balance in a chain of disaster, one, two, a third toppling over the edge, falling, splashing into the stream's deadly embrace, sucked down so fast there were only brief cries as the dark forms of the victims vanished beneath the luminous ooze.

Nuada had only a heartbeat to register all this before the young woman ahead of him was falling too. She'd released the hand of the hapless man before her, but retained Nuada's, flailing out madly with her freed arm to save herself.

She failed. Her feet, too near the crumbled edge, slid out from beneath her. She dropped down, yanking him down after her.

But the brief second she had delayed her fall had given him a chance to react. He went down full length on the narrow path as she dropped toward the stream. She came up short at his arm's length, the jerk nearly tearing her hand from his clasp. Her toes were being licked by the caustic stream.

He hung on desperately, muscles tensed, other arm and legs flung wide to get the most purchase on the ledge.

From up the tunnel there came voices, calls of alarm as the others of the party, stopped now, looked back through the dark, trying to discover what had happened to the rest. "What's wrong?" called one.

"Are you all right?" shouted another.

"We're coming back to help!" promised a third.

"No!" Nuada managed to gasp out through gritted teeth, voice rasping from the strain. "Stay there. Risk no more lives!"

He looked back to the girl dangling below. She was a shadow, no more. He couldn't even see her face. Just that deadly glow behind.

"Hang . . . on!" he told her.

"I can't!" she said weakly, horribly. The burning liquid was eating into the leather of her boots.

"You can!" he said fiercely. "I'll pull you up."

He concentrated, willing all his power to the one arm to draw her up. For long, long seconds nothing happened as he vibrated from the strain. Then he was winning. She was lifting. He was inching back, bringing her ever upward toward the edge where she might get a grip with her other hand.

As if it were a raptor not to be robbed of its prey, the stream below suddenly surged up. A tongue of the fluid lashed around her legs, the thick strand of slime hanging on like a tentacle, dragging her down.

She gave a single short cry of pain and released his hand. He couldn't hold on alone. Her fingers slid free of his desperate grip.

In shock, he watched the figure drop down, feet first, vanishing in an instant beneath the ooze.

He lay for a moment frozen by anger and agony at the loss. Then renewed calls from ahead forced him back to action. With an effort of cramped muscles he got to his feet and edged along, carefully feeling his way past the spot where half the ledge had broken away, finally reaching the new end of the company.

"Who is it?" the last person in the chain asked him.

"Nuada," he barked, still breathless from his effort. "But there were five others between us!" the other said in consternation.

"No more. Pass the word to go on."

"We could have come back to help," said another figure behind the first.

"There was nothing you could have done," Nuada rapped out, "except to get yourselves killed too."

"But . . ."

"No more talk," he said. "Let's get out of here." He lifted his voice to shout up the line: "Move on!"

The line obeyed. Once more they moved along, even more cautiously now as word of their comrades' loss spread up the line. But the worst seemed past. The nearly strangling concentration of acidic fumes lessened. The slope eased. A circle of daylight came into view above. Soon after they were emerging from the tunnel's other mouth into the daylight.

Only in contrast to the blackness of the tunnel could the illumination be called bright. Little more than a faint glimmer of the sun's glow fought through the heavy blanket of

overcast. It gave a grey and dust-hazed light, just adequate
to illuminate the new landscape that faced them. But it was
not necessarily any great blessing that it did so.

For the bleak and barren scene revealed was that of some
nightmare country of complete despair.

The party had come up onto one side of a flat area, a
huge, roughly circular plateau. It was land totally desolate,
devoid of features, its hard, dried, and soot-blackened earth
thickly carved by deep fissures.

This earth formed a border, a broad margin surrounding
a central lake. The lake, which might once have been clean
water, was now a seething wizard's cauldron of yellow-black
ooze, fat bubbles popping up to burst with thick, obscene,
splattering burps of sound, letting off blasts of near-over-
powering stench.

The foul lake, in turn, formed a surrounding for something else: a feature that rose at the exact center of the
plateau.

It was a steep-sided and grotesque cone of hill that
thrust up starkly from the stinking slime. Its seamed black
slopes rose up to a jagged peak, a spike-edged rim surrounding a gaping hole from which a geyser of oily smoke spewed.

There could be no doubt in the adventurers' minds that
the source of the island's poisoning was here, at this looming
cone. The smoke from its awful throat rose and welled out
in all directions, forming concentric rings that rolled away
to cover the whole sky, to carry smothering dust and caustic
rains over all the country around.

Everyone in the party had gone immediately on guard as
they entered this dismal scene, staring around for any sign
of an enemy. There was none. Indeed, there was no sign of
any life at all.

"Where are the giants?" Dagda demanded of their feline
guide.

The cat nodded toward the cone. "Inside. It is their
workhouse, and their home as well. They never come out."

"Then we'll have to go in," Nuada said grimly.

"Hold on there," Mathgen said quickly. "Shouldn't we
consider what happened below?"

"The edge gave way," Nuada simply explained. "We lost
five more comrades."

"And do you mean to ignore it, like some little thing?" the other demanded.

"Of course not. There's simply no place or time to mourn them now. That can come after this is ended."

"But we *can't* go on!" Mathgen wailed in open dismay. "I kept my silence before, but no longer. This is madness!"

"It is our vow," Nuada said.

"Oh, no," Mathgen argued. "It's *your* vow, Nuada. *You* made this choice for us. You talked us into this. You with your fool bravado, your mindless sense of honor, your stupid self-sacrifice. You don't care if you risk everyone."

"That's nonsense, Mathgen," Goibniu said angrily. "Nuada did not make the choice for us."

"He did! He's your leader. You all follow him and you blindly obey! And he's leading you to death."

"I give no orders," said Nuada. "We have no leader. I've said before that all should act only of their free will."

"Before, no one really knew what terrors we'd face," Mathgen reasoned. "Now we mean to enter the lair of these monsters to challenge them, and nearly a third of our force is gone!"

"I can't deny it," Nuada conceded. He looked around at the rest. "It's surely truth that Mathgen's saying. Still, I mean to see this out. I'll give no more reasons or arguments. Follow me whoever will. I'll put no blame on anyone who stays behind."

With that he moved forward, toward the edge of the lake. The others began to follow without hesitation. Only Mathgen, Dagda, and Morrigan held back.

"Stay here, coward," the raven-haired woman hissed to the cunning one. "But know that to ignore what's happening around you is to be a part of it. Do nothing, and it will destroy you too."

She went on after the rest, leaving Dagda, who stepped close to tower menacingly over Mathgen.

"Nuada will lay no blame, but I will," he said pointedly. "With so many lost, we'll need every sword hand in there— even yours. Refuse us, and you're no part of this company. If we survive, I'll see you left behind here to rot away, or to feed our sharp-toothed friends."

Mathgen looked up at the massive man, then sighed in

defeat. "Ah well, even being dead would be preferable to being left alive here," he said bitterly. "Lead on!"

Dagda grinned in victory. He went on after the rest, now at the lake's shore. Mathgen followed, muttering to himself: "At least there's still the wealth."

As with the stream's channel, the bank's edge was sharp, the drop to the bubbling surface of the lake quite sheer. There seemed only one way to cross it—a series of piers, six-sided columns of what seemed stone, sticking up from the goo at regular intervals, like stepping stones across a pond.

They led from the bank before them to a spot at the cone's base where a high, arched opening showed.

"The giants made that causeway to reach the hill," the cat explained. "Took up long shafts of stone from the rock cliffs of the coast, carried them here, and cast them right down into the bottom of the lake as if they were great spears."

This astounding feat had created a simple avenue, save for one thing.

"But they're nearly three strides apart!" said Luchtine.

"Three of *our* strides," Diancecht corrected. "Likely just one for the giants."

"A bit more of a leap for us," said Nuada. "But we can make it. Though, Diancecht, I think that you should stay here."

"I'm not so old or feeble as that!" said the healer, drawing himself up indignantly. "I mean to see what's across there. Besides, you may well need my skills."

"I won't deny it," said Nuada. "Come ahead." He looked to Mathgen. "What about you?"

"Me?" said Mathgen. He glanced aside to Dagda, then said caustically, "Oh, I can't *wait* to go!"

Nuada gave him an odd look, then turned to the big champion. "All right, Dagda, would you go first then? You can steady the next ones who jump across."

Dagda made no delay in crouching and leaping for the first stone. His powerful leg muscles carried him easily across the gap. He turned, braced himself, and spread his arms to catch Goibniu, Diancecht, Mathgen, and then Luchtine as they jumped across.

The shaft's top could hold no more comfortably. Dagda

and his group began to hop onward to the second stone while others followed them on to the first. Nuada led the second group, followed by Morrigan and then the big cat that leaped lightly, almost effortlessly across. Thus, in a leapfrogging manner, the adventurers began a slow, hard, dangerous process of crossing the acid lake.

"You needn't continue with us," Nuada told the cat as they waited to go on. "You've guided us here. That's enough."

"I made a vow too," the creature reminded him. "I'll stay with you until the end."

"At least this part seems to be going well so far," the young man remarked, jumping onto another stone. The front of the party was just passing the halfway point. "So long as no one else falls in." He peered down at the acid lake. "Amazing how swiftly this foul stuff destroys all life."

"Not quite all," the cat remarked, hopping after him.

Nuada turned to it quizzically. "What do you mean?"

"Well, some little very crude life has survived . . . in a way. By . . . change."

"What kind of change?" Nuada asked.

Some way ahead, Luchtine made the leap that would take him to his next stone.

Up from the muck leaped a long, massive, fishlike form, its wide mouth gaping open. It snatched the jumping Luchtine from midair between two stones, like a trout snapping up a fly, arching down to dive again beneath the slime.

Chapter 9

Giants

The initial effect of this new, sudden assault was consternation.

The adventurers huddled back into the centers of their stone hexagons, looking down and around them at the bubbling waters.

"By the gods! Luchtine!" Nuada said in horror. He rounded on the cat accusingly: "Why didn't you give us more warning? You didn't tell us about the burning rain. Now this!"

"It would have made no difference," was the cat's reply.

"We might have made some defense."

"There is none. You take your chances here as with the rain. Your only way to avoid it is to go back." It eyed him challengingly. "Do you wish to do that now?"

"You know the answer," Nuada snapped, then turned to the rest.

"We can't stay here," he shouted. "We have to go on. Let only one jump at a time. The rest of you, keep close guard."

So, with a certain natural reluctance, they began to move again. From each stone, in turn, one made the leap ahead.

The rest kept wary eyes on the lake surface for any sign of rising creatures, their spears up and ready to throw.

Each segment of the party moved on to another stone without a new attack, but it was not cheaply done. Many spears were cast by nervous hands at rising bubbles, the precious weapons lost forever in the mire.

More tragically, another young man was lost, this time by his own fear. His hesitation in jumping threw off his calculation. He jumped short, his chest crashing against the edge, the impact throwing him back before his comrades could grab him.

He plunged down into another rising bubble, bursting it, sinking beneath it as the crater he made in the surface of the dense liquid closed up over him.

As with the others, he didn't rise again.

The rest stoically went on. Another round of them crossed safely to the next stones. A third circuit began. Dagda first jumped on from the lead stone. A young man made it safely on from the next. A young woman leaped forward from the third.

The creature shot up from beneath her as she did.

So lightninglike was the speed of its strike that it had clutched her in its jaws and was dropping back before any of those guarding with their spears could react and throw.

A half-dozen spears still struck the target, but to no avail. Even the keen barbs fashioned by the skilled hand of Goibniu could not penetrate the monster's hide. They bounced away as it slipped back beneath the goo, carrying another victim away.

"As I said," the cat told Nuada. "There is nothing you can do."

"If you always accept that, then you will always fail," he stubbornly returned. He looked across to his comrades on the stone ahead. "Diancecht, what do you say? There must be *something* we can do."

"There may be," the healer answered thoughtfully. He had had a better look at the fishlike thing this time. Its flat, tapered body was covered with a smooth grey skin like that of a shark, and clearly quite thick enough to protect it from the acid in the muck. Save for the enormous mouth and short, broad fins, it had no other obvious features save for bulging eyes set on either side of the wide head.

"Its eyes may be its only vulnerable point," Diancecht said. "They appeared to be filmed over. I've seen that on fish before. It's a protective covering. Though it's likely to be much thicker here to shield the creature's eyes from being burned away. Even so, the covering will be thinner than the skin."

"Then we could blind it," said Nuada.

"Perhaps, if we could strike both eyes. Even damaging one might be enough to frighten it away. But that is only one fish. How many are there?"

"It is the last of the life that once teemed in this lake," said the cat. "Only becoming this . . . 'thing' has kept it alive so long."

"I am amazed by your depth of knowledge," the healer said, eying the beast thoughtfully.

"I have seen these changes come, haven't I?" the cat replied.

"Of course you have. Well, if it truly is the only fish— and I feel there's no reason to doubt our guide—then the attempt may succeed. But it will take a quick and skilled thrower to have any chance."

"Two," said Nuada. He looked to the big champion beside Diancecht. "Dagda, you will be one. You be ready to strike at the eye on that side of the thing when it rises again." He looked around to the raven-haired woman who stood behind him. "Morrigan, you will strike from this side."

"No," she said shortly.

"What?" he said in surprise. "But you have the quickest hand and the finest eye of all of us, even Dagda. No one could have a better chance."

"I cast my spear to kill an enemy or food," she rasped shortly. "Nothing else."

"This *is* an enemy," he reasoned.

"No," she argued. "This is a creature that is trying to survive. It is the last of its kind. I'll not do harm to it."

"It is of no kind," said Nuada. "You heard the cat. It has become a monster."

"Not by its choice. Too much evil has been done to it

already. You know me, Nuada. You must know why I can't do any more."

He looked into those intense, dark eyes, seeing the anguish there, the memories and wounds that now tore at her. Still, he could not relent.

"Morrigan," he said firmly, "I do understand. But don't you see that it is either the harming of this creature or the deaths of some of us? How many? One . . . two . . . ten? Which lives do you say are most valuable?"

"It is a cruel choice you're putting on me," she said bitterly.

"There's no other way," he told her with intensity. "I'm truly sorry. But please, Morrigan Who Was Moire, will you help?"

She stared at him fixedly for a moment, her lean face hard. Then she nodded.

"Good," he said with relief. "Then just be ready to strike when the thing rises again."

"But, Nuada," Dagda called from the stone ahead, "to be certain, we must have it rise right here, between us. How can we do that?"

"The same way one catches any fish," Nuada answered. "By baiting it. Only one person will leap . . . right here, back and forth, and back again if necessary, until it makes a leap."

"Who'll do it?" asked Dagda.

"I'll not risk any more of you," Nuada announced. "I'll do it myself."

"You can't," said Goibniu. "Let me."

"That I won't," Nuada told him firmly. "My life's no more important than anyone else's, and surely less important than yours, Master Smith. And if Mathgen is right, and I did lead you all into this, then it's right I take this risk."

The others saw he wasn't to be swayed and made no more argument. Dagda and Morrigan set themselves to throw. Nuada poised himself, crouched, and made the leap across to the next stone.

There was no sign of the fish.

The two throwers waited tensely. All the others watched in rising agony as Nuada jumped again. Once. Twice. Three times. He paused to get his breath. The lake bubbled beneath him. No small sign of the creature showed.

It was as he crouched to jump again that Morrigan saw it: the faint tracing of the tip of the dorsal fin thrust up through the thick surface of the muck.

"Now!" she cawed loudly as Nuada sprang clear of the stone.

The man and the fish leaped together, arching up toward the fatal joining point.

But two spears were faster, fired by powerful arms, aimed with skill, each striking an eye, piercing through its membrane, puncturing its liquid eyeball as if popping an egg.

The sudden, intense pain of its blinding made the fish jerk off of its course. Instead of striking Nuada, it crashed headfirst into the stone pillar that he was jumping to.

Nuada landed on the pillar's edge just as the collision of the huge fish shook it hard. He swayed, then began to topple backward.

The creature, spears protruding from each eye, dropped back into the acid mire. Nuada, teetering on the brink of his hexagon, was about to follow it down in just one heartbeat more.

A hand shot out to grasp his tunic, hauling him forward to safety.

It was the hand of Mathgen.

Nuada eyed him with both immense gratitude and some surprise.

"Thank you," he said most sincerely.

"My pleasure. And perhaps you can repay me sometime," the other said with a little smile.

For a while longer the adventurers watched the lake surface for other signs of the monstrous fish. But it had vanished. Nuada gamely took a few more baiting leaps from stone to stone, but with no result.

At last believing the danger was likely gone, they began, slowly at first, to send others jumping ahead. When there were still no incidents, they returned to sending several moving on at once, and soon reached the ominous central isle with its cone of black rock.

Their leap from the last stone pillar landed them on a

narrow ledge protruding from the steep and otherwise featureless slope. Just before them was the large opening of a tunnel leading into the hill's depths. They approached it cautiously, weapons ready.

The opening was obviously man-made, hacked rather roughly from the stone. The edges of its round arch had been decorated with enormous faces, crudely carved and forming a continuous chain, the flowing hair and forehead of one blending into the chin and lavish beard of the next. Altogether a score of grotesque faces scowled and leered and grimaced most menacingly down at them.

"No doubt intended to frighten visitors off," Diancecht commented, examining them closely. "Primitive seeming, but really very clever work. Extremely clever, in fact. They imply a most advanced artistic skill."

"Do you think that's what these giants really look like?" asked Goibniu.

"Possibly," said the healer. "Or possibly they simply want us to believe it is. There's no saying what the truth is in this place."

Nuada looked to the cat. "Before we go on, is there anything you'd care to tell us here? I mean, are there any warnings that we might benefit from knowing in advance this time? Little forgotten bits that might possibly help us stay alive?"

"None," said the cat. "I've never been inside. No one has—at least, no one who's come back."

"Most reassuring," Mathgen said darkly. "It gets so much better all the time."

"Well, there's no gate and no guard," said Nuada. "Nothing to keep us from going in." He looked at the others. "What do you say, my friends, is it time we see just what we're facing?"

Now, with their goal finally before them, the fighting spirit and curiosity of the adventurers was fully restored. In two lines they crept in, hugging each side of the tunnel cut into the black cone.

From ahead of them came the sound of a deep and constant roar, growing louder as they approached. A wave of heated air flowed up the tunnel past them, the temperature also growing as they moved. Soon they were all soaked in

sweat running off in streams across their bare skin, streaking
the black soot with pale stripes.

A bright, ruddy, and flickering light became visible,
shining up the tunnel from the far end. They slowed as they
approached it, edging forward the last distance to the tunnel's inner mouth, stopping there to peer warily forward,
letting their eyes adjust to the brilliant glow.

They peeked past the edges of another arch into an enormous space.

Like the outside of the hill, it was cone-shaped, much of
the interior stone apparently having been mined away. Its
sides sloped steeply up and in, the coarse-hacked surfaces
rising to the ragged opening in the peak.

This hole served as a chimney for the space. In the center of the floor below it was a large pit filled with a red-
yellow, incandescent liquid. It was from this that the heat
and light were emanating. It was also clearly from here that
the poison destroying the isle had its primary source.

For a thick, black, greasy cloud was lifting from the
molten liquid, rising up in a constant stream to pour out the
roof hole and foul the sky. And a creeping trail of yellow-
grey slag was running off along a channel from one side of
the pit, sluicing away through a cleft in one wall to defile the
lake outside.

Just beyond the pit there rose a strange pyramid, nearly
four stories high. It was formed from many thousands of
carefully stacked bricks of a dull yellow-brown metal.

Nearby was another, smaller pile, a jumble of various
objects: wood scraps and metal bits, oars, broken spars,
hawsers, clothes, weapons, utensils, and tools, all apparently
scavenged from the wrecked vessels on the coast. And
mixed in with the rest were the broken, scattered bones of
several human skeletons.

But even with such strange and grisly sights, the attention of the invaders was less on the vast chamber than on its
denizens. Nuada and his comrades were having their first
look at the opponents they had chosen to face: the giants.

The beings were three times the height and bulk of
Nuada's people, dwarfing all of them, including Dagda.
They were otherwise shaped as ordinary men, save for a
much swarthier coloring and most rough-hewn features.

One of them was of soft, sagging form and very round potbelly, dressed in leather tunic and trousers and heavy boots. He slumped on a boulder at a table of stone, drinking heavily. At brief intervals he lifted a bulging skin fashioned from the hide of a whole cow and slurped noisily from its stream of greenish liquid. Between his draughts he sat with hanging head and slack mouth, staring blurrily across the room at a companion.

This other one seemed much older. His jut-browed boulder of a head was bald save for a few trailing wisps of yellow-white. He was stripped to his waist in the intense heat, and the red-gold light starkly revealed a body much wizened, the skin splotched and wrinkly like that of a dried apple.

He moved with slow, painful effort to scoop the molten substance from the pit, using a ladle with a handle longer than his height and a bowl that would easily have held two normal-sized men. He carefully poured each ladleful of the glowing liquid into rectangular molds lined up on the pit's edge. It was clearly the hardened ingots resulting from this process that were stacked up behind him.

"Look at them, will you?" whispered Dagda with a certain scorn. "Their likes aren't even a good challenge. One's drunken near to passing out, the other's all but dropping dead from age. Why, we could challenge them man-to-man and likely win."

"I'll leave you to do that," said Mathgen.

"But there are supposed to be three," Nuada pointed out.

He turned to look for the cat. He realized it had stopped some way behind them, as if reluctant to come any farther, and was standing in the middle of the passageway. He moved back toward it.

"You told us there were three," Nuada said to it. "Where could the third one be? You said they never leave here."

"Ah yes," the cat said slowly. "Well, I'm afraid . . . I lied. As I lied when I said I knew nothing more to tell you. There was just *one* other thing I might have let you know."

The figure began suddenly to glow. A shimmering aura surrounded it, and its form began to change. The cat's shape bulged, stretched, distended hideously. It stretched suddenly upward, the swelling body rising upright to stand on two legs.

In seconds the glow was fading, revealing a face grinning down from a towering figure. But it was no longer a cat's face.

"You see," the figure said in a booming voice, "*I* am the third giant!"

Chapter 10
Captives

All in the party stared upward, frozen momentarily by shock.

In that instant of delay, one of the giant's hands lifted to grasp a lever of iron set in the ceiling, yanking it suddenly down.

The square section of floor beneath the adventurers split open down the center as two concealed doors swung down and apart to dump the whole party together and send them crashing into a pit below.

They fell a dozen feet, landing in a tangled heap upon the pit's stone floor.

As they struggled to unentwine themselves and clamber to their feet, the form of the cat-turned-giant appeared, looming above, peering down at them.

Dagda, one of the first to extricate himself, jumped up and drew back his spear to throw.

"Don't!" the giant warned him, its hand still upon the lever to the trapdoors. "If you do, you and your comrades will be sealed away in there and left to starve."

"Better to do as he says, Dagda," Nuada advised, "for now."

Dagda nodded and reluctantly lowered his weapon.

Nuada looked around him at the others, now climbing to their feet.

"Anyone hurt?"

All made a quick survey. Except for some bruises, everyone had survived the tumble unharmed.

"We didn't intend to drop you to your deaths," the giant explained. "Only to make you prisoners. We are not cruel beings."

They examined the pit. It was a simple, square hole cut in the rock, but with sides scraped smooth enough to give no handholds. As they looked up the sheer sides, two more enormous faces came into view above. They were those of the other giants, peering curiously down at their new catches as if they were rabbits in a snare.

In his changing, the third giant had revealed himself as the most formidable. Like the cat he had been, he was lean, strong, and sinewy of build, with a great mane of tawny hair.

"Blonag," he said briskly to the obese one, "lower the pot."

"Aye, Onairaich," the other said in a thick, slow voice. He went to fetch a large iron bucket and lowered it by chain into the pit.

"Just place all your weapons in there," the transformed one ordered those below. "Don't hesitate." His hand tightened meaningfully on the lever.

The captive party had no choice. Dagda collected spears, swords, and shields and placed all in the bucket. It was drawn up. Blonag carried it away to add its load of weapons to the others in the junk pile.

"Very wise," the one named Onairaich told them.

"So," Diancecht said to him, "you have the ability to shift shape. A most miraculous power."

"We find it useful at some times," the giant replied. "But truthfully, at others, it is a curse."

"What about the rest of those cats?" Nuada asked.

"They serve us. In turn we allow them to survive."

"And what about us?" asked Dagda. "What do you want from us?"

"What we have always wanted," Onairaich answered. "Just to be left alone. I warned you not to interfere. You could have sailed away. But you came on. I took you through our worst dangers. Still you came. We didn't mean for your people to be destroyed. That was your own choice. As I told you, we're not cruel men."

"But you're destroying this whole island!" Nuada told him. "You're killing everything. Isn't that cruel?"

"That cannot be helped," the giant replied. "The metal must be refined. That is the only important thing. Nothing must stop it. *You* must not stop it. But you came here, and you left us no choice but to trap you."

"And now what will you do?" Nuada asked.

"That still is up to you," Onairaich said. "We've still no wish to harm you, only be left alone. You are clearly people of honor, fulfilling the vow you made to come here. So make a new vow to us: swear that you will leave here, leave this isle, and never return to it, and we will let you go."

"A chance to leave here!" said Mathgen. "Nuada, we must swear!"

"How can we?" Nuada replied. "If we truly are people of honor, then we can't forswear the quest we came on."

"This isn't honor, you fool," said Mathgen harshly. "It's survival. *Our* survival."

"It's not!" said Nuada. "If we turn away and let the evil of these beings continue, we *haven't* survived. We've given up everything."

"Oh, yes, excuse me," the other replied with exasperation. "I forgot that continued breathing is secondary to mindless heroic posturing!"

"That one seems to make great sense," the giant said. "The rest of you should listen. Just what will you accomplish by defying us and staying imprisoned here?"

"While we're alive, we're not defeated," Dagda said stoutly. "There are always possibilities."

"That we will see," said Onairaich. "For now we will leave you to your new home. Consider being there the rest of your lives. It may change your minds."

With that the giant wrenched the lever upward. The two doors rose, swinging in to close above the captives' heads with a most final-sounding clang.

It left them in a red-grey semidarkness, the only light filtering down from the bright room above through scores of tiny airholes in the doors. Enough to see dimly once their eyes had adjusted. They looked around at their cell and at one another.

"Now what?" asked Goibniu.

"These walls aren't so high as that," said Dagda. "We could form a pyramid, get someone up to the top. Find a way to force the doors . . ."

"No, no!" said another voice irritably. "You can't do that. A waste of time. Waste of time!"

All realized that this was a voice they did not know. In a body they turned toward it, seeing a man rising from where he had apparently been crouched unnoticed in a shadowed corner of the pit.

They peered at him most curiously. He seemed an elderly man, scrawny of build and rather stooped of back. Once-black straggling hair and ratty beard were grizzled. His clothing—a close-fitting tunic and pants of a tight-knit silver-grey—were threadbare with much hard wear, gone completely at his elbows and knees.

"Who are you?" Nuada asked.

"Cuthach, I'm called," he replied in a cracked, shrill voice. "Got caught by the giants just like you."

"I know your dress," said Diancecht, examining the man's worn uniform. "You are from the metal ship."

"I am that," he agreed. "So, you saw it, did you? A storm drove it ashore here, oh . . . some thirty years ago it was. Lost a few lads, but a good dozen survived. Of course they're dead now. All dead. Been alone a good ten years now, I think." The words poured from him, gushing forth as the dam of speech long penned by isolation was burst.

"Explored inland we did, and met the cats," he continued. "They told us to leave, but we didn't listen. An arrogant, strong lot of young men we were then, and well armed too. We came here, planning to conquer this whole place."

"Conquer it?" said Nuada.

"Well, it's the nature of my people," he explained. "We have to conquer everything we find. And then there was this supposed lode of precious metal the giants were mining here. Well, we had to get that! I imagine it's what brought you too?"

"We didn't come for riches," Nuada said. "It was to stop the giants from destroying this island."

"Is that the truth?" the old man said in disbelief. "Well, you are the strange ones then. What's another little island in trade for great wealth was our thinking."

"Your thoughts are as my own," said Mathgen.

"Really?" Cuthach said, giving him a harder, appraising look. "Well, you sound all right. But it's nothing but a torture to think of what we can't have. That stuff they've mined and melted down . . . gold I call it. Nothing but the purest gold."

"Gold?" said Mathgen in vast astonishment. "That whole pyramid?"

"Aye. You can imagine what those giants thought when they found a whole mountain of it. Went right mad from the greed they did. Meant to have it all."

"So they've all but wiped out this island for something so mercenary as that," said Diancecht, shaking his head. "For something that has no real worth to man."

"Speak for yourself, Healer," Mathgen told him, all but slavering in covetousness of such vast wealth. "What power it could give me."

"True enough," Cuthach agreed. "But my mates and I never got near it. We walked in here bold as you please to take the treasure and found ourselves being cast down into this pit. They took our weapons away and left us here. They offered us no choice, as they did you. Oh, no! We'd come to rob them, and we were dangerous. Still they didn't kill us. The rest just died out over the years. But I was youngest, strongest, toughest, and I survived."

"It must have been hard down here, alone, all those years," said Diancecht.

"Not so bad," he said. "Because I knew that one day I'd have my chance. And I had something else."

He held up a strange metal piece, bent and worn down to a small, flat nub.

"They didn't take this. One of my mates had it."

"What is it?"

"A knife. Or, it was. The finest metal my people make. I used it. We all used it, 'til they died. But I went on. The work kept me going. And I finished! Just a year ago. Thirty years work. See here!"

He led them back into his corner. They realized that a scrap of grey cloth was pinned there, all but invisible in the shadows. He pulled it aside, revealing a hole.

"Goes all the way up," he said. "Right to that passage-way."

"You dug this out?" said Goibniu, much amazed. "With that bit of metal?"

"I did," he said proudly. "And big enough even to let a man of your girth slip easily through."

"And the giants never knew of it?" said Nuada.

"They never really looked in here. Never opened the doors but to toss in food or take out the dead lads."

"But if you've tunneled out," said Mathgen, "why haven't you left?"

"To go just where?" he said. "This pit's no worse than this whole isle's become. It's better, in fact. No poisoned streams here. No burning rains. And I couldn't sail away from the isle. I couldn't manage our ship alone. But now, with you . . ."

"I'm afraid your ship didn't survive the years," Nuada said. "It's half-corroded away."

"It isn't!" he said with despair. "Then we're all trapped here."

"No," said Dagda. "Our own ship was only a bit dam-aged. It can be repaired. We can leave."

"You can?" he said with renewed vigor, grinning. "Then, by Balor One-Eye, I'm saved." He stopped, hesitat-ing, looking at them. "That is, if you'll take me with you."

Nuada examined the hole, crouching to peer in, looking along the narrow tunnel that slanted upward. A faint light showed above.

He straightened and looked around to his comrades.

"There does seem to be a way up," he said.

"But do we trust him?" Dagda said. "That ship of his, we all know it was like the one we saw with the Fomor, back at the Blessed Isle. His people must be in league with them."

"If he is an ally of that vermin, he is no better himself," spat out Morrigan. "He deserves to rot away in a place like this."

"I don't know what you mean," the old man said, clearly dismayed by this. "Believe me, please. I've never heard any telling of this 'Blessed Isle.' And I've certainly helped no Fomor there. It's thirty long years I've been here, knowing nothing of what's happened in the world. I'm no harm to anyone. Have pity on me."

"Look here, it doesn't matter anyway," said Mathgen. "If he's given us a way out, I say he deserves to be taken along. He's earned it."

"Thank you for that," Cuthach told him warmly.

"Diancecht, what do you think?" Nuada asked.

"Difficult to say," the healer replied slowly, musingly. "This is all most curious. Everything that's happened—don't any of you find it . . . well, a bit *wrong* somehow?" He shook his head. "It's quite vexing. I'm not even certain what I mean."

"Are you saying we shouldn't do this?" Nuada asked.

"Not that," Diancecht told him. "In a way, I think it all suggests that we *must* do it. As I've said before: there may be no choice for us here but to play things out. All I know is that we must do it without the smallest wavering from our beliefs. We must be completely true to what we are."

"Whatever that means," said Mathgen.

"It means," said Nuada, "that we can escape this pit, but we can't leave here. Not yet. There's a task to complete first."

"You really mean that we're going to get out of this trap and go after those three giants again?" Mathgen cried in amazement. "Are you mad?"

"Certainly not," Nuada answered. "We've been given a new chance. We must take it to stop what's happening."

"May I point out that we're unarmed?" said Mathgen. "Do you intend to wrestle these monstrous beings into submission? Even our bull Dagda might be somewhat over-matched in that."

"I'd not turn away from a chance to find out," the big warrior shot back. "But there's no need. We'll find a way to get our weapons and face those three head-on. They'll surely be no match for all of us."

"Do you think so?" Mathgen said, considering. "Well, if we *could* defeat them, why then . . ."

"We could still get the gold!" Cuthach finished, his own mind running in the same avaricious channel.

"Put that out of your heads, both of you," Nuada said sharply. "It's not for that we've come here."

"Oh, of course not!" Mathgen said, but gave the old man a sidelong wink.

"We can't just attack them," Goibniu said. "It wouldn't be fair. They could have killed us outright."

"Nuada's right," said Diancecht. "They gave us a choice. Violence should be our last resort. Perhaps we can reason with them."

"We'll have to work that out as we go," said Dagda. "First, we must see about the weapons."

"No," Nuada corrected. "First we must see that everyone's safe. We'll make our way up the tunnel and out of this place."

"Let me go first," volunteered Morrigan. "I'll see if the way is clear."

So the raven-haired woman made her way up the passage so laboriously chiseled through the stone. It brought her up to a small opening partly concealed by loose rocks carefully piled into a wall.

She peered out through a crack, seeing she was back in the entry tunnel only a few strides back from the opening to the great chamber. Removing a few stones, she cautiously thrust her head out. She could see into part of the chamber. There was no sign of giants.

She removed all of the rocks and crept out, back over the metal doors atop the pit, back to the edge of the tunnel.

A quick peek beyond it told her all seemed safe. The wrinkled giant was back to his ladling, the fat one had returned to guzzling drink. The third and most hale giant was lying on a stone pallet against one wall, apparently sound asleep.

She lost no time in returning to tell the rest. It was only moments more until Dagda, Nuada, and Goibniu had crawled up to join her.

Together they examined the situation in the big room. Nuada pointed out the pile of salvage and debris beside the pyramid of gold bricks. Their own weapons had been dumped atop it.

They moved back from the entrance to talk.

"I think we can make it about the room to that pile unseen," Nuada said. "That working giant's the only one who might notice us, and his attention's all on his work. Three of us should be able to fetch enough of the weapons back. Dagda, Goibniu, you with me. Morrigan, get all the others up from the pit."

"No," said Morrigan. "I can carry as much as the smith, and I can move with greater stealth. I should go."

"She's right, you know," Goibniu agreed. "I'll see to gettin' 'em up."

Nuada nodded agreement. "Then have them ready here," he said. "And if we fail, Goibniu—get them out of this place!"

"I will that, Nuada," he said. "Good luck to you."

He reentered the tunnel to the pit. The other three approached the opening to the chamber, paused to make certain conditions had not changed, and moved boldly in.

The bright gold-red light bathed them as they crept about the room's outer wall. They slipped from a boulder to a stone bench to a stack of empty molds to a pile of rubble as they made their way along. But there was really little cover, widely spaced, and they would have been spotted easily had the wizened giant not been so totally intent on his tedious but hazardous task of scooping out the molten gold.

Once, just halfway to their goal, they froze, all in full view, as the drunken giant snorted loudly and stretched himself, looking around, swinging his gaze right over them. But the bleary eyes were unfocused, and the gaze swept on. He gave a belch, lifted his skin for a long drink, then dropped his head down on his folded arms.

The three exchanged a look of relief and kept going.

They finally reached the pyramid of metal safely, slipping around behind it to reach the pile of junk.

"Get just the swords and spears," Nuada whispered to his friends. "Leave the shields."

They began to pick over the pile, gathering their scattered weapons. As they worked, Dagda noted a black metal helmet, much dented. Near it, the end of one of the odd weapons Diancecht had found in the metal ship protruded from the debris. He pulled it free, exposing the teardrop-shaped jewel set in its other end. It glowed with a strong blue-white light.

"Look here!" he hissed to Nuada in delight. "See how bright! I could give it to the healer, to make up for the one I ruined!"

"Leave it!" Nuada said firmly. "Too dangerous!"

Regretfully, Dagda nodded and placed it gently back on the pile.

He and the others soon finished gathering enough weapons for themselves and their comrades. They started back around the room, moving even more cautiously, laden as they were.

Morrigan went first, then Nuada. Dagda cast a last, longing gaze at the abandoned power spear, then followed.

The old giant, now engaged in dumping cooled ingots from their molds, was completely oblivious. The younger giant still slept, and the drunken one seemed to have fallen into a stupor, sagging in his chair.

When they reached the passage, they found all their companions gathered there. Quickly they doled out weapons to everyone, except for their elderly savior.

"You should go outside," Nuada advised Cuthach. "There's no need for you to risk yourself in this."

"No. I'll stay with you," he said. "If you fail, where will I be alone?"

"Very well," said Nuada, passing him a spear. "Then we will all face them."

"But you can't seriously mean to try reasoning with them," Cuthach said. "I tell you, you have a chance now of killing them easily. You can take them unawares, kill them all before they have a chance."

"That might be the way of your people, but not of ours," said the healer. He looked around him at his companions, speaking gravely: "Remember how we first banded together under our leader Nemed, seeking only a place to live in peace? That is still our first goal. We will not take life except to save our own. We will not use force unless they leave no choice."

"We'll divide into three groups as we go in," said Nuada. "Dagda, you and five others on the one at work. Morrigan, take five more in about the fat one. Diancecht and the rest, come with me. Those of you with spears, be ready to throw if they attack."

Thus prepared, the courageous band moved forward, into the giants' lair.

Chapter 11

Revelations

Dagda took his group toward the working giant. Morrigan led hers toward the drunken one. Nuada and Diancecht approached the one who slept, leading the rest of the party.

They were all within a dozen paces of their objectives when their presence was at last noted. The working giant, turning from stacking fresh ingots on the pyramid, saw them, stopping to stare in surprise.

"Onairaich!" he called out. "Blonag!"

The giant at the table lifted his head slowly, looking around in a besotted, bewildered way. But the young one reacted quickly, leaping up from his bed.

His quick gaze evaluated the situation. He and his fellows were faced by a band of seven times their number—much smaller certainly, but armed and most determined.

"I don't know how you escaped," he said, "but it certainly won't help you. Give us your weapons and surrender, and you won't be harmed."

"We don't mean to fight," said Diancecht. "We might have come at you while you slept, but we didn't. We mean to talk. To reason."

"Reason?" The giant laughed. "It's our treasure you mean to have. You want to steal what we've worked for.

You're no better than that one." He pointed toward Cuthach.

"We haven't come to steal," said Nuada. "I told you before. Our purpose is to make you stop destroying this isle. We want to save the few trees and creatures left."

"That you won't do. We spent a hundred years of hard labor digging out this hill, melting down its foul ore to find the gold. I say a handful of puny beings like you can't stop us."

"And *I* say that we can," Dagda answered most determinedly.

"Look here, why risk yourselves?" Onairaich said more reasonably. "You're free now. Why not just take yourselves away? We'll even help you get your tree, fix your ship, get you off the rocks and out to sea."

"Just sail away?" said Nuada. "Forget how you've despoiled this isle for greed? Forget all the life you've destroyed, and all our own friends who died in our coming here?"

"We really don't wish to destroy you," Onairaich said, yet more sincerely. "Forget us. Sail away. If you do . . . we'll . . . we'll give some gold to you! Yes. We'll give ingots—two, three . . . five apiece! More wealth than each of you could ever spend! Just sail away from here and let us be."

"Five bricks of gold?" said Cuthach, awestruck. "The ransom of a great chief!"

"Enough to buy a chieftain's land; to have a chieftain's power!" breathed Mathgen.

"No!" said Nuada fiercely. "We want no gold from you. It means nothing to us. Only life does. Don't you understand? Haven't you wrenched enough wealth from this poor dying isle? Can't you stop?"

"There can never be enough," said Onairaich tersely, his patience lost. "And all of you little people are giant fools. No more talk. Surrender now, or run away, or stay and be destroyed!"

With that he started toward Nuada's party, lifting hands, clearly meaning to grasp at them.

"Don't do this," Nuada warned, shaking his spear. "You are unarmed. Don't make us strike at you."

The giant only laughed again, loudly and scornfully. He batted out at Nuada with his open hand, as if to swat a fly.

Nuada jumped back clear of the hand and threw. His spear sailed up to strike the giant's chest right over the heart.

And it rebounded harmlessly, dropping to the floor.

"Don't you realize your little weapons can't harm us?" Onairaich said. "Do you think that we'd have survived here all these years without thick skins?" He looked to the other giants. "Come, fellows, let's crush these troubling mites!"

With a great bellow, the drunken one suddenly stood up. Swinging his drinking skin around, he flung it at Morrigan's lot.

The quick raven-woman ducked, and the swollen bag caught the man behind her, driving him back as it burst against him, all but drowning him in ale.

At the same time, the wizened giant moved. With an alacrity amazing for one seeming so aged, he charged forward, swinging out with his immense ladle.

Two of Dagda's warriors were caught in its path and slammed sideways to sprawl brokenly on the floor.

Now a wild melee ensued. The smaller fighters scattered, weaving, ducking, and bounding about, this way and that, as the giants lunged at them. The adventurers struck back whenever they could, slashing out with swords, casting more spears, but to no effect. Mathgen did his best to stay out of the greatest danger. Cuthach gamely and agilely joined in, though panting with the strain.

The drunken giant, weary of the dance, picked up his stone table with a grunt of effort, lifted it high, then cast it down at Morrigan and her group. They leaped away from beneath as it shattered in their midst, but the flying rubble caught one woman, knocking her down and half burying her.

The old giant's ladle struck out again at Dagda's group, catching another not quite nimble enough. It swept the warrior over the edge into the pit. A single sharp cry, and he was gone beneath the molten ore.

Enraged, Dagda charged boldly in and struck at the giant's knee. But even a sword cut backed by his great strength drew only a shallow trench of blood across the wrinkled skin.

Still, it caused pain. Roaring, the giant struck back. Dagda lifted his sword to parry the swing. The heavy ladle struck his blade, the force knocking the weapon from his grip. It spun away and fell into the pit.

Unarmed, he retreated, the giant lumbering after him. He made for the nearest, most advantageous ground: the pyramid. He began a climb up its slope, using the layers of ingots as steps. It was slippery going.

He ducked as the giant swung at him, and the ladle *swished* over his head. He seized one of the heavy ingots, lifted it, turned, and cast it at his foe. It hit the huge being's shoulder, making him jerk back.

Dagda climbed higher. The ladle swung again, this time knocking away a row of ingots beneath him. More above avalanched down, nearly carrying him with it. He clung a moment, scrabbling with his feet for a new hold. He found one, thrusting himself on up just as the ladle swept through the spot where he had been.

He was high now, nearly eye-to-eye with the giant being. He grabbed up another ingot and stood to face his opponent as the other lifted the ladle overhead in both hands, ready to swing it down on him.

Dagda cast the gold brick with all his power. His aim sent it to strike square on the giant's forehead.

There was a hollow, cracking sound. The giant's head snapped back. Then, overbalanced, the being staggered backward toward the pit. He teetered there a moment, on the brink. But, finally, it was a giant's turn to plunge into the deadly muck that they had created.

A great bloom of the molten stuff rose up around the being, casting a rain of fiery droplets out of the pit to sizzle on the floor around. The wave of incandescent ooze lifted, then rolled back in to close over the huge being's sinking head. A fat puff of newer, blacker smoke welled upward as the body was consumed.

The giant was gone.

Freed of him, Dagda looked out across the room. The obese giant had caught Goibniu, had grasped him around the middle with one hand, and was starting to squeeze.

Morrigan ran up behind him and jabbed him hard in the back of the calf with her spear. The point dented the skin but didn't penetrate. Still it caught his attention and saved Goibniu. The giant released him, only to swing a hand around in a quick move, backhanding her.

The blow lifted her and cast her several yards, where she slammed down on the hard floor, breath knocked from her. Before she could recover, the giant had moved to stand over her. He grinned down at her sadistically. Then he lifted a broad foot to drop atop her.

Dagda cast desperately around him for a weapon. He saw the glowing tip of the strange power rod lying on the junk pile below him. At reckless speed he bounced and bounded down the gold pyramid, crashing onto the debris. But he was up in an instant, the weapon clasped in his hands, and running off across the floor.

The giant's foot had now come to rest upon Morrigan's chest, covering most of her torso. He leaned forward slightly, beginning to put the pressure on. She moaned in pain.

The giant leaned farther forward, putting more weight on the foot. She writhed weakly, unable to pull free.

Blonag laughed and leaned yet harder.

Dagda reached them, rushing right up to them. The giant looked down to see him with surprise. He swung a fist at Dagda.

The warrior sidestepped it and thrust upward with his power spear, driving its glowing tip right into Blonag's groin.

A deadly flower of sapphire light bloomed from the weapon. Lightninglike flares crackled out in all directions from the tip, dividing and spreading to surround his loins in a blazing web, flickering up across the swollen belly toward his heart, sending blue-white tendrils snaking down his thighs.

Blonag jerked up stiffly, immobilized by the power surging over him while also convulsed by it. His head was thrown backward on the taut, straining neck, vibrating violently. His eyeballs rolled upward to show only white. The loose fat on his body quaked with his ague. He voiced a long, shrill, ululating scream so filled with agony that all others in the room looked to him in horror.

But the revenge-fired Dagda did not relent. He kept the weapon thrust into his foe's groin until the net of energy had enveloped Blonag knees to neck. Until flares of the azure fire had lapped upward to the head. Until the giant's hair smoked with the power and his eyeballs boiled in their sockets.

Only then did Dagda yank the rod away.

The lightning died. The huge being sagged like something boneless, crumpling to the floor.

The giant's foot was off of Morrigan. Dagda knelt by her side.

She was very quiet. He gently lifted her. She was horribly limp.

"Morrigan," he said in agony. "My Moire!"

The last giant had seen his first comrade die. Now, as the second fell to the strange weapon, he acted desperately.

In a swift move he swept through his enemies, driving for one in particular: Diancecht.

The healer was taken by surprise. Before Nuada and the others could act to defend their friend, Onairaich had seized him up. Ignoring the warriors who swarmed around him, the giant crossed to the pit in three long bounds. In a heartbeat more he was holding the man out, dangling him by his feet over the smoking brew.

Dagda, recalled from his grief over Morrigan by this move, grabbed the power spear and rose up.

"Stop!" Onairaich cried to him. He lowered Diancecht slightly. The man's head dangled close above the molten ore. "Don't use that weapon or he dies!"

Dagda, scowling in rage and frustration, lowered the spear.

"Give up now, all of you!" the giant cried. "I know this is your most valued one. You will not let him die. If not fear, if not greed, then your honor, your loyalty, your love for him will make you obey me. Now, drop all your weapons!"

They hesitated, looking to Nuada for their lead.

"Quick now!" Onairaich snapped. He lowered the healer even more. Tips of the man's long trailing hair touched the surface, instantly singeing away. He coughed wrackingly from the acid fumes rising into his face.

"We have no other choice," Nuada said in anguish. "We can't kill our own friend. Put down your weapons."

"Don't!" Diancecht managed to gasp out. "Don't let him defeat you. Forget me. Do what you must!"

"We can't!" Nuada said.

"You can!" the healer returned.

And in a swift and unexpected feat of agility, the man swung upward from the waist, striking with the spear that he still clutched.

He drove its point into the base of the giant's thumb where it clasped around his ankle.

The point drove into the thinner skin there. No more deadly than an insect's sting to the giant, but still enough. The healer had chosen his spot well. The pain and surprise caused Onairaich to involuntarily open his grip. Diancecht fell.

Nuada and the others watched their comrade drop into the glowing muck, plunging instantly from sight. Onairaich stared at the spot in openmouthed astonishment at the man's self-sacrifice.

"No!" cried Dagda. Galvanized by fury, he lifted the power spear and made a cast.

True to the mark it went, right into the giant's still-opened mouth and down his throat, its blue-white gem of energy bursting there.

All the stored power in the strange weapon was released at once. Onairaich's head seemed to explode with it. Flares of blinding light shot out from his ears, eyes, nostrils, mouth; combining and growing into a single brilliant globe.

But the effect didn't cease with this.

The globe continued to swell farther, with incredible speed, the sapphire glow like a cool but intense sun in the throes of birth—or death. It filled the interior of the vast cavern in seconds, catching, surrounding, swallowing the adventurers before they could escape.

It grew on until the hill itself, the lake, the plateau, the whole isle, had vanished in the incandescent ball.

The glowing sphere was fading, and it was changing too. The azure light was replaced by a reddish-gold.

Nuada opened his eyes.

He realized that he was looking at the sun, now half-obscured by the scrim of a small, wispy cloud. It was the sun's rays shining on his eyelids that had made the glow.

Impressions sorted themselves out slowly in his disordered mind.

He was lying on his back, staring up at the open sky. A blue sky, clear but for a handful of the soft, scattered, drifting clouds.

He sat up, looking around. It was on a soothing carpet of lush grass that he lay. It covered a broad, gently rounded hilltop. Around it the land sloped lazily, gracefully down to a luxuriant surrounding forest of a vibrant green. A small lake, its waters sparkling clear, marked the center of the hilltop. A pure, rushing stream from it rippled brightly away downhill.

His wondering gaze scanned this, then went to the figures close around him. They were humans, laid out as he was, most starting to move now, stretching, sitting up, staring around them as bewilderedly as he.

They were his comrades.

His gaze went across them, taking in Dagda, Goibniu, and then, unbelievably, Luchtine! And beside him lay Diancecht!

He looked around again, scanning each face. Here was Morrigan, already getting to her feet, as hale and lithe as ever. And here were all the others they had lost, both on the trip to the hill and in the fight. All of their company. Every one. Alive!

But how? What of the cavern? And of their enemy?

A massive figure rose up suddenly into view from beyond the brow of the hill.

It was Onairaich, distressingly alive and hearty too.

Chapter 12

Magh Mell

Nuada grabbed at once for his weapons—sword, spear, and shield—somehow laid out neatly beside him. Dagda, Morrigan, and some others grabbed for theirs as well. The rest, still too dazed to react, could only stare.

"Don't be alarmed," Onairaich said, lifting a hand in peace as he approached. "I'm not an enemy. I'm not even a giant."

A glowing aura rose about him as they stared, enveloping him in a haze of light. Within the haze the giant could be seen as a shadowed form. But that form began rapidly to change. The being was shape-shifting again, but not back to the great cat. This time the general form remained the same, but it shrank down to a less-than-normal size.

When the transformation ended and the glow died away, the adventurers were startled to discover that it was upon a very small young man that they now gazed.

He was barely above waist-height to the average man in Nuada's group. His limbs and trunk were short, while the hands and head were of almost normal size, as a result appearing disproportionately huge. His features, too, were of overly large size, and shaped emphatically. He had a great hooked beak of a nose; long, sharply pointed chin; and broad, outthrusting ears. Only his close-set eyes and bow of mouth were small. A head of stiff and spiking red-orange hair completed the odd assemblage. It was overall the kind of face one might have seen on a comic doll or on a jester's mask.

Though small, the man stood with hands on hips, fearlessly confronting them.

"This time," he said soberly, "you are looking at my real self. That is the truth."

"Is it indeed?" said Diancecht. Having overcome his own initial bewilderment by this time, the healer got to his feet and moved forward to inspect the young man.

"Is there something *wrong* in what you see?" the man said in a tone of offense.

"Oh, no," said the healer quickly, stepping back. "I'm sorry for staring. It's just that seeing you . . . like this . . . is, well . . ."

". . . a bit of a comedown," Mathgen finished for him.

The little man shot him a hard look at the slighting remark.

"What . . . who . . . I mean . . . are you human?" Nuada asked awkwardly.

The man drew himself up to his full height proudly. "I am. And as much a one as yourselves," he announced.

"Half as much, anyway," Mathgen corrected.

The little man colored, clearly outraged now. "You really have set out to give insult, ugly dark one," he growled. "Would you rather be facing a great cat again?"

"Keep your mouth shut, Mathgen," Dagda threatened, "or I'll do it for you myself."

Mathgen subsided, but gloweringly.

"So you really have the shape-shifting power," Diancecht put in in a placating way. "Most fascinating. Can you become anything you wish?"

"Nearly anything," the man replied, his choler settling somewhat. "It is the magic skill of all the Pooka clan."

He raised a hand. From behind the hill's brow, the two other giants appeared, lumbering forward. And after them came the pride of big cats. They all stopped when they reached the little man, lining up. The bright haze rose about each, and in moments the adventurers looked at a group of

other little men, all so similar to the first in features and
coloring that it was clear they were closely related.

"So you . . . uh . . . people are the real inhabitants of
the isle," Nuada said.

"Not really," the first man told them in a clipped, still-
chilly voice. "We only played the part. We do not come from
here."

"And exactly where are we now?" asked Diancecht.

"Where you were," was the reply. "The same place,
transformed as well. The rest was all an illusion for your
benefit."

Nuada looked about him at the scene. Birds flew above
the trees. Deer grazed the meadows, and rabbits scampered
in the brush. Silver fish jumped in the pristine lake, snapping
at dragonflies.

"A great illusion indeed," he said in awe. His gaze fell
upon Cuthach, still an aged man, his look unchanged, except that his grey uniform was not quite so threadbare.

"What about you?" Nuada asked him. "Aren't you a
part of our . . . our dream?"

"Not I," he said. "I am as you see. A shipwrecked sailor,
as I said. My mates and I came here, seeing the isle just as
you did. That much of my tale was true. But we failed the
test."

"Test?" said Nuada. "Is that what all of this has been?"

"Yes," said the little man. "A way to understand you. To
know the truth of you. It was thought to be a necessary
protection."

"So, that's why I had a sense that we were led through
all this," said Diancecht. "That's why it didn't seem quite
right. And you"—he looked to the man—"you were the one
behind it . . . whoever you are?"

"Not the creator of it," the young man said. "I've no
power for that. I was only in charge of things here. I am the
chieftain of the Pooka clan. And I am still named Onairaich,
the 'Man of Honor.' "

"Man of honor?" said Mathgen with a sharp laugh, defying Dagda's threat. "A strange name for one who hides
his true shape and practices deception on such a vast scale."

Onairaich frowned, clearly rankled again by this jab. "It

was not my choice to fool you or to lie," he said defensively. "It was done on command. I do not like—"

"Enough, Onairaich," said a clear, strong voice that pealed in the air about them like a great bell.

It came from above the hilltop. Everyone looked up. The wispy clouds were pulling together, coalescing, forming into a definable shape. Soon the semblance of an immense face could be recognized; a woman's face, its features bold, comely, but very stern.

Bright blue-grey eyes stared down at them. The straight mouth moved.

"Your clan has accomplished its task, Onairaich," the ringing voice said brusquely. "Say no more now. They have succeeded in the test. They will be brought here. At once."

With this command given, the face dissipated, breaking up once more into small clouds.

"Yes, O Queen," Onairaich acknowledged to the sky, but in a tone that was sharp with a sardonic note.

He signaled to his fellows. Without further words, the clan of Pookas instantly began to once again metamorphosize. In moments the auras of light were fading, revealing them all to now be large horses—tall, broad-backed, and muscular steeds, with a special, extra feature: an immense pair of wings sprouting just behind the shoulder blades of each.

"By all the gods of our fathers," Dagda said, most impressed.

"I've heard tales of such creatures," Diancecht said. "I thought that they were myth."

"And they may well be," said Onairaich, now a sleek, majestic, white stallion with red-gold wings, "unless some-one of your world once saw us. But the shape, real or not, suits our needs sometimes, especially now, when we have been ordered to be beasts of burden. So, if you'll mount, please?"

"Mount?" Nuada repeated.

"Yes, you heard our queen's command. We're not to delay. Climb on us—two on each will do it—and we'll be off."

"Can you at least tell us where we're going?" asked Diancecht.

"If I must," was the curt reply. "It's to the place you

seek. The isle of Queen Danu. The temple of light upon the Happy Plain."

The flying horses carried Nuada and his people two by two upon their backs.

Up from the isle they rose, soaring over the land so vastly changed from the wasteland it had been. The awed—and sometimes nervous—adventurers looked down from the heights at meadow and wood streaming by below. They watched as their strange mounts shot past the outer wall of cliffs and across the narrow band of shoreline encircling the isle. These, unlike the rest, had not transformed. The cliffs were still stark and formidable; the shore still rocky and barren and spotted with wrecked ships, including their own.

"I don't much like abandoning our ship here," Dagda said to Nuada, gazing down at it. "It means we've no way to leave this queen's isle if we choose."

"If you wish to leave, Danu will see to it." This came from the Pooka leader Onairaich on whom both men rode. "You're not captives. Your choice to stay or go will be your own. But from this place, there are no ships allowed to approach the isle."

"What happens if they do?" asked Nuada.

"The last barrier," Onairaich explained. "The magic of Danu and her chief druids would send the ships astray. As if some giant hand had lifted them and moved them instantly, they'd find themselves suddenly far away and wandering aimlessly. It's like a glass wall surrounding the whole isle. The only way to pass it is to go over its top, as we will go. Of course, it's never really been tried. No outsiders' ships have come so far in all these uncountable years."

"You spoke of druids," said Nuada. "Who are they?"

"Sorcerers," Onairaich tersely replied. "Learned men, priests, advisors to the queen. The greatest of the great ones, in their own estimation. With Danu they tap the powers of the earth to supply their needs. But ask me no more. Danu will be angered surely if she thinks I've said too much. It's for her to tell these things to you . . . *if* she thinks you're to know them."

So the two men fell silent as the Pooka and his clansmen

flew on over the sea, great wings beating powerfully, rhythmically, carrying their riders ahead without apparent effort.

But the journey was not long. The isle of their testing had barely fallen from sight behind the eastern curve of sea when a new land came into view in the west.

This, the explorers soon could see, was a much larger isle. As they approached, its shoreline rose and spread far to north and south. Wide, golden beaches were backed by hills and cliffs above which rolled a high countryside of meadows and groves, the green upon green of varied trees against the grass creating a softly rumpled patchwork quilt of land.

The flying horses pumped wings harder, gaining some altitude to top the line of coast and the higher ground beyond. They flew inland, across a country that at first seemed to the observers to be quite wild, empty of any signs of people.

Then they passed a rim and began to drop into a wide, shallow, natural bowl in the earth, many miles across. Here, the nature of things changed quite drastically.

The outer slopes of this bowl were like an elaborately etched border, a cross-hatched pattern of tilled fields bright with many crops. Just within this band lay a ring of small villages, scores of them, evenly spaced, each one a neat, round compound of several peak-roofed houses surrounded by a wall. A circling road connected each village to the rest, and another road ran from each one inward.

They flew some way farther in, across the smooth and gently sloping plains, over groves of blossoming trees and fields of flowers making swatches of bright color on the land. The roads from the villages crossed these areas, converged at what seemed much larger towns.

There were four of these towns, also spaced evenly around the bowl, each built atop a rounded hill. Their outer walls encircled many acres of land and many dozens of homes. At the center of each, at the top of its mound, rose a larger structure, high-walled and many-sided. And each of these palaces seemed formed of a different precious material, one glowing in silver, another gold, the third white bronze, the fourth pink-white marble.

"May I ask you what those places are?" Nuada said.

"I suppose there's no harm in telling you that," the

Pooka answered. "Those are the four cities of Danu. Murias is the marble one, Gorias the gold. The silver one is Finias and the bronze one Falias. Each has its own chief druid who teaches skill and knowledge and perfect wisdom to the young." He paused, then added with a definite note of spite, "At least, to *their* young."

Nuada and Dagda exchanged a wondering look at that last remark.

The Pookas swept on, giving their riders the chance for only a brief perusal of these wondrous places. They were headed for the center of the bowl, toward a place where wide roads from the four fortresses converged, toward a most dazzling structure that sat there.

It had a high outer wall of iridescent bluish-white. Within it were set a circle of huge monoliths, rectangular, sharp-cornered blocks that seemed made from burnished copper. These uprights, set several paces apart, were crossed and linked by square lintels to form a unified but open structure. Within it rose a second circle of monoliths, linked in the same way. Within that was a third circle, but this one was roofed over with copper forming a rounded dome.

Massive gates on one side of the wall stood open. The Pookas dropped down onto the lawn outside them, fluttering lightly, skillfully in to land without jarring a single passenger.

The adventurers dismounted to stand staring in through the gateway with some obvious trepidation. The flying horses quickly transformed themselves into human forms again, and Onairaich addressed his charges.

"Danu awaits inside," he said. "But first, you must leave your weapons here."

"You want us to go in there, into something unknown, without arms?" Dagda asked.

"*I* don't want you to do anything," the chief Pooka snapped ill-naturedly. "But if you wish to make a sign of trust and of peace, you'd best agree. Queen Danu much dislikes objects of war."

"After the tricks you played on us, how can we trust you?" Mathgen challenged, again earning a hostile stare from the little man.

"We have no choice," Diancecht put in swiftly. "It is a

gesture we must make to show our good intent. We have come so far, my friends. Let's not hesitate now."

They agreed and began to divest themselves of shields, swords, and spears.

"Is there anything else you can tell us?" Nuada asked the Pooka chieftain as they stacked the weapons by the gate.

"Don't show the queen the least sign of weakness or fear," Onairaich advised.

"Is there a danger?" said Dagda.

"Of death, no," the man replied, his tone of resentment sounding much more stridently now. "Of losing your dignity, your freedom, your spirit, everything else of value to you . . . well, just be warned that Danu is a queen of very great power and very little thoughtfulness toward anything not bending to her will. You may find yourself a slave here, not a guest. Now, follow me!"

Chapter 13

Danu

They strode forward, following Onairaich through the open gates. The rest of the Pooka clan remained outside.

"Diancecht," said Nuada as they passed through the first ring of monoliths, "do you feel anything here? A quick tingling of the skin, as if you were—were naked in a brisk sea wind?"

"Not an experience I can use for comparison," the healer said dryly. "But, yes, I do notice an invigoration. Most intriguing. I feel as if a younger blood were suddenly coursing in me."

They passed the second ring of stones. All now were aware of a new energy, sweeping away the weariness and aches from the days of hard travel.

But they had little time to consider the odd rejuvenation. The inner structure was now just ahead, and before it stood a most impressive entourage.

It was predominantly a group of some thirty men and women, very tall, very slender, very fine of feature, clad in cloaks and plumed hats of purest white feathers. Before them stood four others in feathered raiment of blue and gold.

At their front stood a woman of most striking look indeed. Her tall, lean figure, clad in a cloak and headdress of emerald-green, was poised with conscious majesty. Her features were cleanly chiseled in strong lines, both chin and nose emphatic, giving her a most imperious look. Bright blue-grey eyes swept the visitors with a commanding glare.

Nuada and his companions had seen that face before. It had appeared in the sky over them on the giants' isle. They knew that it was Queen Danu herself who now stood before them.

"You may go, Onairaich," she told the Pooka in a brisk tone as the company stopped before her.

"That's all?" the little man said. "After what we've had to do, isn't there something . . ."

"What you did was for your queen," she said sternly. "There is no need for a reward."

"There *is* a need for consideration," he persisted, bringing looks of shock to the faces of the feathered company. "After having to labor, demean ourselves, deceive . . ."

"Enough!" she commanded with vehemence. "Go now. We have no more need for you."

He reddened in chagrin, but said nothing. Bowing stiffly, he turned and stalked away.

Danu turned to her visitors.

"We welcome you," she said in a voice now slow, rich, and most carefully modulated.

All of them, as if instinctively aware of the superior power they faced, made bows to her.

"We are very fortunate to finally meet you," Nuada returned.

"Fortune had nothing to do with it," she said firmly. "It was Our will and your own virtues that brought you here. Though, I must tell you at the very start that it was not by the queen's own choice that you were helped through the barrier of fog. You were the first ever to be given such aid."

"We understood that others have come into your realm," said Diancecht.

"Others, a very few, have chanced their way through the fog. You were the first to be guided through, the first from the outside willingly let through for many centuries. But that willingness was not gained easily. Save for the arguments of one championing your cause, you would have been left wandering."

She gestured. From behind the feather-robed gathering another figure appeared: a gangly, big-featured man who grinned broadly at them.

"Lir!" said Nuada.

"I am known by that name here," he said. "But there is another name you might know better."

He turned away for a moment, ducking his face into his hands. When he lifted it again and turned to them, he sported an outrageous, scraggly beard.

"Liam!" cried Dagda. Impulsively he charged forward and swept the man up in a great bear hug.

"Umpph! Thank you. That's enough," the other said, getting free of the near-crushing grip.

"This is the man who came to help us in the outside . . . in our battle against the Fomor," an astounded Nuada told the queen. "He saved our people from being totally destroyed."

"Yes, young man, I am quite aware of that," she told him briskly. "It was I who sent him out into your world. It was Our intent that he be on guard for enemies who might invade our realm"—she gave Lir a most severe look—"*not* that he become involved in mortal affairs."

"But, Lia . . . I mean, Lir, we thought you had died in the last fight," said Dagda. "We saw that ship explode."

"I leaped from the ship just an instant before," Lir explained, peeling off the false beard. "My powers saved me from the sea. After that, I kept a watch on you. I saw the rest of your people sailing back toward their old homeland, and I saw you few reckless ones head into the unknown seas."

"He came back here to Us," Danu said. "After abandoning his mission, after defying Us, he dared to come here asking for Our help. Audacious boy!"

"You know it was my audacity that caused you to send me to the outer world in the first place," he boldly argued back. "No others in this too-protected, long-stagnant realm of yours have any enterprise left. It's exactly why we need these people here—to show us what we've lost."

Queen Danu sighed. "You see how he argued with Us,"

she told the adventurers. "While We should have punished him, We gave in instead. His tale of your great virtues swayed Us enough that We gave him leave to help you through the barrier fog."

"But only that," Lir said to his friends. "Afterward, you had to prove yourselves."

"And so, we were tested," said Diancecht.

"Yes. When I met you and brought you to my isle, I gave what warning I could of what would come, of what you'd have to do."

"And you did most admirably," said one of the men in blue and gold. He, like the other three similarly clad, was more elderly in look than the rest, his lean face creased with years, the hair showing beneath his plumed hat turned by age to silver-white. Still, there was an air of great vitality about him.

"Your courage, your strength, your loyalty, your resourcefulness!" he went on with great enthusiasm. "You demonstrated them all splendidly in your journey here."

"This is one of our chief druids, Arias," Danu introduced. "As you can see, he was quite impressed. For Ourselves, We still have reservations. There was a great deal of violence in your confrontation with the giants."

"*We* pushed them to that fight," Lir pointed out. "I think it proved that they will use force only as a last resort."

"Perhaps," she allowed, "but We sense that the potential to use violence, even to kill, is very strong in them. Even the thought of such has not been tolerated among our people for all these centuries."

"There are times, O Queen, when it is necessary," Dagda put in.

"We do not agree," she said austerely. "For people of true reason and good intent, there are always alternatives. Still, We feel that your other proven virtues go far in compensating the single vice. Most especially to be lauded is your respect for life, as you showed on the isle of birds and isle of rams, as well as on the giants' isle."

"It was your willingness to risk yourselves to stop the poisoning that most found favor with us," chief druid Arias put in.

"Yes," said Lir. "That's very important to us. You see,

our people came here to escape a world that had become much like that isle. In fact, it was memories of the past horrors that were a model for the illusions you encountered there."

"Enough," Queen Danu said with a certain sharpness. "These people need not know our history. All that is important is that We find their spirit for preservation acceptable to Us." She looked to Morrigan, giving a rare, small smile of approval. "With this one, most of all, We are greatly pleased. Though her appearance is somewhat strange to Us, her compassion toward living things is nearly as great as Our own."

"Diancecht, too, should be given note," said Arias. "He is a man of wisdom, of careful judgment, of willingness to sacrifice himself for the good of the rest."

"Dagda is the one I most admire. What strength and courage!" This came from the youngest of the druids, one barely a man, slight-bodied, with deep red hair, freckled face, and most high-spirited manner.

"Quiet, Oigear!" Danu snapped, casting a disapproving frown at him.

He flushed and quickly moved back into the shelter of the group.

"All of you seem to know everything that's happened to us," said Diancecht curiously. "How is that?"

Danu hesitated, considering. Then she shrugged. "Well, We suppose it will do no harm to let you see."

She turned and started toward the central ring of monoliths. The druids quickly parted to let her through.

"Go on. After her," Lir told the adventurers, and led them on in the queen's wake.

With the party of druids following behind, they passed between two of the huge pillars, into the space beyond. Here they stopped, faced by yet another wonder.

Beneath the high copper dome that roofed the circle, there hung a lustrous sphere.

Its suspension there was itself miraculous, as nothing seemed to hang it from above or support it from below. It floated free, midway between floor and dome.

It was like an iridescent pearl, but in diameter two times a man's height. Its surface had a smooth and soft white sheen, but shimmering streamers of pink, turquoise, silver, and gold played constantly across the surface. A faint but definite white aura—like that around a full moon on a clear spring night—surrounded it.

"This triple circle of copper-sheathed stones is the focus of our magic," Arias started to explain. "All the power comes from here."

"Really?" Mathgen said with great interest. "How is that?"

"Well, the energy tapped from the earth is gathered here, focused by the—"

Danu cut her chief druid curtly off: "No more of that!"

"Yes, my Queen," he acknowledged. "Enough to say then that this globe is part of the working of our power. Through it, we can see other places within the realm, control events there to some extent, even project certain magic —well, like the illusions you saw. We can even do so beyond the barrier of fog about the realm, but in a way most limited. Only to specific points of power, and only to specific individuals knowing the magic."

"It worked very well for me when I was out there," offered Lir.

"You can see things in this?" asked Diancecht.

"Chief Druid, you may demonstrate," Danu allowed.

Arias stepped forward, lifting arms toward the sphere. He began a low muttered litany of words unintelligible to the outsiders. The other druids joined in, raising a singsong blur of sound that echoed hollowly against the metal dome.

Within the sphere, the drifting colors caught the rhythm of the chant, swirling and spiraling to its cadences, forming, solidifying, bringing into focus a clear scene.

It was the isle of the colorful birds, the blanket of their many bodies seething across the tiny bit of land.

The chief druid shifted to another chant, the sounds and rhythms altering subtlely. The images changed too, the bird isle swept away, the colors re-forming into another view.

This time it was the isle of the great rams. Their flock could be seen in great detail, roaming over the grassy ridge.

The chief druid nodded to the rest. The chanting died, and with it, the image faded away.

"You have powers that are very great and most unfathomable to us," Nuada said, looking at the sphere in open awe. Then he looked to Danu. "But just what does all of this mean to us?"

"We do not understand," she said in puzzlement.

"Well, you've brought us here, but it's very clear from your cautious words that you're not certain of us. What do you intend for us?"

She seemed genuinely surprised. "But We thought you already understood. We intend to grant you exactly what you wish. You talked to Lir of it. He pointed the way to Us. The fact that you are here now is the proof of your success."

"Do you mean that you will grant us leave to stay?" Nuada asked.

"It is a leave that you have earned," she told him, then lifted a hand, *"but* not without qualifications."

Lir seemed somewhat taken aback by that.

"Qualifications?" he echoed. "Why? Just what do you mean?"

"Your friends may have proven they mean us no harm, and they may have demonstrated virtues to make them worthy of Our succor and patronage. Still, We sense too much of mortal failing in them, of barbaric emotions, not always in control. Such things could be most harmful to Our special people."

" 'Special people,' " Lir echoed with scorn. "People who have lost appreciation for the sometimes hard but always thrilling realities of mortal life. People living too long under always-perfect skies and breathing always-perfumed air. Don't you see? That's exactly why we would benefit from having these new minds, new hearts, new spirits intermingling with us."

"Our people have lived here in perfect peace and security and beauty for many centuries," she corrected him brusquely. "That will not be risked. *We* have *decided,* Lir!"

She turned from him to the waiting band of adventurers, addressing them in ringing, regal tones: "We intend to be most munificent to you. As our guests, you will be allowed to remain if you so wish. You will be granted our food, our materials, our help or advice as necessary; but direct contact between our races will be limited. You will have your own community, somewhat removed from ours." She ran a searching gaze over them. "Will that be acceptable to you?"

Nuada looked around him at his fellows. He saw nods and smiles of assent. He looked to Diancecht. The healer nodded also.

"You speak for us, Nuada," Diancecht said.

"I—I think I'd rather not," Nuada said.

The healer gave him an odd look at this unusual reluctance to take the lead, but then stepped forward to make answer for the group.

"Very well, O Queen," he said, bowing again. "We will accept your gracious offer, and your terms."

"But"—Dagda stepped forward to add with a note of pride in his voice—"we will accept your generosity only until our strength is restored and our numbers such that we can be a true people again. Then we'll be wanting to return to our Blessed Land, for it's our great dream to make it a place of our own. Will you also help us do that?"

"We will," she said, "though We certainly do not understand this strange desire that makes you wish to reenter your harsh world." She shrugged. "In any event, with that agreed, We will leave you to the care of Lir and our chief druid Arias. They will help you find a suitable place where your own village can be raised."

She began to turn away, but the aged Cuthach stepped forward, saying with some concern: "Wait, Queen! What about me?"

She looked back to him, her gaze aloof.

"What about you?"

"You're not going to send me back to that isle, are you?"

"You and your people are no friends to Us," she told him. "We might have been lenient, had the test not revealed your most rapacious and brutal nature to Us. We had no choice but to isolate you on that isle."

"For thirty years!" he said despairingly. "I'm alone now. I'm old. I did what you wanted this time, helping the little men in the testing of these ones. Haven't I earned pardon?"

"We feel a sympathy for him," Dagda put in. "He helped us, and he does seem a contrite man. Please, Great Danu, could you let him stay with us?"

She considered. "Well, it is against Our better judgment," she said finally, "but We will put him in your stewardship. And now, good-bye."

She moved away, the flock of her white-feathered druids following. Lir and the chief druid remained with the adventurers.

"I'm sorry," Lir said to them with some chagrin. "My own hope was that your acceptance here would benefit my people as much as your own." He shrugged. "Well, at least *you* have a new chance now, my friends. With us, you'll become a great people again."

"If that's true," said Nuada, "then one day our grandchildren or great-grandchildren may yet return to the Blessed Isle and make it their own."

"It's too bad we'll not see it," put in Dagda with regret.

"Ah, but that you will!" Lir said cheerily. "Right beside your children and their children. And your numbers will grow more rapidly than you think."

"How can that be?" asked Diancecht.

"Because, beyond the advantages of our isle's beauty, bounty, and peace, there is one other," said the chief druid solemnly. "The food you eat here and the air you breathe will grant great benefits to you. Like ourselves, you will retain a perfect health. More, you will not age!"

"That's right," Lir said, grinning broadly at the amazement in the faces of his friends. "That's why there is yet another name for this enchanted isle: Tir-Na-Nog. I welcome you all to the Land of the Ever Young."

Part Two
Land of the Ever Young

Chapter 14

New Home

The great horses trotted forward, muscled silver-white bodies moving powerfully, crimson manes flying as they drew the chariot across the waves and toward the shore of Tir-na-nog.

In the elegant, swan-shaped car behind the trotting steeds rode the gangly one called Lir, his attention focused ahead on the isle of enchantment. His long face, usually cast in amiable lines, was drawn in a musing frown.

The team drew the chariot and its driver ashore in a sandy cove. Then, at Lir's urging, the tireless creatures pulled it up a steep and narrow track to the crest. From here they all but flew inland, across the grassy uplands. So swift was their pace that it seemed little more than moments before they were descending into the great central bowl of the isle where the people of Queen Danu made their home.

He passed through the outer band of farmlands with their crops—full and ripening in the sun—and their arbors —trees and vines laden with succulent fruits. He reached the outer road that ringed the bowl, linking the small homesteads. From here he took another road on inward, toward the city with the shining palace of bronze.

Outside it a small gathering of young women in colorful

gowns sat on a small knoll, listening with great delight to a comely, golden-haired young man playing a sprightly song on a bow-shaped harp.

Waiting with obvious impatience until the tune was finished, Lir addressed them.

"Excuse me, but is Queen Danu holding court here today?"

The young women raised a chorus of bright giggling at this. The young man looked amazed.

"Why, sir, what are you meaning? Everyone knows that in the summer quarter of the year the queen resides at golden Gorias."

"I'm sorry, young man," Lir replied, fighting to keep irritation from his voice. "I've been gone a very long time. It slipped my mind. That's all."

"Gone?" said the youth. "But where? No one . . ."

"Why, it's Lir," said one of the girls. "He who has gone into the outside!"

This raised sounds of wonderment from all the women, and the young man flushed.

"I'm sorry, Lir," he said. "I didn't know. We all have heard of your mission. But, I wonder, why would you so eagerly volunteer to leave our paradise and go into such a terrible place?"

"It might do you good to see something of the real world, young man, instead of wasting your life dallying here," Lir said sharply, and urged his horses on.

He again pushed the team to a gallop and quickly rounded half the bowl, passing by marble Murias to reach the gold city. He rode straight through its gates and up the main avenue to the palace without slowing, whizzing through the residential neighborhoods and past many a startled pedestrian who stared after him.

He pulled the team in as they reached the palace, and the chariot slid to a stop before its main door. He leaped down from the car, tossing his reins to a rather nonplussed young man who happened to be nearby.

"Here, see to them," he brusquely ordered, and stalked on inside.

At the heart of the palace was a large room of a pentagonal shape. A disk of amber light set in each of the five walls reflected from the polished gold surfaces—floor and ceiling too—casting all in a soft, even glow.

In the center of the space, just above a five-sided pedestal, floated an iridescent sphere; a twin in look but half the size of that in the great temple. Before it, on two golden thrones, sat Queen Danu and Urias, chief druid of Gorias, in their feathered robes of state. They were speaking with a small group of men.

"And the crop of grapes promises to provide the finest wine, just as it has these many years," one man was saying in effervescent tones as Lir approached.

"My Queen," said Lir, "I've come."

She only waved him to wait and continued in her conference with the men.

"And how goes the rest of the harvest?" she asked.

"As always, my Queen," said another man. "Perfect."

"Danu," Lir said more stridently, "I've come a great way to see you."

"We know," she answered curtly, "but We have other business first! Now what of the hazelnuts?"

"Abundant!" a third man said. "Limbs cracking under the weight of the ripening crop."

All patience gone, Lir pushed forward.

"Yes, yes," he snapped at Danu. "Abundant, fine, perfect. All perfect, as always! You call me to come urgently here and then leave me standing while you discuss ideal crops that haven't been otherwise in a thousand years?"

"There are proper and polite ways in which things should be done," she told him. "Something which you ignore." She sighed resignedly. "But, very well." She looked to her chief druid. "Urias, please see to receiving the harvest reports. We will go and speak with Our most impudent subject."

She rose and strode majestically away from the thrones, Lir falling in behind. She led the way down a corridor and out a smaller rear door of the palace into a formal garden, a complex living tapestry whose abstract designs were drawn with a multitude of bright and exotic flowers.

Here Lir fell in beside her as they walked a path lined with tall, slender columns of white gold. Insects droned lazily among the flowers and the sun shone with a pleasing light and warmth. A perfect day.

"Now, my Queen," he said, "tell me: why have you re-called me from my travels in the outer world? It sounded as if there were some emergency."

"Not an emergency," she said. "At least, not yet. Just a concern. And it has to do with your friends—Our guests."

"My friends? There has been some trouble?"

"No, no. So far as I know from my chief druids' reports, everything has gone quite smoothly with the outsiders. Much better than We anticipated, in fact. So far."

"And now?" he asked.

"Now," she said with a worried frown, "it seems that *something* may be going to happen."

The wail of new life rose within the round-walled house.

The man known as Dagda ceased his restless pacing out-side and rushed to the house. He threw back its plank door, nearly tearing it from its hinges in his haste, and shoved his huge form through.

After the bright outside, the interior seemed dark at first. Only the glow of a small blaze in a central firepit lit most of it. Beyond the pit, across the single circular room, he could see figures within a chamber partitioned off from the rest by walls of wickerwork. There was much brighter light within it, and through the cracks at the corners he could glimpse the moving forms. The high and strident cry was coming from there.

He peered toward the chamber, his tensed face revealing the anxiety he felt. The wailing sound faded, and his anxious look increased. He drew a breath and held it, listening in-tently, frozen at the spot.

One of the wickerwork partitions was shifted open, re-vealing the chamber, lit by many tapers in tall holders. A large bed sat within, three young women in long, simple, bright-colored gowns around it. One of them completed the careful wrapping of a tiny bundle and laid it in the arms of another woman lying covered upon the bed.

On noting Dagda's massive presence in the house, the

three women said soft good-byes and moved out of the chamber, around the firepit to him.

"It's all right?" he asked quickly.

"It is," one woman said with a smile. "And 'it' is a she. You have a girl this time, Dagda. A fine healthy one too."

"A girl," he said, seemingly a bit stunned by the idea.

"Yes," said another woman. "Everyone has them, Champion. Even you."

"You can go to your wife now," the third woman said. "We'll wait outside until you've seen her and the babe."

They filed out, and Dagda, with some trepidation, moved toward the bed.

A young woman of great beauty lay upon it. Her long hair was the white-gold color of a rich wheat field ripened by the sun, lush and rippling about her shoulders. Her features were fine, smooth, exquisitely drawn, the flawless white skin touched with color by the flush in her cheeks and the deep red of her full lips. If there were indeed any fault in her comely looks, it would be in the sense of their being perhaps too delicate, too fragile, this especially accentuated now by the draining effects of her recent effort and pain.

Long lashes lifted to reveal eyes of a clear and sapphire-blue as she looked up to him. Uncertainty showed in them.

"You know it's a girl," she said in a gentle, faint, but still-clear voice.

"I do," he said.

Her eyes went to the bundle she cradled in her arms. "It . . . doesn't displease you?"

He quickly knelt beside her. "No, no!" he assured her earnestly. "Nothing that you do ever could."

"But you wanted sons," she said, still troubled, "to help rebuild, to make our people strong. I—I know you've been disappointed in our having so few. The two . . . then so long until now. And . . . the others . . . so many children."

He took hold of one of her slender hands in his own massive one, engulfing it. "Boand, my wife, I have never complained," he told her with great feeling. "I wed you freely. You have my full devotion. Believe me, there are no regrets."

With his other hand, he carefully pulled back an edge of

the blanket around the bundled object, revealing a tiny face. It was red, squat, wrinkled, almost hairless, its eyes squeezed up tight against the painful light of its new harsh world.

"It's certainly quite as—as—as handsome as the others," he said, assuming a hearty and approving tone. "Yes, a most healthy, intelligent-looking child. Impressive . . . even for a girl."

Boand smiled for the first time, seemingly reassured. "And what will you call her?"

"Call her?" he said with some surprise. He considered the newborn for a moment, frowning. "A female's name," he muttered. "I hadn't considered . . ." Then he shrugged, looking to his wife. "Well, after all, weren't the sons mine to name? This one should be for you."

She beamed in pleasure at that. "For me? I thank you my husband." She looked down at the baby. "Then I shall call her after my own mother: Bridget, for bright arrow. And may she have all the great intelligence and strength of my mother that never came to me."

"Don't say so of yourself," Dagda told her. He stroked her cheek with his fingertips, lightly, not to discomfort her with their callousness. "Yes, your mother was one of the finest among the women who first came here with us. And you are no less fine a woman, a wife, or a mother."

She smiled again, but wanly this time, and didn't reply. Clearly the fatigue from the long labor was overcoming her. He rose from the bedside.

"I'll leave you now to sleep," he said. "I'll call the women back to see to you. Later I'll return. Meanwhile, a good rest to both of you, my wife."

He went out of the house, telling the women waiting there that they could return to Boand. Then he set off at a brisk walk.

He moved along a graveled path across a level, grassy yard. He passed through several rows of round structures, spaced widely and evenly to form concentric circles. Like his own home, they were of a simple construction traditional to his people in their old homelands. Wattled walls— woven sticks—were covered with a mud and plaster daub painted in whitewash. Cone-shaped roofs were made of thatch—straw bundles tied and neatly interwoven. Most roofs were an older, weathered grey-brown. New ones stood out as a bright gold.

Around the several hundred such structures rose a wall, a high palisade, constructed of logs carefully chosen, cut, smoothed, and set upright in the ground. The wall completed a somewhat primitive but most practical fortress.

He saw other people as he walked, many clad in long robes of fine, all but diaphanous materials and gay pastel hues—men and women alike. The rest, like himself, wore the same kind of homespun wool tunics that had clad the adventurers on their arrival here.

The only change in the traditionally garbed ones seemed to be that the men had given over wearing trousers as a concession to the very temperate climate. Men were bare-legged, their tunics reaching to just above their knees. Women's tunics more modestly reached down to their calves.

He greeted many of these people—mostly the staidly dressed, largely ignoring the brightly attired—announcing with gusto the birth of his new child, receiving congratulations as he went on.

"Have you seen Nuada?" he asked here and there, but got only negative replies.

"No Nuada," he said to himself, "but I know where Goibniu is."

On passing through the outermost ring of homes, Dagda entered a wide area just within the wall. This was a commons area, where many activities necessary for the day-to-day function of the town were under way.

One section of the wall was lined with stalls where food-stuffs, clothing, utensils, tools, blankets, pottery, and the like were being both produced and bartered to a good number of customers.

At one end of the marketplace, a butcher and his young apprentice worked, slaughtering cow and sheep and pig brought from a pen nearby. They gutted and carved the meat upon an immense slab of wood used for their block, hanging the split carcasses up on hooks for viewing. The area and men were a welter of liquid red and dried black blood.

Some few patrons were about there, picking out sections

of meat. But most shied away, instead crowding in to haggle about the stalls piled high with fine fresh vegetables and fruits.

Dagda made his way through the market to a row of lean-to sheds built against the section of wall just beyond. Here the various craftsmen of the village did their work. Though there were very few of them at it today.

He passed a carpentry shop where a single young man was planing and fitting together the thick spokes of a heavy cart wheel. Next to it was a potter's shed where a woman shaped a stout, bulbous urn while a boy slipped another finished one into a stone-walled kiln.

A baker's and a tinkerer's shops were empty. A solitary woman in the weaver's shed worked in a desultory fashion at a plain brown rug upon her loom.

Separated somewhat from these shops was the long blacksmith's shed, actually little more than a sloped roof propped on heavy timbers, open on three sides. A dozen large chimney openings lined the roof, all fitted with broad collars of age-browned copper. But a plume of grey-black smoke rose up from only one. And from within the shed came only a single rhythmic, clanging sound.

Dagda went in. A dozen forges lined the smithy floor. A single one of them was fired with red-gold glowing coals. As the big man entered, a black figure was just lifting a red-hot hoop of metal from it with great tongs.

The figure laid the hoop upon a massive block of black iron, lifted a broad-headed maul, and began to beat a spirited tattoo upon the heated metal. Showers of sparks flew up from it, raining upon the black being who seemed oblivious to their sting.

Dagda waited until the hoop had cooled back to dark metal and the hammering had stopped before approaching the figure.

"I'm not interrupting serious work, am I?" he asked.

The other looked up. It was Goibniu himself, face barely recognizable beneath the layer of soot coating his exposed skin and the long leather apron he wore. The red-rimmed whites of his eyes showed startlingly against the black, and when he smiled in welcome at his friend, his teeth flashed out like sun shining through the sudden rift in a storm cloud.

"Dagda!" he said with delight, tossing the maul down. "Come in! This is only a wheel rim I'm working out. Seems there's no one but me wanting to do these repairing tasks. So what's brought you here?"

"Just the news that I have another child," Dagda replied. "Boand has finally given birth."

"Congratulations to you!" said the smith. "I'd begun to worry after her, it being so long."

"So had I. But she seems fine, and the child too. A fine, healthy girl."

There was just the slightest hesitation from the smith before he spoke. "A girl, eh? Oh, fine. Fine."

"What does that mean?" Dagda said sharply.

"Mean? Nothing at all. A fine thing to have a girl. I've five of them myself, along with the eight boys. And for you . . . that makes three children now?"

"You needn't say it," Dagda told him. "We both know well enough. But we know, too, *why* it's so."

"We do," Goibniu said contritely. "I was being an old fool to forget your long sorrow for the sake of my own bragging. I'm sorry."

"And there's Boand's weakness," the big man added. "So frail." He shook his head. "I didn't know. She is a fine woman. I wanted to . . . to protect her. I needed that, Goibniu."

The smith put a hand of understanding to his friend's shoulder. "Don't think of it. It's worked out well now, hasn't it? You've a new child. A healthy girl, sure to grow up strong and clever and as likely to do great things for us as any man. And you've your two lads. They've certainly grown up well!"

"Both?" asked Dagda.

Goibniu shrugged. "Ah, well not all children call their father's greatest loves their own." He cast a gaze around him at the empty smithy, and a certain ruefulness crept into his tone. "Look at me, then, working here alone, without one son, with most of my older ones off making songs and smelling flowers with . . ."

Here he broke off, realizing he was about to go too far. But Dagda finished for him: ". . . with my son Bobd."

The two men exchanged a commiserating gaze for a moment. Then Goibniu shrugged again and laughed.

"Never mind it," he said. "Come. Look here. I've another one."

A new energy seemed to animate him as he went to a rack near the forge, lifting off a spear with a smooth, sleek, polished wood shaft. Its head was covered with a bag of cloth.

"This is what I've worked on when I'm not about the repairing," he told Dagda with all the smith's old zeal, lifting the weapon and handing it to his friend. "You might call it a newborn child of my own. Let me just pull the cover."

He drew the bag off, revealing a spearpoint whose sleek lines, gracefully curved barbs, and polished silver-grey metal made it an object of beauty and wickedness at once.

"I've never seen the like," said an impressed Dagda, hefting the skillfully crafted weapon.

"It seems a hundred years at least I've studied their wizards' tricks to create and forge the strongest of metal," Goibniu said. "And it seems a hundred more I've spent watching their craftsmen. They make no weapons, of course, but their metal working goes so far beyond ours."

"Goibniu, not you as well," Dagda said scoldingly. "You're not being seduced by their ways."

"That I'm not," the smith said defensively. "But what fools would we be to stay with our old ways and ignore what can be learned from them. Just look at this!"

He took the spear away from Dagda, drew it back, and cast it toward one of the roof supports—a log thicker than his own waist. It slammed into the surface, piercing right through the wood, its tip cracking out the other side.

"See that!" he said with pride. "With a good arm behind it, there's no shield, no armor, even no stone wall that this wouldn't poke right through, and yet it's so light and true it'd fly to a mark a hundred paces away."

"A good weapon indeed," said Dagda, stepping to the spear and yanking it free with a single quick effort. He examined the tip. It showed no damage. "You should make more of them," he told Goibniu, handing it to him.

"And what for?" said the smith. His reborn zest over his creation faded away. He recovered the spear's point and returned it to its rack. "This one's only something I've done for my own amusement. What need is there for more?"

"Why, for our host," said Dagda. "For the time we'll sail out of here and challenge enemies to claim the Blessed Land for ourselves."

"And when will that be, Dagda? You know how things have changed. There are . . ."

"Nothing has changed," Dagda thundered in reply, drawing himself up and speaking with finality. "We have our purpose, and it's never changed." He gestured toward the spear. "Make more of those, Goibniu. Make many hundreds more. Make thousands! Someday soon, we will have need of them! Now, excuse me. I've others to tell about my child."

With that he wheeled and stalked out of the shed. The smith looked after him, shaking his head.

"Thousands, eh, Dagda?" he murmured to himself. "My old friend, when are you going to wake up?"

He cast a look toward the hooded spear, the product of his skill, a supreme tool of war.

Then, with a sigh, he took up the wheel rim and thrust it back into the forge's coals.

Chapter 15

Discoveries

The iron spit was lifted from the firepit.

Its tip, glowing gold with heat, moved closer to stop poised just a handbreadth from the hapless man's nose.

"I dislike using such a crude method to secure my ends," Mathgen told the man, "but I want you to understand fully how truly sincere I am."

The one he threatened was the youthful, fresh-faced druid named Oigear. He wore a shimmering, silver-white robe that was the everyday dress of one of the queen's druids, though it was tattered and filthy from some hard wear. Another, more obvious evidence of the young man's travails was the fact that he now hung in chains suspended from an iron tripod, as if he were a pot.

The tripod sat beside a round, stone-lined pool of liquid as black and smooth as polished iron. It was the central feature in a huge, circular room. Flaring torches set in sconces around its circumference revealed the stark, grey stone curve of wall that rose up some three stories to a raftered ceiling thick with dangling cobwebs. The air within the windowless space was thick with humidity and a musty smell.

Mathgen himself had changed somewhat in appearance

since his first arrival in Tir-na-nog. As with the others of his race, he had ceased to age, but he had taken on a more impressive look. A carefully trimmed ridge of dark beard had reshaped his weak-jawed and chinless face, giving him both a stronger and a more sinister look. He wore a tunic of finest black linen edged in gold embroidery. Over it he wore a long, plush cloak of deep scarlet, fastened at his throat by a large gold pin fashioned as a dagger.

"Let me move the spit closer to an eye," Mathgen told the man, "and have you really feel the searing heat."

As he did so, the young man's face drew tight, his eyes squeezing to narrow slits against the brightness.

"You would be advised to speak to me, Oigear," Mathgen urged. "I could burn out both sockets and leave you horribly blind. Or I might simply shove this brand up a nostril and burn out your fool brain."

"It doesn't matter what you do to me," the young man said bravely. "The secret of our magic is for ourselves alone. It could never be mastered by someone like you."

Mathgen laughed at that. "Not mastered? Why, you really don't understand, do you? I've mastered much of your magic already. Watch!"

He drove forward with the spit, the hot point spearing into the young man's eye.

The youth threw back his head, mouth opening to scream out his great pain.

But there was none. He was unhurt. The glowing point had vanished just as it plunged toward his socket. A maliciously grinning Mathgen now held nothing in his hands.

"You see?" he told the druid. "An illusion. Nothing more. One tiny bit of the magic I have learned from your fellows. And there's much more. Oh, yes. I've been gleaning the knowledge, bit by laborious bit, from their gullible minds for all these scores of years. I've flattered and cajoled and stolen secrets that give me power greater even than yours. You." He sneered. "So trusting! It was really too easy."

He moved back from the captive to a nearby table. He took up a short, thick rod of glass and a small bowl with a lid.

"Here is another little trick of mine," he said, removing

the lid and upending the bowl. Three objects dropped onto the floor and began at once to move about. They were spiders, no larger than a thumbnail.

Mathgen waved the glass wand over them. A light shone out from its end, cool and silver like a shaft of moonlight, fanning out as it fell to play across the insects. They began immediately to grow.

"They'll come for you now," Mathgen said, stepping back from the spiders that quickly swelled to the size of large mastiffs. Their enlarged bodies were wide, squat, and thick of limb, all covered with bristling black hair.

"They'll wrap you like a fly and then they'll devour you," Mathgen went on, savoring the words. "Slowly. And alive. Not pleasant at all."

The young druid stared in pop-eyed horror as they crawled toward him. Viscous, yellow-green slaver dripped from their working pincer jaws.

"I'll stop them, if you tell me what I wish to know," said Mathgen. "Tell me the secret of the greater powers."

"Greater powers?" said the other, voice growing shriller with his rising terror. The spiders had reached his feet now. Hairy forelimbs lifted to feel over him slowly, caressingly.

"Yes," said Mathgen. "I've learned these lesser skills, but it's the great powers I want: the ability to create immense illusions, to raise storms, control nature and men's minds. That's what I have to have."

The spiders had begun to enwrap the druid now, lifting pointed tails to shoot out their sticky filaments, each in turn casting a coil about him, starting at his feet.

"I can't give that to you!" the youth wailed. "There is no access to such powers except through the great sphere. That's the center of the magic power. The chief druids and the queen control it."

"Are you certain?" Mathgen demanded. "There is no other way?"

The spiders had wrapped him to the waist by now. They spun their way on upward toward his chest.

"No! No!" the druid screamed. "I'd tell you if I knew. Please, help me! It's the truth!"

"Yes," said Mathgen, scowling. "Unfortunately, I suppose it is."

He gave a sharp wave toward the spiders with his wand. Instantly they disappeared, taking their half-made cocoon of binding strands with them. The youth sagged in his chains, gasping in relief.

"They were never there," Mathgen said carelessly. "Just another illusion."

He went to the dangling man, slid a stool up beneath his feet to support him, unshackled his wrists from the chains, and stepped back.

"There," he said tersely. "You are free now."

The released druid rubbed at his chafed wrists and looked at Mathgen in surprise. "What? I can go?"

"Of course," the other said in a bored way. "You spoke the truth. I've no more interest in you."

He waved his rod toward the wall. An arched opening appeared in what had seemed solid stone. "There you are. The way out. Feel free to leave. And in the future, be less naive in accepting invitations to dinner from such as myself."

The young man made no reply but only bolted for the opening. Mathgen stood unmoving, seemingly uncaring, watching him go.

The druid reached the archway and started through into a long black tunnel beyond. Something large loomed up ahead.

It was a rodent. A ratlike creature, but of enormous size. Its whiskers vibrated excitedly and its tiny eyes glowed red.

The young man stared at it as it crawled toward him, then looked back to Mathgen.

"Another illusion?" he accused. "More of your magic? Well, this time I'm not afraid."

He went forward. The rodent rose up onto its hind legs, towering over him. Its mouth opened, revealing pointed teeth.

"Yes, it is another creation of my magic," Mathgen admitted as the youth strode boldly on.

The rodent struck, jaws clamping down over the druid's head, closing on his neck. There was a sharp crackling and a spurt of blood.

Mathgen gave a small, cruel smile. "But this time, I'm afraid, the danger is real!"

Dagda marched purposefully out the gates of the fortified
town.

The habitation of his people had been constructed atop a
broad, low hill, and he followed a road from the gates down
the slope. Below, on flatlands at the base, fields had been
laid out for training and for games.

On one rectangle of earth, hard-trampled by many feet,
a dozen youths of ten or twelve played a fast, rough-and-
tumble game with curved sticks, battling to drive a wooden
ball through goals at either end. The flailing sticks struck
home on players' bodies more often than on the ball. As a
training in combat reflexes, slash-and-parry sword tech-
niques, blood lust, and endurance to pain, it was near to
being as good as actual battle.

Not far away, some two score young men of around
fifteen were working with the real and lethal thing—iron
swords. They were blunt-edged, dull-pointed, but still fully
adequate to provide a killing blow as the youths, paired off
for practice, swung and stabbed and whacked at each other
with great energy.

One adult—a young man of about twenty years—stood
by to supervise. It was this one Dagda approached.

"Angus," he called.

The young man turned. "Yes, Father?"

His features alone were enough to identify him as of
Dagda's blood. He had his father's solid, square-jawed
looks, though softened by the influence of his mother
enough to make their effect more handsome, less intimidat-
ing. His figure, too, was similar: not so massive, but broad,
tall, and rock-hard, even more lithe and sinewy than
Dagda's.

"I came down to tell you: your mother's had the child,"
Dagda announced. "It's a girl."

Disappointment showed clearly in the other's eyes.

"A girl is it?" Angus said. "I should have known it. I'd
hoped so for a brother I could train up. At least one more
who'd be a warrior."

"And couldn't you do the same for a sister?" Dagda
asked.

"What chance would I have for that?" his son said bitterly. "Even a boy, my own brother, went the way of the harpers and the bards. Not likely my mother'll be having spear throwing and swordplay for her little girl."

"It's no fault of your mother's that made Bobd Derg what he is," Dagda said sharply. "Boand wants only what I want—for my children and my people. No, it's the soft bright lure of this place, this 'perfect land' that's drawn your brother in. That's what's made him soft."

"How can you say that, Father?" Angus said critically. "Look to yourself." He poked a finger into Dagda's belly. "You've grown soft as well, sitting about the house, dining on beef and pork and swilling ale, telling tales of great adventures no one believes in anymore."

This open and scathing assault seemingly shocked the big champion. He looked down at himself. Indeed, his massive form had become a bit more massive over the years of ease, his belly sagging a bit over his belt.

He sucked it in, drawing himself upright. "It's all muscle," he said indignantly. "If you're saying that I'm soft, whelp, well then you're going to have to prove it!"

Their exchange had by this time drawn the attention of all the lads. They'd stopped their own combats to watch.

"Very well," said Angus. He took up a sparc sword and shield from the ground and tossed them to his father, then got the same equipment for himself.

"Now, boy," Dagda growled, setting the shield firmly on one arm, "now we'll see."

"That we will," Angus agreed, adjusting his own shield.

The two charged in, the huge men like a pair of bulls slamming together. The din of crashing shields and clanging swords echoed from the hill and across the plain, so loud people up in the town stopped, listening, certain a thunderstorm must be on the way.

Down on the field, the lads watched in awe and some consternation as father and son fought. The combat was fast, brutal, and seemed in most dead earnest. They hacked and thrust and hammered, delivering massive blows with both shields and swords. They moved, swung, spun, and ducked with amazing agility and grace for ones so large.

Other parts of the body came into play as well. When

Angus locked sword and shield against his father's and the two were face-to-face, straining together in seeming impasse, Dagda jerked his head forward, driving his skull hard into Angus's face.

The younger man staggered backward and Dagda drove in, launching a furious barrage of hard blows against his son that battered the round shield and sent the sword spinning away.

Dagda stepped back and grinned. "Enough now, boy?"

"Not quite," said Angus, sweeping his foot up in a sudden kick right to his father's groin.

There were gasps of shock from the watching youths as the blow connected. Dagda gasped too, doubling forward in pain.

Angus stepped in and swung his shield sideways against the side of his father's now undefended head. The sound of iron against skull was like the gong of a great bell. Dagda was knocked sideways off his feet, thudding to the ground with a force that seemed to make the entire plain shake.

"*Now* it's enough," Angus announced.

As the disbelieving lads watched, he threw down the now concave shield and went to help his father up. The blow that would have annihilated the skull of any normal man seemed to have barely stunned the champion. He was already sitting up.

He shook his head and looked up as his son put out a helping hand. Then he smiled and took the hand, pulling himself to his feet.

"A good move, son," he said with satisfaction, tossing down his weapons.

"But I don't understand," said one of the youths, clearly bewildered. "Great Dagda, you're not angry?"

"Angus and I like to have little practices like this from time to time," the older man said. "It keeps skills sharp for both of us."

"It's also a good lesson for the likes of you," Angus put in, "to see that real battle's no kind of game, but hard, vicious, bloody work."

"It was a most unfair move you made against your father," said one handsome lad of freckled face and curling, dark red hair.

"No, Cian, it wasn't," Angus told him. "Father taught me that move himself. In a fight for your life, no move that can win for you can be unfair. Remember that and it might save you. Now, lads, get back to your own practice."

The game of sticks and ball began again. Most of the older youths in sword training also went back to their combats. But two of them approached the men.

"Please, Angus," said one boy hesitantly, "we don't think we want to take warrior's training anymore."

"Yes," said the other. "It's . . . well, it's too . . . cruel."

"Too cruel?" Dagda echoed in disbelief.

"We . . . we didn't know until we saw you," the first put in. "We'd never be able to do such things, to . . . to harm someone."

"It's a sculptor my mother's wanted me to be anyway," said the second. "To put my hand to the carving of beautiful things—birds and deer and . . ."

"Yes, yes. I understand," Angus said shortly, cutting him off. "I'll certainly not make anyone take training who hasn't the heart for it. All right, you two, leave your weapons and get on back to the town."

With expressions of great relief the youths dumped swords and shields and scampered up the slope toward the gates.

"There's no place for a warrior who can't be hard," Dagda said in disgust, looking after them. "Just as well."

"Is it?" said Angus, clearly put out by their desertion. "I've few enough in the training as it is. And of this lot, there's only one with real skill—young Cian there."

Dagda examined the youth who had spoken up. He was slender, but wiry and strong and very quick.

"He has some skill," the champion agreed.

"A great deal," said Angus. "Still, only one good fighter out of the scores of boys who could—who *should* be in training . . ." He looked to Dagda, speaking gravely. "Father, it wasn't all in fun when I said that no one believes in your tales of the old life anymore. Few of these younger lads care at all."

"Nonsense," said Dagda stubbornly. "The dream of our people is alive."

Angus shook his head. "The dream has faded. Only you few of the First Ones who were there really know. With each generation it's gotten worse. The vision of this green and blessed land of yours has been replaced by the wonders we can see around us. You know it yourself. You know what it's done to your own son."

"No!" Dagda said stubbornly. "Bobd Derg is only one. They haven't all become like him. Oh, they may well have become fascinated with the life here. But when the time comes . . ."

"When it comes?" said Angus. "And just when will that be? How strong must we become? We're five thousand strong now. There are seven generations all grown up, all still young, all intelligent and strong. Still, where is the word to go? No one raises it. Even you seem to have forgotten."

"That I have not," Dagda told him with vehemence.

"Then why not act?" Angus challenged. "Call for the fulfilling of the dream now. Remind everyone what they were meant to do. Restore the true purpose for our being here before it's too late. Father, listen to me: you have to do it now."

Dagda considered, then nodded. "It may be you are right. The years have flown by like the soft, sweet days of spring, and it may be we've been lulled into a careless sleep."

He slammed a massive fist into a palm, his voice taking on a determined note. "All right," he told Angus. "The time *has* come to speak about these things. Do you know where Nuada has gone?"

"To Filias, I think," Angus said, clearly delighted with his father's new fire, "to visit Diancecht."

"Filias," said Dagda. "Then that's where I go too!"

Chapter 16

Unrest

"Something?" Lir said to Queen Danu in puzzlement. *"Something* is going to happen, but you have no real idea what it is going to be."

"No more than We've told you," said the queen.

They were now seated at a long table in a dining room of the golden palace. They sat on gold bedecked chairs with golden plates and goblets before them, served by young people in flowing golden gowns. Golden light from the lowering sun struck through a large window, gleaming so brightly from golden serving bowls and pitchers that Lir had to squint.

"Look, could we have the shutters closed, please?" he said with some irritation. "I'm very near to going blind."

Urias, the gold city's chief druid, was seated with them, his official duties now concluded. He signaled to the servants who moved quickly to swing golden shutters closed.

"Ah, much better," said Lir, and took up the haunch of pork he was avidly devouring. He tore off a great strip with his teeth and chewed with vigor.

"You seem to have acquired some rather unusual dining habits during your time in the mortal world," she commented, eyeing his eating with distaste. She and Urias were dining most lightly and neatly upon vegetables and fruit.

"Oh, sorry," Lir said around the mouthful. He swallowed. "I traveled a hard, long way here without a meal. Please, my Queen, continue."

"Well," she went on, "as We have said, Our own powers and those of the sphere can give Us suggestions of the future, but only that. Exact events are impossible to foresee."

"Queen Danu could discern only that it somehow involves a drastic change for the ones from the outside," said the druid, "and that the change will involve our people, and also our most ancient enemy."

"This last is the thing of most concern to Us," said Danu. "We certainly want no involvement with those cruel ones we escaped from so many centuries ago. That is another reason you were recalled. You are the only one who has real knowledge of them."

"There seems nothing to fear for us," Lir told her. "I have continued keeping watch on them all of these years, as you asked. A mostly lonely vigil it has been too, I don't mind saying, save for those times when I could slip away to explore other parts of the outside world." Here some enthusiasm entered his tone as he leaned toward Danu. "You know, my Queen, you would be amazed at what things are like out there. The grand passions that those mortals have! Why I could tell . . ."

"Lir," Urias said sharply, "the queen has no interest in any of that. We want only your report on our enemies."

Lir sighed. "Of course. I always forget how truly narrow your thinking is here. A report? Well, there's not much to say. Whatever power they still have they keep concealed. I *have* had a single brief glimpse of Balor."

Danu gasped. "What? That monstrous thing? Still functioning?"

"Balor might say the same of you, my Queen," said Lir. "But he and his people scarcely venture outside of their tower of glass. Those deformed Fomor creatures of theirs do the pirating and raiding for them. The vermin have reoccupied their city on the island, of course. But they're little more than a rabble."

"Then why would Our vision include our old enemies as a part of the events?" Danu asked.

"Quite simple," said Lir. "When Nuada and his people leave us and go back to take their Blessed Land, they'll certainly confront the tower's forces again."

"Indeed?" Danu said. "Would that have to be so?"

"Of course," said Lir, surprised by her ignorance. "Nuada and the others expect it. That's why they've needed time and a place to rebuild strength, to prepare. Didn't you ever know?"

"We have not discussed their needs or their desires since they first came to Us," she said in a haughty way. "It is not for Us to deal with mortals. We have Our own people, Our own affairs."

"This *is* our affair," Lir argued. "Don't we share a common foe? Isn't their battle going to be our own?"

"*That* is something they must never know," Danu said sharply.

"You mean, our past is still being kept secret from them?" said Lir, aghast. "Don't you think they have a right to know? Since they'll be fighting a battle we ran away from, shouldn't they know the whole truth about what kind of terrible powers they might face?"

"Their choice to face these powers is their own," she said sternly. "But when they return to their world, We will not have them carrying knowledge of our magic or our past. No one out there must know who we are. For all this time We have kept Our children safe and hidden away. That will not change."

"But we can't live out eternity isolated here," Lir shot back. "With our help, Nuada's people can succeed in having their own land. They can finally destroy the evil we've feared so long. We can all go out . . ."

"Enough!" she said. "Even from you We will tolerate only so much insolence. We have bowed to your will in letting these mortals come here to live and to rest themselves. It is enough. Your task for Us now is to talk to them. It is you who are their closest friend. Find out what is happening. Make certain it will have no effect on Our people."

She rose from the table and lifted a finger toward him. "Do not fail Us in this, Lir," she admonished as if scolding a small child. "This is most imperative. We have not said so before, but Our forebodings were a most disturbing thing. Never since coming here have We had such feelings of dread. They *will* be resolved!"

With that, she turned and swept grandly from the room. Lir looked to the chief druid.

"Well, it certainly seems as if *I've* been told," he said with some chagrin.

"Yes. Our queen is most definitely not one to be denied," Urias said, smiling in sympathy.

"Then I suppose I should get right at the task of speaking with my old friends," Lir said, rising from the table. "Perhaps they can shed some light on this."

The druid rose too. "Um . . . Lir," he said with some hesitation in his voice, "before you do . . . I think there are a few things that you should know."

"Things?" He gave Urias a curious look. "What do you mean?"

"It's just that . . . well, it's not all as Queen Danu believes it is with the mortals."

"Aren't Nuada and his people faring well?"

"Yes, yes," the druid said quickly. "They're all doing quite well. Their numbers have increased to several thousands. Their first village has developed to a town rivaling one of our own in size. It's just that they've not stayed quite as . . . as separate as Danu wished."

"They haven't?" Lir said with delight. "You mean my hopes may have been realized after all? They actually may have infused some fresh, robust, free spirit into this idyllic and indolent little realm of ours?"

"No," Urias said. "Sorry. It's actually quite the opposite."

"Opposite?" Lir echoed, taken aback.

"Yes. That's why we've allowed it to go on, you see. They were so friendly to us, and they seemed so eager to learn our ways . . ."

"So . . . you taught them?" Lir said, still disconcerted by this unexpected revelation.

"Just little things at first. And slowly the relationship has developed. Nothing dangerous, of course. Some skills in the arts and crafts and in agricultural things. A bit of harmless magic. But mostly appreciation of our view of life: the peaceful, pleasant contemplation of natural beauty, philosophy, art, music, poetry."

"What you're saying is that you've been subverting an adventurous, independent people into becoming useless dreamers like yourselves," Lir told him angrily. "What kind of favor is that? They have a wonderful, most viable character of their own."

"I take great offense at that," said the druid. "Life in their harsh world made them dependent on their bodies, not their minds. We've rescued them from pain and suffering and death. We've made them aware of a new, greater reality. How can they not be the better for it? Oh, some of the First Ones—that large one called Dagda especially—seemed much opposed, and the earlier generations were somewhat reluctant, but the later ones have been increasingly keen. They join our classes, mingle with us, dress and live as ourselves. Some spend more time in our cities than their own! Even Queen Danu couldn't tell many of their people from ours now."

"Speaking of our queen," said Lir, "just why doesn't she know?"

"You know her decrees: complete separation of the two peoples. No knowledge at all of our ways to be passed to them. Though this was most harmless, still, we felt that she . . . well, she wouldn't understand. She has lived a very long time, don't you see. She's become set in certain ways. Protecting her children has become her one obsessive goal. We certainly didn't want to arouse her ire. So we determined to . . . protect her from the news. It wasn't difficult. Except to pass from city to city at the seasonal changes or to visit the great sphere, she rarely goes abroad. Everything was fine—until you arrived."

"The rotten grape cast into the vat of fine wine," Lir supplied. "Able to spoil the lot. I see."

"So, you'll not say anything?" Urias asked with a certain anxiousness.

Lir considered. "I'm not sure I like keeping anything from Danu," he said. "For all her stubbornness, there's a great wisdom that goes with her great age. Still, I wouldn't like to see her roused, especially against Nuada's clans."

"Good," the druid said with some relief.

"Hold on," Lir said. "I *might* keep silent, but only if I'm convinced there's no danger in it. What about this foreboding she's had?"

"A misreading of the signs," Urias said dismissively. "All the other chief druids agree with me on that. None of us saw or felt anything. We couldn't call up any evidence through the great sphere. Perhaps it was some tiny fluxuation in the lines of force. Perhaps it was only the queen's nightmare." He shrugged. "Who knows? There is no way that it can be of any matter."

"It can when the people of Nuada return to their Blessed Land."

Urias laughed at that. "Return? That will never be. With their new attitude, I think they'll be quite content to stay here."

Lir shook his head. "You may think that's true, but I can't credit it. So self-reliant a nature . . . for it to be changed so drastically? It just can't be!"

"You'll see it can," said Urias. "There's been no talk of their going for . . . oh, many scores of years. No talk at all. It's my belief they'll stay, and if they do, how can there be a reason for concern?" He smiled smugly. "After all, how *could* anything troublesome ever happen here?"

He picked a plump, red, perfect strawberry from his plate and popped it in his mouth.

Then he grimaced, gagged, and spit the pulped fruit out.

"By good Danu!" he said, staring at the bloody-looking mass where something half-chewed still writhed. "Worms!"

Rats of a normal, though well-fattened, size swarmed upon the pile of bones and rags in the dim tunnel.

The one called Cuthach edged by the remains and went on, peering apprehensively around him into the deep shadows.

He looked little different than on that day when he had first met Nuada's party. Like his saviors, his aging process had been suspended on the enchanted isle. The rub in his case was that the miracle had left him cursed to go on through the years unchangingly old, unchangingly bent.

Still, his scruffy look had vanished with the cutting of his straggling hair and beard; and his long-since disintegrated uniform—the last physical link to his past life—had been replaced by new, if plain, trousers and shirt of wool.

He came on slowly through the tunnel, finally emerging into the vast, circular room that was Mathgen's lair. He stopped there, gazing around him at the rather gloomy scene, breathing the dank air.

Not far away, Mathgen himself sat perched on a stool at the side of the central pool, squinting down sullenly at his own reflection in its smooth black waters.

Cuthach waited a moment to be recognized. When nothing happened, he cleared his throat loudly and called to the man.

"Ahem. Cap'n? I've come here, sir. As you asked."

Mathgen looked up from the water to see the older man. His mouth attempted a warm, welcoming smile and he rose to his feet.

"Cuthach. My good Cuthach. Welcome!"

He crossed to the other, slipped an arm about his shoulders, and ushered him forward.

"I'm so glad you could come," Mathgen said. "It seems so long since I last saw you. Just how long has it been?"

"Since the day after we came to Tir-na-nog, I think," Cuthach said.

"So long? Well then, it was certainly time to get together. Here. Sit down."

They had reached a long plank table set beside the pool. Mathgen offered his guest a stool at one end and went to sit at the other. Cuthach sat down, but continued to look about him a bit uncertainly. His gaze took in the rather ominous-looking metal tripod with its dangling chains.

"It . . . it's a . . . an unusual place that you have here," he ventured.

"It's simple," Mathgen said, "somewhat stark, perhaps, but it serves me admirably. I am well separated from everyone else on the isle, I'm totally independent of that overbearing Nuada and his precious lot, and I can work quite undisturbed. Now, why don't you go ahead and eat." He waved an arm over the table. It was loaded down with an array of foods—heaped platters of meats and vegetables and fruits, brimming pitchers of wines and ales. "I hope there's something that you like."

Cuthach's eyes went ravenously over the lot. "Everything!" he said with deep feeling.

"Fall to then," said Mathgen. And while the older man was piling up a plateful, he asked idly, "So, they're not feeding you very well?"

"I can't complain, really," Cuthach said, pouring out a mug of ale. "They're good people in the town. I do my little tasks for them, and they give me enough food, though plain it is. The really fine eating's in the cities of Danu's folk. 'Course there's none of that for me." He took a deep draught of the ale.

"Why not?"

"Well, her people, they don't like me, do they?" he said with bitterness, drinking again. "Too grand to have me around. All of your folk are free to visit. They even get invited in. But not this one. I just stay in my place and do my work and eat my simple fare alone."

He lifted the mug and poured another long draught down his throat.

"So you don't feel you're being treated fairly, is that it?" Mathgen asked.

"I said I can't complain!" Cuthach returned, refilling the emptied mug.

"Oh, come now," Mathgen said. "It's just the two of us. I know what your life is: a servant's! You muck out their stables, clean up their rubbish, change the filthy straw on the floors of their homes, and in exchange they feed you their old scraps. Don't you resent that?"

The older man drank again. Then he met Mathgen's eyes. The fire of the drink was clearly kindling a blaze in him. Old energies and old passions were flaring up, flickering brightly in the time-clouded eyes.

"Yes, by Balor. That I do resent. I'm as good as any of that fancy lot. As good even as your folk. I've rights to as fine a life as them."

"Well said," Mathgen told him, smiling in satisfaction. "Then I believe that we may be able to help each other. Let me show you something."

He rose from the table, signaling Cuthach to rise as well.

The other obeyed, though already with a bit of unsteadiness from the drink, and followed his host to the edge of the pool. They both peered in.

"What do you think?" asked Mathgen.

"It's very . . . black. It must be deep."

"Oh, it is. But do you know *what* it is?"

Cuthach looked harder, frowning as he tried to fathom the depths. Then he shrugged. "It's a pool, isn't it?"

"Wrong, my friend," Mathgen said with a grand air. He waved both hands over the water and murmured a chant of unintelligible words. Instantly the dark surface came alive.

A light, like a glowing bubble, rose up from the black depths at the pool's center. It touched the surface and spread, rushing out in all directions like the ripples from a dropped stone, radiating waves of light, pushing the darkness backward as it expanded.

In moments it had reached the pool's stone edge. The surface had been in those moments transformed to a sheet of softly glowing, iridescent white. Streamers of pale color—turquoise, saffron, tangerine—played through it like liquid hues poured in and gently stirred.

"There, you see?" he said with pride. "This is the equivalent of one of the spheres of energy. Not the great one, I'm sorry to say, but certainly one of the four lesser ones, and with fully as much power."

"It can't be so," Cuthach said.

"Oh, but it can. Watch here."

Mathgen waved again, uttering another chant. The drifting bands of color gathered together, twined and looped and twisted into shapes, coalesced and brightened and clarified into a sharp image of the isle's central ring of copper-clad monoliths.

Mathgen waved. The image changed. The view was rising from the ring, swinging, soaring over countryside, swooping down to focus on the log-walled town of Nuada's clans.

"By all the powers," breathed Cuthach, much impressed.

"It's more than this," said Mathgen. "I can draw the magic from here to use elsewhere."

With a magician's flourish, he produced a glass rod as if

from thin air, shining with the pool's same iridescent light.
He pointed the rod's tip toward the dining table. He uttered
a single strange word. Furniture and food vanished away,
leaving Cuthach staring at empty space.

"My food," the older man said in dismay.

But he was quickly distracted from the loss as Mathgen
lifted the wand and swung to aim its tip at a point high
above the pond.

A geyser of light spouted from the water's surface, rising
and pooling to form a surging mass just below the ceiling.
The mass swirled slowly, its bottom growing flat. Its top
billowed upward into the rafters. Forked bolts of golden
lightning crackled back and forth within it. Some flashed
down toward the pool's surface from the base of the boiling
cloud. Rumbles of thunder—diminutive but still potent in
the enclosed space—shook the room.

"I can create storms too," said Mathgen. "Small ones so
far, I grant, but still strong enough to destroy one little man
like you. Another practical use of these powers that Danu's
people haven't considered, the pacifistic fools."

Cuthach stared up in terror as a tongue of lightning
licked far out toward him. The acrid smell of ozone was
strong in the air.

"Please, not me," he pleaded to Mathgen. "You didn't
really bring me here just to kill me, did you?"

Mathgen gave the glass rod yet one more little wave.
The storm receded, shrank away as if sucked back into the
spout. The column of light shrank back down into the pool.

"Of course not," Mathgen said, smiling and turning toward the man. "I have a great need of you, my dear old
friend."

Once more he slipped an arm of comradeship, of assurance, of conspiracy around Cuthach's bent shoulders.

"Together," he said, "we are going to conquer this entire
isle!"

Chapter 17

Arguments

"Conquer?" Cuthach echoed in astonishment.

"Yes," said Mathgen, "unfortunately."

He dropped his arm from about the old man's shoulders and began a restless walk about the pool as he went on.

"You see, I've gone as far as I can alone. It's taken me all of our years here just to gain the knowledge to create this." He swept a hand out over the water.

"What is it, exactly, if you don't mind me asking, Cap'n?" Cuthach said. "I mean, how does it work?"

"It's far too complex an explanation for you to understand in detail," Mathgen said in a superior way. "To put it simply, there are lines of a magical force that crisscross the world. Places where many of these lines cross are points of immense power. This . . . supernatural energy, if you will, can be harnessed by the human mind. By the *proper* human mind, I should say. One both sensitive and strong enough to control rather than be controlled. Through the energy, a man can become as potent a sorcerer as one of the chief druids. Or more so."

"A chief druid," repeated the old man, caught up by the idea. "What I wouldn't give to be one of them."

"Yes. Well, I'm afraid your mind wouldn't qualify,"

Mathgen said dismissively. "The energy would destroy you. In any case, it took half my years here to discover that secret and understand how it worked. Here. Look."

Now on the opposite side of the pool from Cuthach, he stopped and gestured over the surface. The colors shimmered and re-formed. Once more an image of the central monoliths was shown.

"There," said Mathgen. "That ring of copper-sheathed stones is the key. Four extraordinarily strong power lines join there. One of the surrounding cities sits right upon each. The ring itself serves to store, concentrate, and focus the magic power. The great sphere is the focus point."

He gestured again, this time using the wand. He murmured a quick spell. The images re-formed to show, incredibly, Mathgen himself! He was walking across a meadow, carrying a curiously shaped stick. It formed a fork, the two short tines held in his hands, the long end thrust forward. Its tip vibrated with some violence, and seemed to be actually pulling him along.

"I devised an instrument sensitive to the lines," he explained. "Our shamans in the old country used a like hazel rod in dowsing for water sources. With it, I managed to trace the most powerful of the lines—the one running through Murias."

"That . . . that's you!" said Cuthach, looking from the image to the present man.

"What a quick intellect! Yes. Me many years ago."

"You can show the past?"

"Quite easily," Mathgen said offhandedly. "Mine, or anyone's. Even yours. It's showing the future that's a bit hard. But to continue: I traced the line to this place, the most isolated spot it passed through. Perfect for my plan. I dug down and tapped into the stream of energy, just as if I were digging a water well. This pool serves to disguise it admirably."

At his next wave of the rod the image altered yet again, showing a sharp promontory thrusting out into the sea. Atop the point, high above the waves, rose a circular tower, looking stark and lonely there. It was a featureless turret several stories high, seemingly made from a smooth and seamless metal of a dull brown.

"That's the very tower we're in now!" said Cuthach.

"Yes. And it took me many more years of hard toil—alone naturally—to construct it over the pool. I took my basic concept from Danu's people, and improved on it substantially, I believe. I sheathed the exterior completely in copper. This entire building is a storehouse for the energy, vastly increasing its potency, and my own power."

"But all of this is going right against the queen's decree," Cuthach said with some anxiety. He looked around him as if her wrath were about to fall upon them. "I mean, stealing their secrets, building this, doing magic. Haven't you been afraid of her people finding out?"

"Them?" Mathgen laughed scornfully. "They're so honest, so trusting, so absurdly innocent. They made the mistake of believing me as pure and honorable as Nuada and the rest. I simply declared I needed a place alone for my arts and contemplations. They were eager to let me go where I wished, and paid me no heed after that. Of course I took other precautions. And with the magic skills I've developed, I've put up some very effective shields." He smiled arrogantly. "Even Danu and her great sphere couldn't spy out what I'm doing within these walls."

"So you've fooled and cheated these people and you've gained yourself some power," Cuthach said. "Very admirable indeed. But it still doesn't say why you need me."

"Because I've reached a point where I've no other way to act. I've rather pushed things to a head, and I must move swiftly. I believe they may have finally begun to suspect me."

"Why?"

"My own fault, really. Frustration drove me to it. You see, I have some power, yes. But control of *The* power is denied me without control of the main temple and the great sphere itself. I tried siphoning it off to here—and failed. I tried using magic to shift control to me—and failed. I even used my skills to probe the sphere itself for clues. It turned my spell away. I've a feeling my interference has made them aware something is wrong. And then there was my last, most desperate attempt. I lured a druid here, hoping that he might know some trick or some key that might help me. Again, I failed."

"I saw the remains," said Cuthach.

"That may have been a little foolhardy. His disappearance will be noted eventually and an alarm will likely be raised."

"Especially in a land where hardly anyone dies."

"Exactly. That's why I was forced to my last resort. I realized I'd have to seize the temple, physically take control of the sphere. Then I could have the power."

"Not likely they'd let you walk in and take that," Cuthach said.

"Ah, there's that quick mind at work again. No. Not even they are so naive. I knew I would need help. But I also knew I'd have no chance of raising a suitable force among either Danu's people or my own. I'd have to find someone else; someone who shared my desire for wealth, my need for power, my ruthlessness. That's why I called for you."

"Once I did share those things," the other said. "But long ago. Now I'm only a poor, weary old man. And I'm alone. What good can I be?"

"You can help me to secure a host strong enough to seize and hold Tir-na-nog. You can take me to your own people."

"My people?"

"Yes. Those of that tower of glass. You said they were a warrior host, eager to subjugate and pillage. They sound ideal men. Perfect allies."

"It might be that they are. But to conquer this whole isle . . ."

"What? You don't think they'd have the strength? The will?"

"I can't be certain. I can't tell you much about them of the tower. I was only a simple, ignorant sailor all my life, or near to it. I went into the training as a child. Don't remember much before it but a huge, bright room filled with squalling brats. And afterward, well, my world was either on a ship at sea or in the docks that were underneath the tower. Like a cavern that was. Only our officers went into the upper floors, and they hardly spoke to us."

"But you must have at least heard something."

"Oh, there were tales, certainly, of the life upstairs. Mostly wild rumors of wondrous things as hard to believe as . . . well, as the things I've seen in this enchanted land."

"Still, you know the ships and the men were real."

"Oh, aye. Dozens of ships and hundreds of men. At least, there were all of those years ago."

"And you could guide me to the tower and get me in."

"I could do that."

"Good!" Mathgen said with elation. "Then I can do the rest. I'll win their help. I'll show them what they can gain here."

"Now, hold on there, Cap'n," Cuthach said. "I told you I *could*. I didn't say I *would*. A long time has gone by. I've lost track of how long. Things may well have changed. My friends will all be dead. I'll be a stranger to them as much as you. Why should they trust us?"

"We'll make them trust us," Mathgen said determinedly. "It's the only way. We have to take the risk."

"You mean *you* do. It's too risky for me. Look here, I may not live a grand life, but it's comfortable and safe, and surely better than those years being marooned."

"But think of the riches," Mathgen cajoled. "Think of being a hero to your people for leading them to such a prize. Think of the power!"

"And what good will those be to me now?" the other said with bitterness. "Do you see what stands before you? A crabbed and ancient man. It's too late for any reward to tempt me."

"I don't think so," said Mathgen cunningly. "There is still one. You help me win control of Tir-na-nog, my friend, and with the power I'll have then, I will be able to make you young again!"

A gleam of blended astonishment and hope came into the old eyes. "Young?"

"As young as you'd like, with all the spirit and passion and strength that you ever had. Youth—eternal if you wish —and riches—beyond any you could imagine. Now, my friend, what do you say?"

Cuthach's consideration lasted only an instant. Then he bared his old yellowed teeth in an avaricious grin.

"How soon do we make a start?" he said.

The fire from the tiny brazier licked at the base of the delicate glass retort.

The liquid bubbled furiously, turning from a pale yellow to a shade of dark red-brown. Diancecht peered at it and nodded with satisfaction.

"You see?" he said to Nuada. "It will make the proper combination in a few moments now."

They were in a large, rectangular, open room, well lit by sun through a row of high windows along one side. All the walls were of a polished grey-white marble, lined at precisely spaced intervals with slender, neatly fluted columns.

The room's look of balance, proportion, and harmony produced a sense of pleasant rationality. This was, however, in contrast to the seemingly random and jumbled masses of complex paraphernalia filling tables, stacked on shelves, even piled on floors.

Diancecht, his long tunic of plain white linen covered by a protective apron of leather, hovered over the retort and a dozen other glass containers of varied kinds cooking away on as many other braziers. Some of the receptacles were linked by tubes that also seemed of glass. Liquids of many hues were scooting or bubbling through the tubes, dripping out here, whooshing out there, altogether making a colorful, fascinating, and somewhat noisy show.

Nuada watched it all with great interest.

"I always love visiting you," he told the healer. "Always something going on. What is it you're about now?"

"Well, if I do the whole process correctly, I'll have an elixir that can cure the plague," Diancecht said.

"What, a plague like the one the Fomor put on us in the Blessed Land?"

"Yes. I always wanted to know just how Liam . . . Lir, I mean, produced it for us. Leigh, the chief healer of Murias, has been teaching this to me. Ah! It's ready!"

The liquid in the single retort had now turned a deep golden brown. Diancecht carefully lifted the container from its stand over the fire with metal tongs and poured the contents into a pottery mug.

Then, before Nuada's shocked gaze, he lifted the mug and drank!

"Diancecht, what are you doing?" Nuada cried. "You're drinking the cure?"

"This?" said the healer, lowering the mug. "Oh, it's not the cure. All the rest of this is making that. No, this is something else. It's a distillation from the beans of a strange plant I found growing here. A little experiment of my own. It has a most unusual, most intriguing taste." He held out the mug. "Try it."

Nuada took the mug, hesitated over its brown contents, then sipped. He considered, then sipped again.

"Hummm. A rich, deep, full-bodied taste," he said critically. "Not bad. But it has much bitterness to it. Some sweetening might help. Honey?"

"Perhaps this finely granulated substance I found would help," the healer suggested, taking up a bowl of golden crystals and a spoon. "I'll stir some in, and . . ."

"Is this what you call work?" came a booming voice.

They turned to see Dagda crossing from the door toward them, moving with purposeful stride.

"Dagda!" said Nuada in surprise. "It's most unusual to see you here."

"I come all the way here to find you, expecting to find you deep in some crucial, most difficult work," the big man growled. "Instead I find you toying with some new kind of drink."

"I sense that some of us are not in a good mood," Nuada said.

"And why should I be? With this easy, carefree existence taking us over. With everyone giving up the old ways. I expected better of at least those few of us who were the first. But look at you, Nuada. You've even given up our manner of dress."

Nuada glanced down at himself. He had changed from the simple homespun such as Dagda wore to a fine tunic of pale green fringed in gold and a light wool cloak of white and emerald plaid. A silver brooch of delicate spiral shape fastened the cloak at his throat. A matching pin caught up his long fair hair behind his head.

"These clothes are well made, comfortable, long-wearing," Nuada said by way of defense. "I like their look as well."

"But they aren't ours," Dagda said. "That is the point. It's *their* style, produced by *their* skills and magic. One more way we've become dependent on them, become more them and less ourselves. What's wrong with our own good wools?"

"They itch," Diancecht said simply.

"Maybe your skin's just grown too soft, Healer," Dagda returned scathingly. "You're worse than Nuada. You've given up our town entirely to live here, among them, surrounded by their luxuries, soaking up their ways."

"I object to that," Diancecht retorted with uncharacteristic heat. "I work very hard here—all day and often through the night—sharpening my skills and learning new healing methods and new cures. It is all most valuable. How foolish it would be to live in a land of such knowledge and not to make any use of it."

"That's the same excuse that Goibniu made," Dagda said gruffly. "Even he's been seduced by this land of wonders. And now my son tells me I have been growing fat and lazy too, forgetting about my duties to my own."

"So *that's* what it's all about," Nuada said with sudden understanding. "Angus has been goading you again."

"Well, maybe," Dagda admitted. "But isn't he right to do so? Look at what's happened to so many. Look at my own other son, Bobd Derg. Can you say the kinds of things he's learning are doing our people any good?"

"They are things of value," Diancecht said reasonably. "They can do us no harm."

"They can if they make us lose belief in our own values," Dagda argued in return, "if they destroy our hold on our own dreams."

"My friends!" came a new voice. "How have you been?"

They turned to see Lir coming through the door into the room. Their own argument for the moment forgotten in their delight, they moved to meet him with expressions of warm welcome.

"Lir, it has been too long," said Nuada, shaking his hand.

"We wondered if we'd ever see you again," Dagda said.

"Oomphh," said Lir, submitting to another of the big

man's near-smothering hugs. "I'm glad to see you all as well."

"How do things fare in the outside world?" the healer inquired.

"Much as you left them," he said. "Men still war and raid and enslave. Things are still harsh, but they are exciting too. Your Blessed Land still awaits you. The Fomor have returned there, but they are no match for the large nation you've become. You'll win your land easily when you go back."

"*If* we go back," Dagda corrected.

"Dagda feels we are losing touch with our true goals," Nuada explained.

"And are you?" Lir asked him bluntly.

He exchanged a look with Diancecht. The healer considered, then gave a nod of agreement.

"All right," Nuada also agreed. "A little, perhaps."

"Much more than that," said Dagda forcefully.

"I must truthfully say, I have to agree with Dagda," Lir told them. "Perhaps my having been gone makes me somewhat more objective, able to see changes that have crept gradually upon you. But I've done a bit of looking since I returned. I went to your own town. That's where I heard that Dagda was coming here. What I saw was . . . well, it was disappointing."

"Disappointing?" Nuada repeated, taken somewhat aback. "Is that really how you feel?"

"I'm afraid so." Lir shook his head unhappily. "I had such hopes of your bringing some vitality to this place, shaking these people out of their cushioned, sheltered bed of apathy. Perhaps it's my own fault. You leave a place for a century or two, and things just fall apart."

"A century or two?" said Dagda.

"What are you saying?" asked the healer. "Surely it hasn't been more than eighty years or so that we've been here."

"I'm sorry," said Lir. "You don't know, do you? The nature of this place makes time seem to go by more quickly. It all becomes rather a single pleasant blur. But outside the Enchanted Isles, the real days pass more ponderously. Out there, it has actually been nearly three hundred years since you entered the barrier fog."

"Three hundred years!" Nuada said in shock.

"By Good Danu," said the healer. "Even the bones of our comrades who returned to the old lands must be dust by now."

"Long since," said Lir.

"So many years," said Diancecht. He looked at his friends. "Maybe we have let the spell of this place come upon us too much. Maybe it is time to act."

"Time to renew our pledge," said Dagda. "Time to make ready to return. Nuada, you must take command. Order preparations to start."

"No," said Nuada. "I'll not order anything."

Dagda looked at his old comrade in surprise. "What do you mean? You are our leader. They'll listen to you."

"I've never claimed to be leader," he returned sharply. "And if I was, it still wouldn't be for me but for all of our people to decide what course we are to take. There are many more of them whose opinions must be included now. They have their own lives and desires. We can't force ours on them."

"We're forcing nothing!" Dagda said forcefully. "Their desires are as our own."

"That we will see," said Nuada. "All the families must be gathered. Everybody must be notified."

"All the First Ones especially must be contacted," said Dagda.

"Some are scattered," said Diancecht. "Mathgen lives somewhere on the coast. I've no idea where Morrigan is."

"I have," said Dagda. "I'll fetch her."

"Wait," said Nuada. "What about Boand? Should you be leaving her when she is so near her time?"

"Oh," said Dagda, reminded, "her time's come. She had the child. A girl."

"Then you should most definitely be with her," said Nuada.

"No," he said firmly. "My new child only makes my need to act all the greater. I'll not have another of my blood growing up in a world that is not our own. What we need to do right now is the most important thing. Boand understands."

"All right then," Nuada accepted. "You contact the other First Ones. Tell your own sons as well."

"I'll tell Angus," said Dagda.

"What about Bobd? He must be told. He has become a figure of much influence among the younger ones."

"You see to it, Nuada," Dagda said. "Please? I . . . well, I can't seem to even talk to him anymore. It only ends in arguments."

Nuada sighed. "If you wish it, I'll tell him. And I'll notify all the families in our own town. Diancecht, you should spread the word to all our people in their cities and to our students in their schools."

"I say we tell them all we'll meet in three days," said Dagda. "That should be long enough for gathering."

"It is a very good decision you are making, my old friends," Lir told them. "I think that it is coming just in time."

"We're all agreed then," Nuada said. "Three days from now, our people will decide upon their fate."

Chapter 18

Meetings

The two birds flew up suddenly from the treetops as Dagda's huge form pressed through the bushes toward the clearing.

Startled, he looked up toward them. He watched as the pair lifted gracefully away, their brilliant crimson plumage brightly visible against the blue of the clear sky until they had shrunk away to tiny dots. Then he went on, forcing a passage through a last screen of brush and into the open.

The clearing was roughly circular, about two dozen strides across. The high pine trees of the dense forest surrounded it like a palisade. There was no sign of life in or about it.

He stood for some moments scanning it with his eyes. No movements. He listened intently, holding his breath. No sounds. Finally he lifted his voice to call out: "Morrigan, where are you? It's Dagda. I want to speak to you."

He waited. No response. He raised his voice to bellow out the name: "Morrigan!"

It rolled away through the forest like a thunderclap. He waited again. Then, a sharp *caw* from above drew his attention.

He looked upward to see two specks there, high overhead, but rapidly dropping down toward him. He thought at first that they were the same birds that had flown up at his approach. But as they swept down nearer, he realized that they were both jet-black.

They came yet closer, sweeping ever lower in broad, lazy spirals, gliding on outspread wings. Ravens, he could now see. Very large birds, even for their type, rivaling a hawk in size. Enormous wingspans supported long, sleek bodies covered with feathers of blue-black so deep and glossy that the birds flashed gold, green, and crimson highlights in the sun.

They sailed on down, flapping as they reached close above the ground to settle gently in. Wings furled, they stood fearlessly, meeting his gaze with their glinting black eyes, heads cocking from side to side.

Dagda stood staring, uncertain of what he was to do. But the quandary was solved for him. An aura of shimmering light rose about one of the birds. It grew quickly larger, brighter, enveloping the whole creature in a translucent haze. The bird's form within it was only a shadow, indistinct. Still, it was obvious from Dagda's viewpoint that its nature was most definitely changing. In moments the shadow had expanded, shooting upward and altering radically.

When the transformation ceased and the encasing cocoon of light faded away, the figure of the little chieftain of the Pooka clan was revealed.

"Onairaich!" said Dagda. "I should have guessed at once that it was you."

"So, you wish to see Morrigan?" the other curtly replied.

"Yes. I heard she was living here in these woods somewhere. I've been searching without any luck all day. Do you know where she is?"

"I do." He gestured to the raven still standing beside him.

A similar aura of light rose to swallow it. The bird figure shot upward, shifting into a long and lanky shape. The glow died, and Morrigan stood there.

She was even more wild a figure than before. She had aged no further, but she had become yet more bizarre. Her body and her limbs—much revealed by the brief leather shift she wore—were lean, sinewy, and as hard as any man's. Her thick billows of black hair surged about a long, almost cadaverous face, chin and nose and cheekbones sharply, almost painfully pronounced.

"Why did you find me?" she asked in a voice that had become a low rasp.

"Things are happening," he said. "Urgent things. We have to talk."

She nodded sharply. "I'll get my cloak and weapons."

She went off toward the clearing's farther side where the trunk of a large tree lay. The two men watched her.

"Has she learned to shift shape herself?" Dagda asked the little man.

"Only from human to raven," Onairaich said, still in his brusque way. "It was her choice. She seemed interested in no other. She is a very strange woman. It's something I don't understand."

"I do," said Dagda. "Her heart and mind have become like those of the raven. Why not her body too?"

She was reaching into a hole in the log now, pulling objects out from a hollow space within and donning them.

"I had thought it impossible for one not of Pooka blood to develop the skill," the little man said. "It took our clan many centuries of labor and sacrifice to learn the magic transforming arts, to make them part of us. She, an outsider, learned in only a few score years."

"I've always wondered," said Dagda, "why was it your clan decided to become shape-shifters themselves?"

"You see what we are and ask that?" Onairaich asked him, looking up the form that towered over his. "One so powerful as you? We wanted what you and everyone here has: to be strong and beautiful and proud. While the rest used magic to make their lives easy, we worked hard. My father who was chief before me died in the attempt to make more perfect forms. Now, I'm forced to give up our hard-won secrets."

Deep resentment was so obvious in these words, that Dagda looked to him wonderingly.

"Forced? What do you mean? Did Morrigan force you?"

"No, no. Not she. It's not her I feel ill will toward. In some ways, I even feel a kinship with her. No, it's the queen at fault, as always. Our Great Ruler," he said sarcastically, "so gracious to her own, and even to you outsiders. So domineering to us. It was she who ordered me to just hand away the one skill that gives us identity. Just because she felt your raven-woman had earned her special favor, she granted her a boon. Of course, it was my task to spend these long years carrying it out. Great Danu's grateful slave. Great Danu's little tool."

Morrigan was coming back to them now, a cloak of black about her, a sword belted at her waist, a casting spear and a shield in her hands.

"You wanted to talk," she said to Dagda. "Then talk."

"Look here, this doesn't concern me," Onairaich said. "We're finished for today. I'll leave you."

The glowing cocoon rose instantly about him as his shape-shifting once more began. In seconds he was a bird again, but a handsome peregrine falcon this time, flapping up from the clearing on broad wings.

"See you at dawn tomorrow," he called down to her as he winged out of sight beyond the circling trees.

"Amazing skill he has," Dagda said, looking after him.

"A good man," she cawed out tersely. "A good teacher."

"Also a man of much anger," said Dagda, "much hate."

"Yes, I sense those in him too. And much pride as well. That makes him feel great humiliation."

"Because of Danu's treatment?"

"The way he sees it, yes. His people came to Tir-na-nog with Danu because of her pity for them. They were cruelly treated in the outer world. They hoped to change that here, becoming equal to the rest."

"So they learned the shape-shifting art."

"But it failed them. The new skill only made them all the more objects of curiosity, of amusement. Worse, the queen saw uses for them, and began giving them tasks. They saw themselves as being turned into slaves, and their resentment grew."

"Couldn't they leave?" asked Dagda. "Fly away anywhere?"

"Where?" she replied. "You know the mortal world would treat them no better. Likely worse."

"True enough. And being trapped here would also chafe

after so many years. In fact, Morrigan, that's why I've come to you. Our people are going to meet. I'm meaning to propose that it's time to prepare for our leaving."

"Finally!" she said. "We are ready to return then?"

"Well . . . in numbers, yes," he said with some hesitation. "But in other ways there will have to be some changes and some labors to be done. For one, we must see that all the younger ones are properly trained as warriors."

"That hasn't been done?" she said, aghast. "What's been going on? What have you been doing these past years?"

"There has been a lessening of interest," he explained defensively. "And then the drive to enforce the training has been . . ." He stopped abruptly, shrugged, then said irritably: "Oh, I'll just say it out! Things have been let go. I'll make no excuses. Much of the fault is mine."

"*You* let it go," she said accusingly.

"Look here, I didn't see you helping to keep a spirit for fighting alive," he pointed out. "You hiding out here and learning magic ways."

"I had to do it," she said. "How could I ignore a chance to learn such a great power? Think of the help it can be against the Fomor when we return."

"You, Goibniu, Diancecht, all learning the magic skills of Danu's people. All saying that it's useful, that it's for our good. But the truth is that you've become so concerned with gaining knowledge for yourselves that you've let the others go astray. Morrigan, what good will all the skills and magic do us if we never return?"

This took her aback. "You think that that could be?"

"It could, but not if we act quickly and definitely. I think the desire is still strong in our people. Maybe sleeping in some. We just have to reawaken it. That's why I need you."

She shook her head. "Not me. I'll be no use to you. I have no place among people anymore."

"You have to come!" he said earnestly. "I need all of the First Ones to face the rest, to remind them what we want, to raise the old fire in them. I need you, Morrigan. We can't take any chance of failing."

She considered, then nodded. "All right. I'll help you."

"Good," he said, relieved. "We meet at the central hall of the town at dawn in two days time."

"The town," she said. "I can't think how long it's been since I was there."

"Since my wedding to Boand," he said. "I've not seen you from then 'til today. Many things have happened. I . . . I have had children."

"I know. I have asked Onairaich about you. Two boys, already grown, and a girl just two days ago."

"So, you do still have some feelings for me," he said.

"Not feelings," she said impassively. "But there is still . . . an interest."

He leaned toward her, speaking with sudden intensity: "Those children should have been ours, Moire."

"Not Moire," she said, unmoved. "I am Morrigan."

"No," he said, putting a hand to her shoulder. "Moire still lies in there. She is alive, some tiny part of her. It's for her that I'll always feel love. I married another, but . . ."

Firmly but gently she removed his hand from her. Her glinting dark gaze and her rasping voice were both emotionless. "It was right that you married, Dagda. Your other wife was dead. You were a man who deserved a companion, who deserved children. You have them now. Give all your love to them."

He sighed resignedly. "Through all these years I have hoped that, someday, the woman you were might return. I hoped that maybe the healing nature of this place, the peace, the magic . . ."

"Would restore the one you loved?" she finished. "No. Instead, it's Morrigan that the powers here have made stronger. Now the heart of the raven is truly mine. When we meet the Fomor again I will sweep over them as a black sign of the death that will come upon them. Hold out no more foolish hope, Dagda. The only love I will ever feel now is for my sweet revenge!"

"The beauty of pure poetry is the only thing to love," said the young man of fine features and loosely streaming golden hair. "In poetry we find the real truths of life. It soothes the heart and it delights the mind. It answers all questions and it drives away all cares. Only in total surrender to its powers can we be completely free."

The other young people gathered around him on the flower-carpeted hillside sat listening, clearly rapt by his words. Like great blossoms themselves, they sat with colorful gowns spread out about them on the ground. In appearance they were a lithe and lovely assembly, men and women both, their faces lit with their adoration for the speaker and his speech.

Nuada approached the base of the hill and stopped on the fringe of the group. He listened without interrupting as the young man continued, his clear, strong, melodious voice soaring out over the hillside like a bright bird.

"It's truly a land of the blest we've come to live in, where basic needs can be supplied without toil, where there is peace and absence of pain and the whole of our spirits can be given to the art of weaving words. For it is like fine weavers that we are, you know, intertwining the warp of purely musical sounds and cadences of words with the woof of their most subtle and precise meanings. The looms for this are our own voices; the weaving hands are our own separate minds. With them we can fashion grand, glowing tapestries. What thrill, what joy, what magic, can be any greater than that?"

He caught sight of Nuada then. It seemed to break his concentration on his subject, his look of intensity replaced by one of curiosity.

"I think we've had enough talk of this today," he told his audience. "Go out now each of you and find some song of your own within you. Tomorrow, come and share it with us."

They rose and moved off, some tarrying to share a final word, a touch, a smile with him. Nuada waited patiently until he was alone and then approached.

"Nuada," the young man greeted. "I'm surprised to see you at a gathering of ours."

"You have come very far in a short time, Bobd Derg," the other said. "Once a student of Danu's teachers, now a teacher yourself."

"I hold no such grand image of myself," Dagda's son said humbly. "We are all equal here. I merely say what seems of value to me. It is they who choose to listen to my words."

"But if they choose to listen, then you must have something wise to say," said Nuada. "And they know it. I could hear the sound of authority in your voice. A leader's voice it is, with a power like that of your father's."

"I am no leader," Bobd said sharply. "I told you, we are all equals. In such a land there is no need for authority. Now, why did you come here?"

"Your father has asked that all of our people meet," he said. "We are taking word to everyone."

"A meeting? Why?"

"Dagda wants to discuss the beginning of our preparations for return."

"Return?" Bobd repeated. "Where?"

"To the Blessed Isle," Nuada told him. "Come now, you know that as well as I."

"Yes, yes," the other admitted. "I suppose I do. It's just rather difficult to believe. And what has prodded my great bull of a father to lift his head from placidly grazing the lush grass of the meadow and go charging about again? A sharp stab from my iron-hard goad of a brother, perhaps?"

"Your father is not the dull, plodding fool you make him," Nuada returned. "You'd know it if you two would talk together."

"Oh, really?" said Bobd, a touch sardonically. "And just where is Dagda now? Why hasn't he brought me this news?"

"He is . . . busy," Nuada hedged. "He is taking word to the other First Ones."

"Busy. As he was too busy to bring me word even of the birth of my own sister."

"I'll not hide that he's uncomfortable with you. He feels he can't talk, that you won't understand. Is that more his fault or your own?"

"He thinks of no one but himself," Bobd said harshly. "Didn't he leave my mother not half a day after her giving birth to my new sister? Wasn't *I* the one who went to see her, to sit by her and give her comfort, to coo to the baby and feel its first grip on *my* finger? *He* should have been there."

"You're not fair to him. He is more openhanded than any man I've ever met. He only wants good for all of us.

That's why this is so important to him. He has tried to be tolerant of the new ways. He has tried to let everyone live as they wish."

"Oh? Like me?"

"You are his own son," Nuada reasoned. "Of course he wished for you to be a warrior. Of course he was disappointed when you turned another way. Still he did not stop you. But now he feels things may have gone too far. He is afraid our purpose and our values may have become . . . well, let's say confused. Diancecht agrees."

"And you?"

"I assume that most of the rest—all offspring of the First Ones—will agree as well. Still, I think everyone should have a free choice. What we do must be decided fairly, by consensus. We won't force any decisions on the whole. We don't even mean to force you to take part in this meeting."

"Oh, I'm going to take part," Bobd Derg said most decisively. "My father is going to meet me and he's going to listen to me this time." He gave a little smile. "And I think that he's going to have a very great surprise."

Lir pulled in the reins on his silver-white team and the chariot carrying himself and Dagda rolled to a halt.

The two men stared out at the narrow promontory to where the strange round tower sat on the peaked tip, far above the sea.

"That's where Mathgen lives?" asked Lir. "Are you certain?"

"So I was told by Morrigan," the big man replied. "She was the only one who seemed to have paid any notice to where he had gone."

"No one else cared that he had left you?"

Dagda shrugged. "He's never really been one of us. Always aloof, usually nasty. I think most of us in the old group were relieved when he left. The generations that came after us, well, they know little or nothing about him. Even Morrigan only noted him out here by chance, when she was practicing her flying as a raven."

"But you know Mathgen is a most cunning man," said

Lir. "I never fully trusted him. Didn't it bother you to have him separate from you? Out of your sight?"

"I never really thought about it," Dagda said. "What can he do out here, all alone?"

"I don't know," Lir answered thoughtfully, looking at the blank tower with its seamless, dull-brown sheath of metal. "He's somehow managed to build himself a most impressive—and most curious—abode."

"You can ask him about it, if you want to," Dagda said. "Come on, let's waste no more time. The meeting's tomorrow morning."

Lir nodded agreement and snapped the reins. His team started forward, drawing the chariot toward the promontory.

But near the cliff's edge, where the thin neck of land began, the animals came up short.

"What's wrong with you?" Lir said in puzzlement. "Go on!"

He snapped the reins again. They took a step, then balked, trying to turn sideways.

"It's as if something there is blocking them," said Lir. "As if they'd run against a wall."

"I'll look," offered Dagda, turning to jump down from the car.

"Never mind," said a voice. "I'm here."

Surprised, they looked around to see Mathgen not far away, standing with Cuthach in the car of another chariot.

The vehicle rivaled Lir's own for impressiveness. The car was fashioned as two twining serpents' heads arching up in front, with the bodies looping around to form the sides. They were a polished, gleaming ebony all decorated with golden trim. The pair of proud, powerful stallions in the traces matched the chariot they pulled. Their coats were glossy black, their flowing manes like molten gold.

"Where did you spring from?" Dagda asked.

"Oh, I was just out, riding," he said vaguely. "I saw you driving up. It's really good to see you both after so very long."

"Is it?" said Lir neutrally. "That's nice. We've come . . ."

". . . about a meeting of the clans?" Mathgen supplied.

"Yes," said Dagda. "How did you know?"

"Just a guess on my part," the other said. "What else would bring you out here? Well, I'm ready to follow you right now."

"Very well," said Lir. "What about him?" He nodded to Cuthach.

"Oh, he'll just come along with me, if that's all right."

Dagda shrugged. "No matter to me. I didn't know that you were friends."

"Oh, a long time," Mathgen said breezily. "Shall we get on?"

They set out, the two chariots rolling side by side.

"Don't you want to know what the meeting is about?" Lir asked.

"I'm sure you'll tell me as we ride. Frankly I'll welcome any excuse to visit the town. It's so long since I've seen many other human faces."

"Just what is it you've been doing here so alone?" asked Lir.

"Oh, contemplation, meditation, communing with the sea and stars."

"Really?" said Lir. "If you don't mind my saying so, I never thought of you as a solitary philosopher. Don't you find it just a bit dull?"

"On the contrary," Mathgen told him most gravely. "It's been quite enriching. Yes, indeed. Great insights have been opened up to me. Do you know, I really think that someday soon I'm going to be a whole new man."

Chapter 19

Decision

At dawn the central commons area of the town of Nuada's people was thronged with their full numbers.

Those in the assembly were of two clearly identifiable groups. There were the adherers to the old styles in their traditional homespun woolen clothes of greys, yellows, and browns. In striking contrast there were those who had adopted the ways of their long-time hosts, clad in bright-hued cloaks and robes and gowns of many finely textured materials.

The distinction between the factions was further amplified by their groupings. The two did little intermixing. The crowd was thus a living quilt of bright- and dull-hued patches. And the bright patches were in definite predominance.

There was much hubbub. Voices were raised in excited speculation, discussion, sometimes argument. Between members of some of the opposing groups the exchanges were quite hot.

From out of the large oval hut that served as the town's meeting hall came Nuada, accompanied by Dagda, Diancecht, and Lir. They climbed onto a log platform that had been hastily constructed by the chief carpenter Luchtine so that speakers might be clearly heard by all. He, Goibniu, Morrigan, and others of the First Ones were gathered close by. Mathgen, as usual, stood somewhat separately, Cuthach at his side.

"Nuada, you address them first," Dagda urged. "Tell them what we think."

"I can't do that," said Nuada with a force that drew a startled look from Dagda.

"What? Why not?" the big man said.

"Well, I . . . just don't feel I should . . . should do the speaking here," Nuada told him somewhat awkwardly. "It's Diancecht who has the wisdom and the eloquence. Please, Diancecht, you speak for us." He put a hand to the man's shoulder, pressing forward firmly, all but shoving him ahead.

So it was the healer who stepped out from his friends to first address those gathered. Their own talk ceased as his voice carried across the yard.

"My comrades, it has been many years since we gathered here together," he said. "Then it was no more than a handful of you that I addressed, and they were all well known to me. Now, in what seems all too short a span of time, I face many times that number, and many I look upon are unfamiliar. I see that I have grown away from you, that you have grown away from each other. I realize that we may have been adrift for too long, letting ourselves be carried by the prevailing breeze. I understand that no matter how pleasant that breeze has been, no matter how wonderful are the places it has blown us, we have ceased to steer ourselves."

"You see," Nuada murmured to Dagda, "how much more movingly he speaks."

"From our beginning," Diancecht went on, "from the time of Nemed—that brave leader only we First Ones knew —our choice has been to make our own destiny, to go and do as we wished. It seems that now the time has come for us to gather and to decide as a people just what that destiny should be."

He gestured to Dagda who stood behind him.

"This man is the greatest champion of our people. He has risked himself to save us many times. It is his concern that caused us to call this meeting. It is right that he tell you what his feelings are."

He stepped back and Dagda moved forward. The big man silently scanned for a moment the upturned faces with their intent gazes, clearly feeling awkward at having to address them. He saw his wife Boand, standing outside the door to their house on the edge of the central yard. Though still wan from childbirth, she had gamely joined the throng. She held their infant Bridget cradled in her arms, rocking her gently. She smiled encouragingly at her husband when their eyes met. With this help he finally steeled himself and spoke, his voice hesitant at first, then growing stronger, booming out.

"It's only a simple fighting man I am," he said, "not one of words. I can only tell you what's in my heart in the best way that I can. We came here, to Tir-na-nog, with only a single goal: to rebuild our strength for the day when we would return to the Blessed Land. To have that isle *is* our destiny. To settle a place that we could make our own. To live and grow there. To be free. We have a chance to do that now. The time has come to return."

"Return to this so-called Blessed Land?" called Bobd Derg from the crowd. "Return to a place we know of only from your old tales? How can we believe in that? Each time you tell it the isle glows more brightly, more greenly, more richly, *and* more impossibly. Why should we trade that dream place of yours for this perfect reality?"

"Because this is not our land," Dagda pointed out. "That could be."

"*This* could also be our land," Bobd countered. "We have only to accept it."

"What, become like the people here? Give up what we are?"

"What *we* are—myself, my friends, all of our most recent generations—is what *this* land has made us. We have already become as the people here. Why shouldn't we stay?"

It was Lir who spoke up in reply to this. "You have no way to make a judgment about that honestly. You call Tir-na-nog reality? I say you've lived your whole life in a fantasy. Listen to me: I am from here. I have also seen the outside. Outside there's purpose, there's meaning to life.

What good is there for all your knowledge, all your arts and skills if they stay isolated here? My own people won't listen to me. I pray that you will. Please, go back outside!"

"It is a hard and a deadly life outside," Bobd Derg replied. "We have heard the tales from Danu's people. Their own first ones came here as ours did, to escape. They were content to stay. Why can't we be?"

"They were cowards," Lir said sharply. "They chose to run from the evil rather than to fight. I thought you would be different."

Morrigan now leaped up from the crowd onto the edge of the platform. She swept her black cape to furl around her as she wheeled to face the crowd, a tall, gaunt, and eerie figure as her glinting gaze swept over them.

"Is it frightened, weak children that you've all become?" she chastized in her harsh voice. "How can you even speak of staying here? Great wrongs we suffered at the Fomor hands. They warred upon us, poisoned us, set monster and plague upon us, stole our children. We were tortured, massacred, and nearly destroyed. Those who did these things still survive. They still hold the land that should be ours. How can we have honor until we have repaid what they have done to us? How can you say that you have any value if you do not take revenge?"

"Revenge?" said Bobd Derg, unswayed by her words. "There is no need for that. In this land of peace there is no place for violence. These horrors you speak of—if they truly happened—happened to you, to a very few of you, not to the many of us. And they happened many, many years ago. It seems to me that the existence of these terrible Fomor creatures only makes a return to your outer world even less desirable."

"I can't believe what you're saying," Dagda said in outrage. "You can't be people of our blood. You're not of us. You're something alien."

"Come, Father, how can you say that?" said Bobd. "Look at Morrigan. Look at yourself. You First Ones are all that's left of our tie to the outer world. Only you still cling to the harsh, ugly, primitive ideals of that terrible place. In this gentle and carefree land it's you who are the aliens. Worse, you seem like freaks here, completely out of place."

Dagda's other son, Angus Og, had stood in a group near his brother's during all of this, Cian and the other youths in warrior training around him. He had seethed through the first parts of Bobd Derg's tirade, holding himself back from action with obvious difficulty. But at this last insult he pushed through the intervening crowd to confront his brother.

"It's time for you to keep quiet," he said. "We're tired of hearing from you."

"Ah, the perfect example of the ways of the old ones," Bobd Derg pointed out. "See, my friends? The primitive values at work."

Angus grabbed a handful of his brother's robe front and wrenched him close.

"Quiet, brother, or I'll . . ."

"Thrash me senseless?" Bobd concluded for him, smiling. "Of course. That's the way you always deal with matters. It's a good thing that most of our people have evolved into something much finer, much improved."

Angus released him, snorting derisively. "Improved? Is that what you call becoming simpering fawns and cooing doves? Why don't you flitter away, bright butterfly? Let somebody else here have a voice. Let's hear what the rest of the people have to say."

Bobd tugged his robe back neatly into line, speaking with a certain haughtiness: "My brother, I *am* speaking for the rest. Or all that count, anyway. Haven't you realized yet? Look around you. The ones who support my beliefs are vastly in superior numbers here."

Angus gazed about at the masses of brightly garbed figures clustered supportively about his brother and staring at him with a decidedly unsympathetic air.

Bobd Derg pushed by him and approached the platform, the crowd readily making way. He climbed up to face his father and the others there boldly, making it clear that he was moving to the offensive now. Though he spoke to Dagda, his voice rang out, carrying his words to all in the audience.

"Let me be very clear to you, Father," he announced. "While you and your old comrades have drifted along, holding on stubbornly to your dusty, worn-out dream, we have

been active. There are many hundreds of the younger generations who adhere with fierce loyalty to me now. Many
more have given me their support. Very few but yourselves
will truly support your cause any longer." He turned to look
out at the assemblage, shouting: "Am I right?"

A great cheer of agreement rose from the people in response.

"No!" Dagda shouted desperately. "You are *not* right.
The dream is still alive." He appealed to the crowd. "Show
him, my comrades. Show him all of you who still want to
return."

A handful of voices were raised in shouts of positive
reply. A few score faint murmurings that may have been of
affirmation joined them. But many more of the people exchanged glances of uncertainty, shrugged, shook heads, or
simply looked uncomfortably away.

Dagda stared around at them in dismay. "You can't
mean this!"

"Oh, yes. They do," Bobd Derg confirmed. "This is not
something that has come about just now. We have been talking for a long time about what we should do. Thanks to you,
things have been brought to a head at last. You have
brought us together. You have demanded a decision. Now,
as you said, is truly the time. We will determine our destiny
today. But *I* say that destiny should not be to leave this
place. *I* say that we should here agree that we will proclaim
ourselves the Tuatha de Dannan—The Children of Danu—
and ask the queen for rights as full citizens of Tir-na-nog!"

Another roar of acclamation rose from thousands of the
crowd, but Lir spoke up again with deep concern.

"Wait now," he said. "You move too quickly. This re-
quest may not be a welcome thing to the queen."

"How do you mean?" asked Bobd in puzzlement.

"To present Danu with this proposal also means that
you must reveal to her how much like her own people you
have become. This . . . this 'incorporating' is a clear viola-
tion of the terms under which she let you stay. She may be
angered at discovering it. Remember how fiercely, almost
blindly protective of her subjects she is."

"Angered that we have adopted her ways as our own?"
said Bobd in disbelief. "Angered that we wish to give all

praise to her?" He shook his head. "I don't think so." He looked to the people. "We will discover here and now. We will make up a delegation who will march directly to her from this place and put our petition humbly and respectfully before her."

"No delegation, Bobd Derg!" someone shouted. "Let's *all* go. Show the queen by our numbers how great is our support!"

Once more a wave of shouts and cheers surged up in agreement.

"Very well, my people!" Bobd shouted. "We will march to Gorias and the queen. Come on!"

He jumped down from the platform and moved through the crowd. They poured after him, flooding out of the commons area and toward the main gates.

Caught totally aback by the speed and totality with which the spontaneous decision had been translated into action, Dagda, Nuada, and those still loyal to them stood staring after the others.

In moments the noise of the crowd's exuberant uproar was fading as the thousands emptied from the fortress, streaming out the gates and down the hill. Dagda looked around him at the few hundred who were left.

"It didn't turn out exactly as you supposed, did it?" Mathgen called to him. There was just a hint of amusement in his voice at the big man's defeat.

"By all the gods my fathers prayed to," the big man said, still in shock, "I never thought to see this." He looked to Nuada, anguish in his eyes. "It's my fault. I brought things to this."

Nuada put a comforting hand on his shoulder. "It would have come to this sooner or later anyway. Perhaps we all caused it, by neglect, or selfishness, or ignorance. Or perhaps it was just meant to be."

"Meant to be?" said Dagda, staring at him in disbelief. "How can you sound so accepting?"

"There is no time to be arguing that now," put in Lir. "We've got to go." He hopped down from the platform and started off across the commons area toward the stables. Then, realizing he was alone, he stopped and looked back to them. "Well, aren't any of you going with me?"

"Where are you going?" Diancecht called.

"To get my chariot and follow them to Gorias," Lir called back. "I have to be there too when they see the queen. It's going to be a bit of a shock to her. I'm not certain how she's going to accept it. And the First Ones should be represented there too, don't you think?"

"I suppose that some of us do have to go as well," said Diancecht, climbing from the platform to join Lir. "It was we who made the agreement with Danu and accepted her conditions for all our people."

"I'll go with you," said Nuada. He started after the healer, but then paused and looked back to the big man. "Dagda?"

"I have no heart to see it," he said heavily. "My people, led by my own son, abandoning what we are." He looked across to his Boand, still standing by the door of their house, tears glistening now in her eyes. "I'll stay here with my wife."

He left the platform and started across the yard toward Boand, plodding defeatedly, not looking back. Morrigan watched after him. The gleam of her own anguish for him showed for an instant in her own dark eyes. Then she was leaping down from the platform to join Lir, Nuada, and Diancecht.

"I'll go as well," she said briskly. "I surely don't want to be left here."

The others left in the commons area declined to go. All looking as disheartened as Dagda, they moved slowly, solemnly off toward their own homes. All, that is, but Mathgen.

"What say, Cuthach," he said to his new henchman with a certain gaiety, "shall we follow too?"

"You want to see this?" the other said. "See your old companions' spirits being smashed? Watch them be dishonored?"

"It does promise to be most entertaining," he replied. "And it might present us with some useful possibilities. Go quickly then. Fetch my chariot."

Chapter 20
Defeat

"My Queen," said chief druid Urias most hesitantly, "there are some . . . some . . . uh . . . visitors?"

Danu looked around from the rosebushes. She had been in the process of directing several young apprentice gardeners in the precise method of pruning them. She clearly disliked being disturbed.

"What are you talking about?" she said.

"A . . . a contingent is approaching the palace. It's . . . well, it's rather large."

"Contingent?" she echoed in puzzlement. "Large? Who is it? Why?"

"I think you should see for yourself, my Queen," he suggested.

She gave a humpf of irritation, but followed the druid out of the gardens and through the palace to the front portico. They stopped there to stare down the road through the city. Several thousand people were indeed visible below, moving purposefully upward from the gateway toward them.

"This . . . this *rabble,*" she said aghast, "can they be *Our* people?"

"I'm afraid that they are not, my Queen," the druid said in obvious distress. "They are the . . . the . . . the . . ."

"The what, man?" she snapped. "Stop your babbling."

"The . . . outsiders, my Queen," he forced out.

"It can't be," she said disbelievingly. "So many? It was only thirty mortals who first came here."

"They have been multiplying rather prolifically, my Queen," he said.

"I should say so. Well, what do they want with Us now?"

"I can't say, my Queen, but I believe that we are about to find out. It would seem they are seeking an audience. They will surely not fit into the throne room. Better to receive them here."

"Here? Now? But We should be in Our proper robes."

"No time, my Queen. I'm afraid they have arrived."

The van of the contingent was just spilling into the yard before the palace. Bobd Derg, at their head, strode on forward, boldly approaching the queen. The others spread out, filling up the space behind him in a densely packed crowd.

Bobd Derg stopped a few paces before the queen. He raised a hand to the crowd, and they fell silent. He turned to her and made a deep, respectful bow.

"My great Queen Danu," he said. "It is the grandest honor of my life to finally stand before you."

"Is it, young man?" she said, her regal manner not wholly disguising some apprehension at this most extraordinary and near-overwhelming occurrence. "And may We ask just who it is that you are?"

"I am Bobd Derg, my Queen. A humble servant to you. A most loyal subject."

"Subject? But you are not of Our people."

"Not by birth perhaps. But I have worshiped you and your high ideals all of my life, as I have steeped myself in the knowledge of your poets and philosophers. The same is true of all those here with me."

"I . . . I don't understand," she said. "Steeped? *Our* knowledge?" She looked to her chief druid in perplexity. "Urias, what does this mean?"

"Well," he said without relish, "to speak the truth of it, my most gracious, kind, and understanding Queen, it means that we, your own druids and craftsmen—all your people, in fact—have been . . . have been . . . well, have been, let's say, nurturing the outsiders somewhat over the years."

"Indeed?" she said coldly. "And why were We not informed?"

"We were afraid that . . . that you might not . . . understand, my Queen," he said, wincing slightly as he spoke as if he were already receiving the expected chastisement.

"Don't let your anger overwhelm you, my Queen," came a new voice.

It came from Lir, whose chariot was moving forward through the crowd. The vehicle pulled up close by Danu. Lir and his passengers—Morrigan, Nuada, and Diancecht—alighted from its car.

"Lir," she said. "We are glad to have your presence here to help unravel this most bewildering affair. But what do you mean by Our anger?"

"Well, the outsiders broke the rules you set down for them," he explained. "I thought surely that your temper would be roused."

"We are not certain," she said thoughtfully. "We are somewhat vexed, certainly. But We are also greatly flattered." Bobd Derg beamed brightly at this, and she favored him with a little smile.

"But you *should* be angry," Lir argued. "At least to some extent. They deserve some punishment."

At this an astonished Nuada pulled Lir around to him.

"What are you saying?" he murmured. "Are you mad?"

"There may still be one way to stop this," Lir murmured back. "Just listen."

He turned away and strode toward Danu, speaking forcefully: "My Queen, you know now these people can't be trusted. They must be forced to leave."

A look of realization filled Nuada's face. He exchanged a gaze with Diancecht. The healer's quick nod said that he understood the desperate tactic too.

But the tactic was not working.

"It would seem it's Our own people who cannot be

trusted," Danu countered, looking accusingly to her druid. "They appear to have accepted our guests most willingly."

"They were very fine pupils," he said by way of defense. "Very eager to learn, very quick to adopt our ways."

"Obviously so," she said, looking over the silent, watching throng. "They are a most handsome group. In manner, look, and dress they are barely distinguishable from Our own." She bestowed another, larger smile upon Bobd Derg. "And this lad is particularly impressive to Us. He is most eloquent."

"My Queen, aren't you disturbed by this at all?" Lir said more stridently. "These people have been mingling with ours, invading our cities, even learning our secrets, just as you feared."

"What We feared was that the crude and violent aspects of their natures should infect our people, not that the opposite influence would take place. We see clearly now that they have true sensitivity and intelligence. We were unfair to judge them as primitives."

"No finer words could come to our ears, my Queen," Bobd Derg said with great fervor. "If you are truly pleased by us, then could you consider granting us a boon?"

"What kind of boon?" she asked.

"A simple one. We ask you to make us truly your people. It's our intent to take the name of Tuatha de Dannan. Great Queen, would you accept us as your children, and give us a home forever in your enchanted land?"

"Don't listen to him," said Lir. "Don't give them leave to stay. That cannot be their destiny."

"*Why* can it not?" she demanded. "We are most pleased with them and with the gift they wish to bestow on Us. Why should We not grant this boon?"

"They were meant to be mortals!" Lir told her. "They were meant to be out there, in a real world!"

"Why should they face the terrors of that world if they are happy here?"

"If you let them stay, you destroy them," he said angrily. "You condemn them to the same stagnant, useless lives that the rest of our people already live. They will languish here forever in these perfumed fields, dreaming millennia away. You must save them. You're their only chance now. You must send them out of here for their own good. You must give them back their own challenges again!"

"No more," she said commandingly, deeply outraged. "We will not listen to more of your blasphemy against Us and Our realm. It is only you who find this life at fault. We now realize that your thinking has been twisted by your exposure to the horrors of the outside. We can no longer feel favor toward you!"

She looked toward Bobd Derg and his followers, this time bestowing a most benign smile upon them. "As for these people, their actions have earned them *great* favor from Us. If they are willing to accept this life and Our leadership, they may become true citizens of Tir-na-nog. We are generous. We will share perfection with them."

"My Queen, then you will accept us?" Bobd Derg said excitedly.

"Yes," she told him, "but it must be properly done. Not here and now in this highly improper way. The beginning of the new season, the harvest time, will be here in twenty days. That will be the proper time to make a proper ceremony of your declaration of loyalty. We and all Our druids will gather with you then at the central temple. But for now, We wish that you all return to your normal lives. Please disperse. This gathering here is a most unseemly spectacle for you and for Ourselves."

Grinning with his victory, Bobd Derg bowed again. He turned and waved to his people.

"The dream is ours!" he declared to them. "We will do as our queen says now. Let us depart."

They obeyed at once as he led them, moving back out of the yard and down the avenue through the city, making sounds of rejoicing, but in a proper, subdued way.

The queen nodded in satisfaction, then turned and strode grandly into the palace, Urias behind her. Lir looked to Nuada and his friends.

"I'm sorry, Nuada," he said dismally. "I tried. It was a last chance."

"I understand, Lir. You did what you could. Just take us home."

"I will go my own way," said Morrigan as the others climbed into the chariot. "Things are over here. I wish my solitude again to ponder what has happened."

She waited until Lir had started the vehicle away. Then she began the process of transformation. The shimmering light rose about her.

On a far edge of the palace yard, Mathgen and Cuthach watched the departure of the crowd, Mathgen quite gleeful at the announcement of the queen.

"This is quite perfect, my friend," he told the older man. "In twenty days the queen, her druids, and much of Tir-na-nog will all be gathered at one spot—the very spot I must seize. How easy it will be to capture them all at once! It's time to act."

"But quickly, Cap'n," Cuthach said. "Twenty days will barely give us enough time."

"Yes," he agreed. "We must act soon. There is only one problem still to work out."

His gaze fell upon Morrigan across the yard. Her shape-shifting was nearing completion. The aura of light was fading away, revealing the glowing black raven.

"There's a problem," he said thoughtfully, watching the huge bird flap up into the sky, "but I think I may have just found its solution!"

"So that was the great change that Danu sensed," said Lir.

"But was it?" said Diancecht. "What about the sense of something direful you said she felt?"

"Yes," put in Nuada. "And what about the involvement of the Fomor?"

Lir shrugged. "It seems that the chief druid was right. She simply misread the signs. If your people stay here, there will be no more encounters with those pirates."

"Unless *we* choose to go back and face them," put in Dagda fiercely.

The four men sat in the big champion's house, glumly sipping ale around his fireplace. Boand, modestly choosing to be out of the men's way, sat in the chamber partitioned off by wicker walls, nursing the infant Bridget.

Lir, Nuada, and the healer had returned from Gorias to

tell their huge friend of the debacle. Though Dagda had been expecting the outcome, having the details described to him had certainly not improved his mood. He had sat silently, sullenly listening until this empassioned outburst.

Nuada looked to him in surprise. "We? Go back?" he repeated. "What, do you mean just us?"

"I mean all those still loyal to our dream. Not everyone has joined my . . . *that* traitorous whelp's mutiny."

Out of sight behind the partitions, Bobd Derg's mother winced in anguish at her husband's harsh words.

"There is no reason why we must be held by the decision the rest have made," Dagda went on. "Danu will not keep us from leaving if we choose to go. We can still return to the Blessed Land."

"Dagda, there are scarcely six hundred who did not join Bobd Derg's march," Nuada pointed out. "Even if all of them chose to go back, it wouldn't be a host large enough to secure the isle or defend against our old enemies."

"And I've a strong feeling many of them wouldn't choose to go back now, knowing the new odds," added Diancecht. "There are families, small children to be thought of. They all know that here they will be safe, if not wholly free."

"Yes," said Nuada, "and after a bit more time here, what little sparks of the old dream that are left glowing in them will be extinguished, too."

" '*Our* dream,' Bobd called it," Dagda growled. "It's well I wasn't there to hear him say that. I don't know what I might have done." He slammed a huge fist powerfully into his other palm in his outrage. "That ungrateful, arrogant . . ."

Lir held up a staying hand. "Don't be so hard on him," he said. "It's not entirely his fault. It's this place. It's deluded him. Enchanted him. I've seen its powers work on my own people. Magic is most dangerous when even the magician ceases to recognize that it's being worked. Only you few who have kept a memory of the outside world's realities living in your minds know the truth. But now you are in the minority."

"We *are* freaks here," said Dagda, "as Bobd Derg called us."

"It's my fault," Lir said, angrily shaking his head. "I should have realized the danger. I should never have left you for so long. But I thought your people were strong enough to defy the seductive spell, even reverse its effect. I was wrong."

"It wasn't wrong for you to bring us here," said Nuada. "You did save us."

"I ruined you," he returned uncompromisingly. "I helped my people rob you of all the reasons why your lives in the outside had such great value. We stole the one greatest reason when we gave you immortality. No more struggle to survive, to accomplish, to battle pain and death. No more chance to take that greatest risk, make that greatest sacrifice only mortals can. And then we gave you a protected paradise where you no longer had to want for anything. No more need to fear, to strive, to grow. No more reasons left. The end of you."

"I refuse to accept that end," Dagda said, standing up. "I will go back to the Blessed Land with whoever will go with me. I'll go alone if I have to. Better to die there quickly, alive and fighting, than to go on forever here in this changeless place."

"And what of us?" said the voice of Boand.

They turned to see her at the opening to the partitioned space, the baby in her arms. She spoke to her husband with an uncharacteristic spark of defiance: "Would you leave us? Abandon me . . . abandon *her* alone here? Or would you take us into these dangers and to this likely death? You have family too, Dagda. You must think of them."

"You're right," he said contritely, looking at the tiny form of his daughter. "I forget that I'm no longer just my own fighting man. I'm sorry, Boand."

"Running away from this is no answer anyway," said Diancecht. "We have to stay here and find some way to act."

"Must we?" said Nuada. "I mean, are you all so certain this choice of theirs is wrong? Maybe it's the way things should be. Maybe it's for the best. Maybe *we're* the ones who are wrong."

"Do you believe what you're saying?" Dagda said, aghast. "What's wrong with you? You've been saying foolish things like that right along. And you've been strangely reluctant to take the lead in this. It was your command, your bravery that brought us safely here. It's you that should be rallying us now to lead us back."

"I don't want to lead you," Nuada said fiercely. "Don't you understand? On our journey here, my decisions led us into dangers. They killed our comrades. They killed Diancecht."

"Those were illusions," the healer said.

"Still, the agony of watching you die was real. When a miracle saved us from the consequences of my foolhardy moves, I counted myself blessed. When we came to this place of peace, I was blessed again. No more need to make decisions. No more need to lead. I didn't have to be responsible for the lives of my fellows anymore, and I liked the feeling. I felt . . . free."

"This is not the Nuada I fought beside who's speaking now," Dagda said in disbelief. "This man sounds like a coward!"

"I'm sorry to hear you say that," Nuada said sorrowfully. "I had hoped that you, of all people, would understand. I'm sorry. I'm no good to you anymore."

With that he rose and strode from Dagda's house.

"This place has poisoned his mind too," Dagda said, staring after him. "I never thought it might happen to him."

"We can't be concerned with him right now," said Diancecht, practically. "If there's any way to save him and the rest, we have to concern ourselves with finding it, and very quickly."

He and Dagda turned to Lir.

"No use you all looking at me," he told them. "You heard the queen. I'm no longer in her favor. I'm no better off than the rest of you."

"I suppose that's true enough," said the healer. "There's really nothing you can do."

"Still," Lir said thoughtfully, "I've a very strong feeling that something here is wrong. What if Danu *wasn't* wrong in her feelings? What if something else, something dreadful, *is* going to happen?"

"Why should she be concerned with that any longer?"

said Diancecht. "For her, the thing is settled. Your task for her is over."

"She hasn't said it is," Lir pointed out. "She told me to search into things and settle them for good. Well, my friends, I mean to keep on doing just that!"

Chapter 21

Suspicions

The sleek peregrine falcon settled lightly to the ground. It transformed swiftly into the small human figure of Onairaich, chieftain of the Pooka clan. He stood looking around with curiosity.

There was just the lonely tower of Mathgen on its point of rocks. No living beings in sight.

"Hello," said a voice behind him.

He wheeled about to see Cuthach, smiling at him in an ingratiating way.

"I've been sent to take you in," the aged man explained. "Please, follow me."

He led the way around a low outcrop. He pressed a certain knobbed rock and a portion of what seemed a solid face of stone swung back, revealing a tunnel.

Cuthach started in. The other hesitated, peering into the rather sinister, dark space.

"It's all right," Cuthach assured. "It's just the way into his tower. He has only the one. Much safer, you see. No one can come upon him without their being known."

"And just who is it he's afraid of?" the leader of the Pooka clan inquired.

"Save all your questions for him," Cuthach advised. "Come on. He's waiting."

They went down into the tunnel. It was both a high and wide passage, but rough-walled, as if a shifting in the earth had forced open a crack through the living rock. The way was very gloomy, lit only at wide intervals by torches. There were sounds of small movements ahead of them, of things skittering away out of sight. Several times the visitor glimpsed ratlike beasts and bizarre large insects ducking into holes.

"Quite a warm welcoming place your Mathgen has," Onairaich said, brushing past an obese, hairy spider that hung down before him. "Makes me feel as if I were itching all over."

"It's all just for fun, really," said Cuthach. "Just to fool visitors. You know, throw a good scare into them. All harmless . . ." he paused and qualified, ". . . at least to us."

Once a much larger shadow shot past before them, vanishing into a side passageway.

"What was that?" asked a startled Onairaich. "Was that thing harmless too?"

"Nothing to worry about," Cuthach said cheerily. "One of the cap'n's pets. That's all."

The little man glanced down the side tunnel as they passed. A huge, shapeless mass of something loomed in the black within, and they could see the sharp red gleam of eyes.

More light showed ahead. They stepped over some rubbish—shreds of rag and a chewed bone or two—and came out of the tunnel into Mathgen's lair.

That cunning man himself came forward to greet the Pooka chieftain eagerly.

"Very good of you to come," he said with a grin. "It's quite like a reunion, isn't it? You, me, Cuthach here, together after so many years."

"Not quite a reunion," said Onairaich. "We weren't such great friends before."

"Then we must remedy that right now," Mathgen replied. He took filled goblets from a table and passed them around. "You've nothing against drink, have you?" he asked.

"I've been known to have a drop of it from time to

time," said the little man. He eyed the red-gold contents of his goblet questioningly. "Depending on just what it is, of course."

"Oh, it's a fine ale," said Mathgen, picking up his own goblet. "A fine, heady stuff. You'll like it. Please drink."

Onairaich shrugged in assent. He touched glasses with Mathgen and Cuthach and then drank.

It was only a small taste that he took first. But after some smacking his lips and consideration of flavor, he lifted the goblet again and drained it.

Mathgen and Cuthach exchanged a look of triumph.

"Very warming," the Pooka chieftain said. "I feel . . . I feel . . ."

"As if we were old friends?" Mathgen supplied. "Yes, I always have that congenial effect on people." He waved around him. "Do you like my simple abode?"

"It's . . . very private," Onairaich hedged, looking around at the cheerless space.

"And very separate," Mathgen added. "Here, let me get you more ale." He took up a pitcher from the nearby table and poured another gobletful for his guest.

"Do you know why I keep so separate?" he went on in a confiding tone. "Why I've stayed away from the rest of the outsiders all of these years? Because I am shunned by the rest of them. To them, I am not as good. I am of a different sort than they—too dark, too clever for their liking. So they try to keep me down, making sport of me, abusing me, giving me servant's tasks."

"Really?" said the little man, drinking again, and eying Mathgen in a new, interested light. "I'm surprised to find such a thing happening to the likes of one of you. I can tell you that I certainly understand."

"Of course you do," Mathgen said. "I know you do. Queen Danu speaks of her great paradise. She speaks of the great freedom here. But that doesn't apply to you, does it? No. You, too, are separate, as I am."

"And how do you know that?" Onairaich asked.

"Oh, I've learned a great deal about you in my researches into Tir-na-nog's past. Come here."

He led Onairaich to the pool. Cuthach followed. They stood at the edge, and Mathgen drew his glass rod out from within his cloak. He began to make passes with it over the water.

"Watch this now," Cuthach advised the little man in a whisper. "You'll be properly amazed."

And Onairaich was, staring in astonishment as the dark waters came alive with the shimmering, colored lights.

"How does he do that?" Onairaich whispered back to the old man.

"The cap'n's got more power'n one of those chief druids," Cuthach answered with a note of pride. "It's just the start. Look now!"

The streamers of light were forming into a clear image. It was a view of a band of some dozen of the small people, men and women both. In one young male and female, standing arm-in-arm, could be seen characteristics distinctively like those of the Pooka chieftain.

"Why, those are my people when they first came here!" Onairaich said. "That one is my own father. And that my mother. They were little more than children when they came."

"It wasn't easy for your clansmen then," said Mathgen.

"It's never been easy for my family. In the outer world they were treated with great cruelty, or so my parents said."

"So they left that world, along with the rest of Danu's people," said Mathgen.

"The rest?" the little man said with a bitter laugh. "We were never thought of as 'Danu's people.' They only brought us away out of pity. Saved us as they saved other poor threatened creatures from the ravaging ones that meant to destroy them."

"Yet it seems those creatures now live a life of more dignity and freedom than you do," Mathgen prodded.

"Yes," Onairaich agreed, increasing rancour in his tone. "They have a place, a life, an identity of their own. But not the Pooka clan. Here we're still scorned and used as slaves, just as we've always been."

"And you deeply resent that, don't you?" Mathgen said.

At this Onairaich looked to him sharply, suspiciously. "What is this all about?" he demanded. "Your warming ale hasn't muddled me that much. There's some greater reason for your asking me here than a drink for old time's sake."

"There is," Mathgen admitted. His eyes fixed on those of the young chieftain. He spoke with a new intensity. "I do believe we are of a kind, we three. All outcasts, all mistreated, all seeking for what should rightfully be ours. And I believe that we can help you. We can all help each other. But before I tell you how, I have to know just how deep your feelings toward Danu's people go. Tell me: how much do you hate them?"

"Hate?" Onairaich hesitated. "It's a harsh word to use. I . . . I can't tell you something like that."

"You can." Mathgen's dark eyes bored into the little man's. The voice coaxed and commanded at once. "We're friends. I need to know. And you need to tell me. Let it out."

"All right!" Onairaich said as if a cork had popped, letting the words spurt forth. "I hate them! Yes! All of us hate them. We live with humiliations every day." With the spigot opened, a stream of long pent-up venom now poured forth. "For centuries it has rankled. Today it rankles many times more. Now we'll have to watch *your* people being accepted, being drawn into Danu's open arms as her own children, while we are still ignored."

"I hoped that might be the case," said Mathgen. "But you can change things, you know."

"Change? How?" said Onairaich, still wary, but now intrigued as well.

"The power is not in Danu," Mathgen explained. "It can be held by anyone who can command the spheres. That is what I . . . what *we* are going to do."

"You mean to take control?" the little man said in astonishment. "But the magic skills . . ."

"He has them, my lad," Cuthach assured him. "I've seen the proof. I told you, he knows more than the highest druids."

"Even more than Danu herself," Mathgen immodestly put in. "As I've planned it, it will need only a small host to seize the temple. Cuthach, here, can supply us such a host."

"From where?" asked the Pooka. "Not from within the enchanted isles. Do you mean to go outside?"

"That needn't concern you," said Mathgen. "The force

would be totally under our control. And when its task is done, it will be gone. Only we will rule."

"This sounds too dangerous," the little man said.

"You run no risk at all," Mathgen explained. "Your only part will be to ferry our party up over the last barrier around this isle. The great sphere itself generates that. It's one thing my powers aren't strong enough to overcome. Fly them here as you did my people. The rest is up to us. If we fail, your part will never be known."

"Maybe," the other said. "Still, to challenge Danu, to bring in those from the outside, these are the greatest evils that can be done in Tir-na-nog."

"And they bring the greatest rewards. You can be rulers here, not servants. You can humble them all."

"Or we can be found out and destroyed by Danu for threatening her realm," Onairaich added. "I can't risk my people in a plot like that."

"She can't find out," argued Mathgen. "Why do you think we're meeting here? Her powers can't penetrate my shields."

"I don't have that much trust in your powers," the little man said. "I think that our talk is finished. I'd better leave."

He handed the goblet to Cuthach and turned to start away toward the tunnel.

"I can give you your greatest dream," Mathgen called after him.

The little man stopped and looked back. "Dream?"

"Your father's dream. I can give it to you. I can make you as tall, as strong, as handsome as the finest of Danu's people. No one would ever torment you again."

"You cannot," the little man said. "We never found the skill. My father died trying to achieve it. The effort needed is too great. We even appealed to Danu. She told us it was not possible even with her powers."

Mathgen smiled. "She lied. I know. She wanted to keep you in your place."

"She could have done it?" said the little man in dismay.

"She has been even crueler to you than you thought," Mathgen went on. "She has the power, and I could have it too. Let me show you."

He lifted his rod to point at Onairaich. A light like that

of their transformation rose about the young man. It swallowed him. Within it, his shadow stretched upward, broadening as well. When the glow faded, it revealed a tall, lithe-bodied young man of most even, comely features and thickly curling, deep red hair.

"This can't be," said the Pooka chieftain, looking down at himself.

"Look into the pool," Mathgen advised.

They moved to the edge of the water. A wave from Mathgen's rod soothed the waters to a glass. Onairaich looked down wonderingly at himself. He put a hand up to his altered face, running fingers over the strong, clean lines of chin and nose, flicking at well-formed ears that no longer protruded.

"It's true!" he said in amazement. "You *do* have the power!"

"Alas, for the moment only," said Mathgen.

Even as he spoke, the Pooka's image shivered in the pool. His form grew hazy within another rising aura of light. In instants more, he had shrunken back to his normal self.

"Without the sphere's power, my spell is temporary," Mathgen explained. *"With* the power of the sphere I can raise the magic to change you and all your people permanently. But *only* with the sphere. Will you help me win it?"

Onairaich looked down at his short body. He looked down at the reflection of his odd-featured face now gazing back at him from the pool. He looked up to Mathgen and nodded.

"Yes," he said determinedly. "I will."

Mathgen smiled in satisfaction. "Good. Then in eighteen days' time, I want you to come to the same isle where we first met. You must bring all of your clan that you can truly trust. Do you agree?"

"I do."

"Good, my friend. Then Cuthach will take you out of here and see you on your way. We've no time to waste." He put a parting hand to the little man's shoulder. "Just remember: succeed in this, and you will have what you most desire."

Cuthach led the Pooka away up the tunnel. He soon returned to find Mathgen filling a leather pouch with food.

"Will that one really obey?" the old man asked.

"I can read his heart," said Mathgen. "I can see the rage, the resentment, the desire there. They'll bring him and his fellows to that isle."

"I surely hope so. Because if they don't, we'll have no way of getting back here with a host."

"Don't worry about that," Mathgen said sharply. "Worry about what you and I must do first. We have to move quickly now. We don't know what complications we might face. We have to be certain we have time to go and return." He threw his henchman another bag of food and a bulging water sack. "Take these and come on."

He led the way around the pool to a section of the seemingly blank stone wall. He stepped up to it and it seemed to turn soft before him, allowing him to step through.

A nonplussed Cuthach stopped and stared.

An arm came back through the stone to gesture him in, as Mathgen's voice came brusquely from beyond.

"Hurry, man!"

He gritted his teeth and stepped ahead, passing through. Beyond the wall was a narrow stairway spiraling down into the natural rock on which the tower sat.

"This takes us to the base of the pinnacle," Mathgen said. "Our transport awaits us there."

"Tell me, Cap'n," said Cuthach as he followed Mathgen down, "can you really give those little ones this great beauty?"

Mathgen shrugged. "Who knows? What he saw just now was no more than an illusion I put on him."

"And what you said about Danu being able to do it . . ."

"Was a lie," the other finished. "It was a little extra fuel for the Pooka's fire of rage. Coupled with the promised reward, it was enough to sway him to me."

"And afterward? If you can't deliver?"

"It won't matter then. They'll have done the work for us. I'll be in control."

"You certainly know ways to shift a rudder and make a man sail your way, don't you?" said the old man insightfully.

"It's another skill I've mastered, certainly," Mathgen admitted with a certain pride.

"The same skill you used on me?"

"I couldn't fail with either of you. I offered youth and beauty, two of the greatest rewards. Next to pure power, that is."

"And did you lie to me the way you did to him?"

"Certainly not, my friend," Mathgen said assuringly. "He and his little people are only tools. You and I are full equals in this."

"Still, I shouldn't trust you."

"Maybe you shouldn't," the cunning man agreed, "but look what you might lose. Can you say the possibility isn't worth the risk?"

Cuthach said nothing, but he did continue to follow Mathgen on down.

They came out at last into a small area of sand just within the mouth of a cave. They were at the base of the high cliff now. Outside the cave a section of the ocean could be seen stretching away. Drawn up on the sand was the serpent chariot with its black-coated team.

"You mean for *that* to take us?" Cuthach asked. "Across the sea?"

"I told you I had as much skill as any of them," was the reply. "If Lir can have a wave-skimming chariot, then so can I. Get in."

They climbed into the car, depositing the food bags and waterskin. Mathgen took up the reins, giving them a shake. The team set out at once at a brisk pace, carrying the chariot off the sand and into the surf.

Cuthach tensed, squeezing his eyes shut as they came off of the beach, but the stepping hooves of the horses and the rolling wheels of the chariot stayed atop the water, as if it were dry land. He peeked, then opened his eyes wide to look about. They were already pulling away from the high pinnacle of rock at a swift rate.

"With a moderate pace, we can be at your glass tower in perhaps five days," Mathgen said. "My powers are sufficient to get us safely through the enchanted isles and past the barrier fog. Then you have to guide us to the tower."

"That's well and good, Cap'n. But first we have to get

through that barrier around Tir-na-nog. We can't fly over. Or can these horses do that too?"

"No. We can't fly over. But we can go under. This chariot does have one other ability."

He gave the reins a yank. At once the team began to slant down through the waves, drawing the car after.

"What?" Cuthach said in panic as the horses' rumps went under and the car began to sink. "We're going to drown!"

"Nonsense," Mathgen said easily. "We're quite protected. Just trust me!"

And, with that, they vanished completely beneath the waves.

Chapter 22

The Tower

Dagda and Angus Og slammed away at each other with sword and shield. It was a vigorous fight, a hard fight, a brutal fight. For both men it was a way of venting their near-maddening frustration.

Nuada stood looking on from the side of the training field. Beside him stood the youth called Cian. There was no other audience. The rest of the few lads once in training with Angus were now departed, leaving only the single loyal pupil. So he and Nuada alone watched the sparring match, admiring the complex interplay of weaponry and bodies, the effect of subtle moves mingled with brute force.

The two huge men, muscled bodies agleam with sweat, great chests heaving with long exertion, stepped back from a last furious exchange and eyed each other.

"Shall we call that enough?" father asked son.

"Enough to limber me up fairly well," the cocky son replied. "Shall we have a real fight now?"

"Oh, it's more of a thrashing that you want?" Dagda said. He looked around to his old friend: "Nuada, Angus needs more exercise. Why don't you step in and have a turn at him?"

Nuada shook his head emphatically. "I can't do that. I

wouldn't give him a fair fight. I haven't even had a weapon in my hand for . . . for . . . well, I really don't know how long now."

"I know it," Dagda said. "That's why you need the chance. Let's see if you've anything left . . . any of the old warrior spirit alive."

"Ah, can't you see that by looking at him?" Angus said scathingly. "Too many soft years. He's surely lost it all . . . if he ever had any of it."

"Watch your words, arrogant pup," said Dagda. "Nuada was the very best of us. Even more than my own match if he wanted to be."

"If you say so," Angus said with obvious skepticism. "Still, that was very long ago."

If these gibes were intended to rouse Nuada's fighting will, they failed.

"What need is there for testing such skills now?" he said spiritlessly. "They'll not be needed again."

"You actually sound as if that's a relief too," Dagda accused. "So you have cast off all your courage along with your will to lead?"

"Are you making a challenge of my bravery?" Nuada said, some fire entering in his voice for the first time.

Dagda took up an extra sword and tossed it to him. "Prove me wrong."

His old comrade grabbed the weapon by its hilt. He weighed it in his hand. He swung it experimentally. He nodded.

"I will then."

While he took off his cloak and slipped a shield on his arm, Dagda and his son exchanged a wink of victory.

"All right," said Nuada, striding toward Dagda. "I'm ready."

Dagda started for him, but was stopped by Angus.

"No. Let me try, Father. If he is such a warrior, I want a chance at him."

Dagda stepped back and Angus moved forward, setting himself before Nuada, smiling smugly.

"All right, old man," he said. "Let's see what you still have."

They closed, circling each other first, gauging strengths, looking for openings. Then they both leaped to the attack.

There was a preliminary exchange, but very weak and uncertain on Nuada's part. Angus had no problem knocking his opponent's sword from the way and swinging in a hard blow of his shield across the side of Nuada's face.

The man staggered back, recovering. Blood trickled from a split lip and one cheek was bruised.

"Sorry, old man," Angus said, still grinning. "Shall I be easier on you?"

Nuada's eyes narrowed and his face grew taut with battle fury.

He charged in at Angus suddenly. The younger man's smile was abruptly swept away as Nuada bombarded him with a series of swift and savage blows. He backed away, on the defensive now. Though very agile, stronger, and much larger than his attacker, he was still overwhelmed by Nuada's energy and skill.

Before he could return a single blow, his sword was knocked from his hand, spinning away. His shield dropped down.

"Is that enough?" Nuada asked him, lowering his own guard.

"Not quite," he answered, kicking out suddenly for Nuada's groin.

This time, his trick failed. Nuada anticipated, sidestepping the kick. The leg swung harmlessly past, throwing Angus wildly off balance. Nuada stepped in, using his shield as a ram, driving forward, slamming the other fully off his feet. Angus crashed down, and Nuada was over him instantly, the point of his blade at the younger man's throat.

"Was I too easy?" Nuada said sarcastically. He pulled back to let Angus, vastly humbled, climb to his feet.

"I'm sorry," Dagda's son said sincerely. "I should have believed my father's tales of you."

"Well, you've certainly not lost *that* ability anyway," Dagda announced with great satisfaction.

"Is this what you two were plotting here to make me do?" said Nuada, throwing his sword upon the ground. "Do you think that it proves something to me? Well, it doesn't."

He cast the shield down too. "It's over, Dagda. Accept that. There is nothing more to do."

"You said once that if you always accept that, then you will always fail," Dagda reminded him.

"And as your son said," Nuada returned, "that was very long ago!"

He wheeled from them and strode angrily away.

"So, we are wondering if there have been other peculiarities," said Lir.

He and Diancecht stood in the marble-walled hall of the palace at Murias, talking to its white-bearded chief druid Senias. Behind the druid floated the smaller satellite power sphere of the city, glowing with its soft iridescence.

"Peculiarities?" repeated the druid. "How do you mean?"

"You don't find this young druid Olgear's vanishing a little strange?"

"Come now," Senias said dismissingly, "you say it's only been a day or two since anyone recalls seeing him. What does that mean? He is an inquisitive lad. He loves communing with nature. No doubt he's out meditating in a field or a grove somewhere."

"So you're not concerned at all?" said Lir.

"Why should I be?" said the druid. "What can happen here?"

"How truly innocent of the realities have you people become?" Lir said with exasperation. "By Tir-na-nog, man, even here people are hurt. And even here they can die."

"There are the occasional accidents, yes," Senias grudgingly admitted. "But those are extremely rare. Too rare to even really consider, I assure you." He gave Lir a hard, questioning stare. "In any case, what has it to do with you?"

"I was told by Danu herself to find out if anything disturbing was happening here. That's one possibility."

"Pfaugh," the druid said in a disparaging way. "You're not needed by Danu any longer. Her premonition was a mistake. Why don't you cease to bother us and go back out into that outside world you seem to prize so much?"

"It's only your own opinion that there's nothing

wrong," Lir returned. "I still have some doubts. This odd power fading you've had here, now, what about that?"

Senias seemed much taken aback by this. "How did you know about it?"

"I questioned the chief druids in the other cities. One said you had remarked on it."

"Arias it was, I wager," Senias said irritably. "He wasn't to say anything. If Danu was to hear of it, it would be most embarrassing to me. And I have nothing to do with it. Nothing!"

"I'm sure not," soothed Lir. "And there's no reason for Danu to know. Just tell *me* what it is."

"It's really so little. Just a certain drain upon this sphere's power, as if something were interfering or blocking a part of the energy source. A negligible change by the time all the lines converge at the temple's main sphere."

"Is this blocking coming from here? I mean, from this isle?"

"There's no way to tell. The energy lines run outward from here and all about the earth, interconnecting with who knows how many others. An earthquake, an eruption, even a great storm in some far country could possibly disrupt the flow."

"Where does the line that feeds this sphere come from?" asked Lir.

"Up from the south."

"The last time Olgear was seen, he was heading toward the south," Lir said. "You didn't by any chance send him out investigating this thing?"

"I told you, I don't know what happened to the lad," Senias said, his patience lost. "And I don't believe this energy fading means anything. I'm tired of you pestering me about it. Go away."

"Senias," said Lir, feigning shock, "where is our perfect peacefulness and bliss? You sound almost like a common mortal."

"I said go away," Senias demanded. "And I don't care if you tell Danu of this or not. The way she feels about you now, she'll not believe anything you tell her anyway."

"A fine day to you as well," Lir returned. "Come on,

Diancecht, let's get out of this marble crypt for long dead minds!"

He led the way outside. The healer, who as an outsider had prudently kept quiet through the whole exchange, now made comment: "It's no wonder he's so ready to accept that Danu's foreboding was false. He likely thinks this energy drain of his was its cause."

"Could be," said Lir as they climbed into his chariot. "Diancecht, just how much do you know about the workings of the lines of power and the spheres?"

"Very little. It's one thing your people have kept fairly secretive about. And I've not pried."

"Too bad. I don't know much about the workings of all that myself. I always left it to the druids. Still, this odd little problem might be worth following along, if we could trace the power stream back from here. But I'm not certain how that could be done."

"A 'stream' of power you call it," the healer said musingly. "You know, I think I might just know of a way."

The chariot carrying Mathgen and Cuthach hove steadily ahead beneath the sea.

The team of muscular stallions at its front galloped ahead through the enveloping water without seeming care or strain, their broad, paddling hooves drawing the car along at a good pace.

The two within the car rode in complete dryness and security. The entire passenger section of the chariot was encircled by a large bubble, like a sphere of glass, keeping the water well away. The men munched on fruits and nuts and watched the underwater world slipping by.

Mathgen seemed only intrigued by the unusual prospect. Cuthach looked at the fish swimming so close around him with an apprehensive eye.

"I really don't like traveling this way," he complained. "I feel trapped, suffocated, as if this shield you've made us is about to give way and let all that sea rush in."

"I am not going to tell you again," Mathgen said impatiently, "it is perfectly safe."

"I don't see why we've got to be staying down so much,"

the other grumbled. "We've been underwater for half the trip."

Mathgen gestured to the ocean surface not far above their heads. It appeared as a grey-white overcast of rippling clouds. "The surface is still choppy. We make better time below."

"So you say. But I'd rather be a bit longer in the voyage and have a real sky above me, and real air to breathe, and the fishes all swimming *under* me, where they belong!"

Mathgen gave a sigh of resignation. "All right then. I'm tired of your whimpering. We'll go up. Your tower should be getting close now anyway. Time you were taking another estimate of our position."

He tugged back on the reins. The team obediently lifted their heads and began to move upward, slanting toward the surface. In moments they were breaking out through the swells, the air-filled bubble simply dissolving away as they emerged.

They rolled atop the water now, horses' hooves and wheels cutting across the cresting waves. Cuthach contemplated the position of the sun.

"Still headed right, I'd say," he announced. His eyes scanned the eastern horizon closely, moving back and forth and back. Then, suddenly, they fixed.

"Look there, Cap'n!" he said excitedly, pointing. "Birds!"

A number of tiny flecks could be seen swooping about just above the curve of sea.

"Head right for 'em," Cuthach told Mathgen. "It's not far away now, I'm certain. Just past that rim."

He was right. They had not gone very much farther toward the flocking birds when a gleaming point of light popped into view on the horizon.

"That's it!" said Cuthach triumphantly. He looked to Mathgen, grinning. "Not bad reckoning for the old man, eh? I pointed us right here."

"You're certain that's the tower?" the other asked.

"Certain as I'm breathing. Like a beacon star it always is when it comes into view. We know that the place is still there, at least."

Mathgen urged his team to a greater pace. They swept

on toward the gleam. It grew rapidly larger as they approached, rising like a glowing sword blade of ice being thrust upward from the sea. The blade became a spire, the spire a pinnacle, the pinnacle a massive tower. Mathgen stared at the amazing structure in open awe.

"The Tower of Glass," said Cuthach pridefully. "Quite a nice piece of work, isn't it, Cap'n?"

This was a decided understatement.

The tower soared upward over thirty stories above the ocean surface, its flat top seeming to scrape the bellies of the clouds. Each sheer face of the square building seemed composed of a single sheet of glass so smoothly polished that it perfectly mirrored the sea and sky, making the tower almost disappear. But as the chariot drew closer, its passengers could detect that the sheets weren't unbroken. Fine black lines segmented the tower into precisely equal parts from bottom to top; and vertical lines divided each level into a dozen rectangular panes.

The full length of the glass-walled portion of the tower had by this time risen into view. Now its base could be seen —a small, rocky isle and a three-story-high foundation section of smooth, grey stone that thrust up from it.

Cuthach directed Mathgen to circle the island. On its south side a natural bay cut back into the rocky shoreline, letting the sea lap right against the tower's stone base. A pair of immense black metal doors were set in the foundation's smooth face. Their lower portion disappeared below the waterline. The doors were closed.

Mathgen steered his team to draw the chariot right up beside the doors. He pulled them to a stop there. The two men gazed up at the vast plates of metal rising twenty feet above them. Their dull black surfaces were streaked with red-brown lines of rust.

"Now what?" Mathgen asked. "I don't see a way past these."

Cuthach shrugged. "Dunno, Cap'n. Usually they just opened up when our ship approached. Must have been someone looking out for it from inside there."

"Then someone's watching now? They've seen us here?"

"Could be. That is, if there *is* anyone still inside."

Mathgen looked hard at his companion. "What are you saying now? You don't think they could all be dead?"

"Or gone, or just not carin' anymore." The old man shrugged again. "Who knows? I told you, it's been a lot of years."

"I'm certainly happy to find you such a great help to me," Mathgen said bitingly. "Well, let's try to get someone's attention anyway. Hand me a spear."

Cuthach pulled one of the weapons from a rack of several fixed to the side of the car. Mathgen took it and began to slam its point against one of the doors. Each stroke produced a sharp, hollow clank that echoed away inside.

There was no reply.

"I can't even tell if this is loud enough to be noticed in there," Mathgen said. He looked at the spear's tip, already badly blunted. "That's hard metal. Likely thick too. Oh, well . . ."

He tried again, banging out a spirited tattoo on the door.

"Ah . . . Cap'n," Cuthach said, glancing behind them. "I think you can stop now."

Mathgen looked around. Two small skiffs of grey metal bracketed them. Each carried half a dozen grey-uniformed men. Several of the men carried heavy spears, also of grey metal, all cocked back to throw.

Chapter 23

Balor

"We're not enemies," Mathgen told them, hastily lowering his own weapon. "We only want to talk."

There was no response from the grim-faced men. A pair in each skiff wielded metal oars to push the boats in close to the chariot. One man jumped across to the car. He drew a short, wide-bladed sword from its scabbard and pressed its keen tip into Mathgen's ribs, poking meaningfully.

"Inside," he said tersely.

"Inside?" Mathgen echoed. "How?"

As if in response, a creaking, clattering sound arose. The two doors shuddered, then parted, swinging inward to open a space just wide enough to admit the chariot and skiffs. The place beyond the opening looked very dark.

The sword point prodded again. Mathgen made no delay in lifting the reins and urging the team forward. The chariot passed between the doors and into the tower's base.

Its interior was indeed cavernous, as Cuthach had said. But it was also clearly man-made. Ceiling and walls were flat and square-cornered, composed of what seemed a smooth, grey, seamless stone.

Around three sides of an artificial bay were massive quays of the same stone where a score of long, sleek, metal ships were tied up. Their design was a familiar one to Mathgen. They were like the wrecked vessel they had found on the so-called isle of giants.

Though gloomy in contrast to the brightness outside, the interior still had adequate light to see clearly, once the eyes had adjusted. The light came from rows of square panels running at intervals across the ceiling. They emitted an even, bluish-white glow—those that were working did, that is. Many of the panels were completely dark. Some were cracked and stained, only half their square alight. Some flickered in an irritating, sputtering way.

There were other signs of deterioration visible too. Several of the ships were heavily streaked with rust. A few were partially dismantled. One, in fact, had been completely taken apart, its gutted hulk floating at the quay, its pieces scattered on the platform above. A swarm of men picked over the jumble like ants on a carcass.

"Looks like they're cannibalizing that one," Cuthach observed. "Getting parts for the rest." Looking around at other decaying craft and up at the broken lights, he shook his head. "Things have certainly gone far downhill since the old days."

At the continued prodding of the man with the sword, Mathgen brought his chariot up to an open spot at a quay. They climbed from the car and mounted a short flight of stone stairs to the quay's platform. Three other grey-uniformed men awaited them there. Two of these wore black helmets with flaring neck pieces. They carried long, thick rods of metal, each with a glowing, sapphirelike stone set in one end. These weapons, too, Mathgen had seen before. He was well aware of the lethal effects of their power.

The third man—a bull-necked, stocky man of swarthy complexion and greasy black hair—examined them with a supercilious gaze. His uniform was made distinctive by a silver, triangle-shaped badge affixed to his barrel chest.

On seeing the badge, Cuthach snapped to attention with an alacrity surprising for the old man. He lifted a hand palm outward in crisp salute.

"Seaman Cuthach reporting to you, Captain," he rapped out.

The officer addressed lifted an eyebrow in surprise. He looked them over closely once again.

"Just *what* are you?" he said with insolent tones. "And what is that preposterous conveyance that brought you here?"

"I came as a friend," Mathgen explained again. "I came to talk. It's quite safe. Cuthach here brought me. He's one of yours."

"What, this?" the officer looked the old man up and down.

"I am, sir," Cuthach said, still at attention. "I was a crewman of the *Raider,* sir."

"The *Raider*?" The man gave a harsh laugh. "Now I know you're mad. That vessel was lost over three hundred years ago."

"It was, sir, and I was on it. We ran aground in a storm. Marooned we were. Those who didn't die in the wreck died off over the years."

"Except for you," said the officer. "Somehow you've kept alive for all this time?"

"He's speaking the truth," Mathgen put in somewhat impatiently. "Don't you understand? He's been on an enchanted isle, a place of magic, just as I have. It kept us from aging."

"Don't take that tone with me," the officer threatened. "Look here, I don't know what kind of game you're playing, but what you're saying is impossible."

"It's not, man!" Mathgen said, all but shouting now in his frustration. "We've both just come from there. Riches and power beyond anything you can imagine lie just beyond that barrier fog."

"The barrier fog?" the man said, his haughtiness replaced by a look of open astonishment. "Is that where you've come from?"

"It is," said Mathgen, noting the abrupt change. "Why? Do you believe us now? Will you let us talk to someone in high authority?"

The officer's gaze went from him to Cuthach to the miraculous seagoing chariot at the quay. He frowned, pondering hard. Then:

"Watch them," he ordered the two guards with the power rods. He turned on his heel and strode rapidly away.

Mathgen and Cuthach waited somewhat anxiously as long moments dragged by. They waited silently, looking around them, or at each other, or at the impassive guards. Finally the officer returned.

"Come with me," he told them. "Guards, follow us."

He led them to an opening in the wall behind the quay. A narrow stairway took them upward for several flights, where they emerged from cramped gloominess into space and light.

"By Balor," said the overawed Cuthach. "So this is The Upstairs!"

They were in a room that took up the entire base level of the glass tower. It was a single, enormous space, made to seem even larger by its outer walls of glass. They offered an open view of the sea and sky in all directions, and let the outside daylight flood in.

As the glass exterior was only a curtain wall, offering no support, the ceiling was held up by pillars evenly spaced about the room. Square, massive, and strictly utilitarian in look, these pillars were a dull silver-grey metal. Floor and ceiling were more of the smooth grey stone.

Many scores of men, all in the same grey uniforms, were bustling about the room. Most were in long lines stretching away from barrel-shaped kiosks in each corner of the room. Men at counters within were dolling out either small packages or baskets or boxes or jugs. Those in line waited patiently, silently, soberly for their goods.

"What's all that about?" asked Mathgen.

"Rations," the officer snapped. "Food, clothes, drink. Goes on all day. This way now."

He led them to a much larger square pillar that rose up in the center of the room. Two open, metal-railed staircases angled up and around its sides to reach openings in the ceiling. More men were streaming up and down, coming to join the lines or carrying their meager portions of supplies off to the tower's upper floors.

In one wall of the central block were set four metal doors. All were closed, but as Mathgen's group approached, one slid open, and a dozen men came out, emptying a small chamber behind.

Other men on the floor started for it. The captain stepped up to the doorway before them, signing them away.

"Priority," he told them tersely. "We go right to the top."

The men looked curiously at the officer's guards and their two charges, then obediently moved back. The five alone entered the chamber.

A man stood in one corner of the small, metal-walled room. One of his hands gripped the handle of a lever seemingly hinged to the floor.

"Top level," the officer ordered him.

"Sorry, Captain, they're only functioning to level twenty-five today," the man said flatly. "You'll have to walk from there."

"Can't they keep anything working properly up here?" the officer growled. "All right, take us as far as you can."

The man pulled his lever back. The door slid closed. The room began to shudder.

"I . . . I feel a most peculiar sensation," said Mathgen. "As if my stomach were dropping out. What's happening?"

The officer shrugged. "Nothing. We're just going up."

"Up?" wailed Cuthach, turning pale. "I think I'm going to be sick."

But he was saved from this by the ending of their ride. The shuddering stopped, the driver pushed his lever forward, and the door slid open again.

"I'd heard of things like this being in The Upstairs," the old man told the captain, "but I thought they were only fables."

The officer said nothing, just leading the way again.

They stepped from the lifting room into a small vestibule. Corridors lined with doors stretched away in several directions. They were low and narrow and the light—from more glowing panels widely spaced in the ceiling—was poor. Mathgen and Cuthach glimpsed what seemed to be women and children peeping out through the cracks of a few doors. Then they were being hustled around a corner and up another staircase.

Around and up, around and up for five more floors they

went. Finally they came out into another vestibule-type room. Without any pause, the captain led them up a single corridor from there, marching ahead of the visitors, the two guards following behind.

The corridor opened into another large room. It was high—some three stories—and it was long—running the length of one side of the tower. The outer wall of glass offered a spectacular view of sea and sky stretching far away.

But something even more spectacular claimed Mathgen's and Cuthach's attention as they entered: a figure of dark metal who stood before the windows.

It was a massive figure, seemingly a giant nearly three stories in height, clad totally in heavy armor. The metal covering was most skillfully made, without an obvious seam or rivet on its smoothly rounded surfaces. The limbs were jointed, and the gauntleted hands had fully articulated fingers.

The helmeted head—alone taller than a man's height—was like a cask, cylindrical and featureless save for a half-moon–shaped visor at the front.

Cuthach came up short as he first saw this figure, exclaiming in astonishment, "Balor!"

One of the guards behind prodded him roughly forward with the butt of his power rod.

"Who's Balor?" Mathgen asked, himself staring in amazement at the being.

"Supreme Commander of the tower," the old man breathed. "Alive, after all these years."

The captain strode forward to stop a few paces before Balor. He signaled the two visitors to stop beside him. The guards drew up at attention close behind.

There was a long silence, as if the seemingly blind being were somehow examining them. Then a deep voice boomed out to them, reverberating as if from within a metal drum.

"You are the two from beyond the barrier fog?"

"We are," said Mathgen, an assertive tone not quite covering his nervousness in the giant's presence. "We've come here to ask you . . ."

"*I* will do the asking," Balor thundered. "I want to know precisely who you are."

"I told the captain here, my Commander," Cuthach began timorously. "I was a seaman aboard . . ."

Balor cut him off. "Silence! I don't mean you, old man. I mean the dark one there. What is your name?"

"I am called Mathgen, Commander," he said, giving a small bow.

"From the fineness of your dress, I judge you one of some position. Do you come from this magic isle where no one ages?"

"Well, no," Mathgen hedged. "Not exactly. I've been . . . well, a guest there, I suppose you'd say, along with Cuthach."

"How did you get there?"

"I sailed there, actually, through the barrier fog, like Cuthach."

"When?"

"When? Is that important? I mean, we want . . ."

"*When?*" Balor repeated, clanging out the word.

"I don't know exactly. Perhaps, around, say, three hundred years ago?"

"Three hundred years ago you sailed into the barrier fog," the giant said. "And from where?"

"Oh, just somewhere off east of here," Mathgen said vaguely. "No place you would know of, I'm certain."

There was a metallic rasping noise. The visor on Balor's helmet lifted up, opening a hairline crack to expose the fiery glow within. Cuthach and Mathgen winced back at the sudden brightness.

"Behind this lid lies my single eye," Balor said. "It is a weapon of great destructive power. With the lid fully open, the blazing sphere could incinerate whole armies, whole fleets. Even a slender beam of its light would turn you instantly into a flaming pyre. So, make no more pathetic attempts to lie to me, Mathgen. Tell me exactly where you came from or your skin will begin to cook."

Mathgen quailed before the threat. "I came from that isle which lies south of here," he admitted very readily indeed. "My people . . . the people I was with . . . they tried to settle there. They had a fight with the ones called the Fomor. Some of your people were there. We were nearly wiped out. A few survivors determined to sail into the western sea. I went with them. We entered the barrier fog. Eventually we reached the enchanted isle. It's inhabitants call it Tir-na-nog."

"So, you *are* the ones," said Balor. "After all this time. And exactly what kind of powers do these inhabitants have?"

"They can use magic to create, to change, to control. They have mastery over weather and growing things. They have made a paradise."

"A paradise, using magic powers," Balor said musingly. "Tell me, did any of their number help your people in defeating the Fomor?"

"Yes," said Mathgen. "One named Lir. He also helped us through the fog and to the enchanted isle."

"Then I was right," Balor boomed triumphantly. "Your people were a clue to *Them.* Now, thanks to you, we have at last discovered our Departed Ones again!"

The ball of polished hazelwood dangling from the length of twine swung in small circles for a time, then settled into a pendulum motion, swinging back and forth along a line.

"There," declared Diancecht, who held the twine. He straightened up to point as the swings indicated, out across smoothly rolling meadowland. "It goes right on that way."

"Amazing how that works," Lir remarked as he and the healer climbed back into his swan chariot.

"Your remark about a 'stream' of energy made me think of it," the other explained. "It's a type of dowser one of your own sorcerers told me about. It can locate almost any kind of substance buried in the earth."

"Fascinating," said Lir, snapping the reins to start the team ahead.

"Apparently all things emanate some sort of power," the healer went on, warming to the subject. "It's enough to cause something as sensitive as the suspended ball to begin a pendulum swing at a certain precise distance from the source."

"Diancecht, I don't really need . . ." an obviously bewildered Lir began.

But the healer, now fully involved in his dissertation,

ignored him. "All substances are different, you see. And your energy line, as I hoped, emanates a particularly strong and distinct power. I located the point where it passes under the sphere in Murias and heads on southward. Then I simply determined the length of twine needed to suspend the ball always the right distance from the ground that's needed to make it swing." He showed Lir a fat knot in the twine. "You see? I only have to hold it there, walk around a bit until the pendulum motion starts, and there we are—right above the line."

"Well, I certainly thank you for that explanation," Lir said with a hint of amusement, "little of it though I really understood. In any case, the thing is very helpful. Too bad it requires our stopping so often. Three days we've been crawling across the countryside."

"Yes, but we really haven't a choice," said Diancecht. "We must stop often to determine the exact course."

"I don't know," said Lir. "The line's gone straight as a spear pole so far."

"But what if it turned?" asked the always exacting healer. "We might go on unknowing and lose the track completely. No, slowly and carefully—that's the most sure way."

Lir sighed and nodded and steered the chariot on.

They crossed the meadowland and passed over a low ridge of hills, pausing at the crest for yet another reading. As they rolled down the farther slope, a movement in the sky not far above them caught Lir's eye. He looked up to see a large bird swooping down at them.

"Look there," he said to the healer as it whisked by close overhead.

"A raven," said Diancecht as it flapped in to land before them.

"Morrigan," both said together as Lir pulled the chariot to a stop.

The bird was already glowing with the aura of transformation. The men watched the shape-shifting within the cocoon of light and were soon looking at the black-haired woman.

"What is it that you two are doing out here?" she demanded. "I caught sight of you by chance earlier while I was flying about. I've been watching from far up there for some while. I would have ignored you, but what you were doing looked too strange. Like my namesake, I have a fierce curiosity."

"We are following an energy pattern in the earth, using this ball and twine," Diancecht explained, holding them up. "You see, everything emanates a special kind of power, and . . ."

Lir hastily cut in. "No need to go through all of that again. Enough to say that we're tracing the line to see if anything has interfered with it."

"And you think this could be some kind of problem?" she asked.

Lir shrugged. "We don't know. It's merely a curiosity for now, but still one that needs an explanation."

"We may not find it," said Diancecht. "Morrigan, can you tell us how far we are from the sea?"

"Not very far at all. That's why I saw you. I'm often doing my flying along the coast. There are fine updrafts there. Good for gliding."

"It looks hopeless then," the healer said, disappointed. "Once the line passes out under the sea, we'll have no way of knowing where it goes."

"That may be," she said, "but I can tell you where it's going to go first."

"What do you mean?" asked Lir.

"Well, if your line continues straight on the way you're headed now, it'll reach Mathgen's tower."

"What?" said the healer. "Are you certain?"

"See for yourself. It's only a rise or two ahead."

She climbed into the chariot with them and they rolled forward. As they topped a second ridge of low hills, the sea came into view. So did the pinnacle of rock and Mathgen's tower.

"I thought this countryside was familiar," said Lir, reining in his team.

Diancecht quickly climbed down. He held out the ball suspended on the twine. It went in circles for a brief time, then shifted to a strong pendulum swing.

"She's right," he announced. "The line must run straight out that promontory and right beneath that tower."

Lir eyed the sinister structure. "I was afraid of that."

"You think he has something to do with the energy fading?" asked the healer. "How? What could he be up to?"

"I don't know, but I've a feeling it could be very bad. I've never really trusted him."

"Nor I," said the raven-woman.

"I suppose he *could* be capable of anything," admitted Diancecht, "if it meant gaining power."

"I should have guessed there was something going on when I saw him with old Cuthach," Lir said, angry at himself. "Danu's said that in her premonition of something evil happening, those of his kind played a part."

"His kind?" said the healer. "But you told us that it was the Fomor who'd be involved."

"Oh, them as well," Lir told him. "But it was the ones of the metal ships and strange weapons who she most greatly feared. By her order, I didn't tell you about them."

"Her order?" said Morrigan. "Why?"

"It was a secret of our past she thought you shouldn't know," he answered. "You see, those people of the glass tower are our most ancient enemies."

Chapter 24

Agreement

A huge image showed upon a silver-white square. It was a dramatic image of a sun rising to silhouette a complex skyline created by scores of soaring structures.

"It has been many hundreds of years for us since the fall," echoed the metallic voice of Balor. "Before that we were a thriving society, controlling the whole earth."

The image shifted, showing the structures from closer and below. The many types of buildings—of glass and stone, of pyramid and pinnacle and cylinder shapes—rose up on all sides like the sheer cliff walls of a deep canyon.

"There were many cities of towers like these," Balor went on, "built on many continents. Broad, paved roadways connected them. Great engines gave them heat and water and light."

A new image showed the city at night, the towers all glimmering with bright dots and lines of light, creating a spectacular show.

Cuthach and Mathgen stood watching the display with interest, while the guards and the captain kept a close watch on them. They all stood a few paces before Balor, now seated on an immense, square-cornered throne of metal.

The room had been darkened, the outer wall of windows

covered. The moving images were showing on a section of the inner wall.

The picture shifted again, lifting to shoot downward as if from far above the city. Below could be seen a crosshatch of avenues running at right angles, cutting sections of the tall buildings into exact squares. Many small objects—looking like tiny beetles from the heights—scooted briskly along the avenues. For the two visitors it was a rather heady perspective.

"Amazing how they show these things, eh?" Cuthach murmured to Mathgen. "You didn't know my people had a magic like yours."

Mathgen looked up to a hole in the ceiling above the screen. A beam of light shone out from it, clearly delineated by the dust motes trapped and floating within. The beam widened rapidly into a pyramidal shape, casting its square base and the images it carried upon the section of wall. A faint clattering sound came from beyond the hole.

"It's not magic," he murmured back. "I think it's a device of some sort."

"Still, no matter how it's done," Cuthach said with a certain pride, "those pictures are fantastic, aren't they?"

"Hardly the quality of my own," Mathgen said deridingly.

Which was quite true. The images were often hazy and colorless. White and black lines whizzed irritatingly through them. And sometimes there were rather violent jerks and shudderings.

"Quit your whispering," Balor rumbled warningly. "Watch and learn."

One scene faded away and another brightened into view, showing a fleet of ships much like those of the glass tower in shape. But these were much larger, and their sleek hulls glowed with the soft, silver sheen of polished pewter.

"We had thousands of ships plying the world's oceans then," the giant's narration went on, "carrying our culture to other lands, bringing back the raw materials to make us yet greater, yet more powerful."

There was a scene of a ship docked at a quay while a swarm of dark-skinned people in bright kaftans loaded bulging sacks.

"We gathered the world's resources to us," Balor clanged out, "and we used them!"

Now there came a flurry of images: huge furnaces belching flame, flowing red-hot slag, great hammers pounding, sparks and steam and smoke billowing away. Then a view of a seemingly endless row of metal objects—hulking, ominous masses of dark metal rolling on thick, black wheels—as they passed down a line and off a ramp.

"At last we became a force like no other," Balor said, and the lighted square showed ranks of grey-clad troops, massed together thousands strong, then line upon line of more marching troops all armed with the power weapons.

The presentation was unexpectedly interrupted.

There came the sound of a loud snap. The image was suddenly rent apart and vanished in an instant, leaving a blank square of white light. A flapping sound came from beyond the ceiling hole. Then the projecting beam went out.

"Sorry, Commander." A most contrite voice came from somewhere above them. "I'm afraid it's broken. It's very old, you know."

"Keep your excuses," Balor snapped to the invisible speaker. "Let's have light!"

There was a rattling, humming sound and the metal panels that had shuttered the windows slid upward, vanishing through slots in the ceiling. Outside light flooded the room again. The captain, guards, and visitors turned to face the seated giant.

"I've shown you these things so you know how great was the damage done by those we've come to call the 'Departed Ones,'" Balor said. "We needed their help to sustain our world, and they abandoned us."

"Why?" Mathgen asked.

"They were greedy," the giant answered bluntly. "They had developed powers and skills beyond ours. They refused to share them."

"That does seem most unfair," Mathgen said.

"Of course, what happened was our own fault to some extent," Balor allowed. "When the potency of our own science and machinery was at its height, we paid no serious notice to their dabblings. We thought their claim of harnessing this earth power—'magic' as you call it—was the ravings of demented or misguided ones. But then our problems began to develop. Errors were made. Flaws discovered. Little things at first, but quickly worsening. We came at last to realize the powers of these . . . these 'sorcerers' could correct the problems. But, by then, we were too late. Rather than help us deal with the decay, they had disappeared. All of their kind had fled from us, sneaking away with the secrets of their powers, leaving no trace. And, not long after, our society entered a period of total collapse."

"All your cities," said Mathgen, "your people, your resources . . ."

"Gone. Except for us. We are the last bastion, the last tower, the last people. We have survived here, isolated, waiting for a time when we might become strong again. Now, we have a chance for that. We can reverse the affects of past disasters. We can rebuild our numbers and our skills until we're once more unbeatable. We can take power in the world again."

"No. Not you," corrected Mathgen. "You seem to be missing one key point here. I intend for this power to be mine. I didn't come here to make you a gift of their isle, I came to ask your help in taking it for myself."

"Then you make a great mistake in coming here alone," Balor told him. "You will tell us how to find this Tir-na-nog."

"That wouldn't help you. Without the magic I've spent so long mastering, you'd never even make it through the barrier fog, much less the hazards beyond it."

"You will take us through them."

"No," said Mathgen stubbornly, crossing his arms before him. "I won't."

"Don't forget the eye blazing behind this closed lid," the giant warned. "Things could be made most painful for you."

This threat no longer appeared to disturb Mathgen. His own arrogant, flippant nature had returned. "A wonderful idea. Torture me, then," he challenged. "I still won't help you. And if you happen to kill me, then you'll have nothing."

"If you don't have help from us, then so will you," Balor countered.

"True. I need your help as much as you need mine.

Therefore, there seems only one way. I offer a compromise: we share the effort, and we share the power. Half of the world is more than enough for me."

Balor considered. Then the massive head nodded. "Very well," his voice rattled. "Equal rule. You will take us safely to the isle. We will supply a fleet to conquer it."

"No. No fleet," said Mathgen. "Too dangerous. Even I couldn't keep Queen Danu from detecting it. One ship would be safe. Cuthach tells me one can carry a hundred men."

"One ship?" Balor said incredulously. "Against the thousands you say live there?"

"Those thousands are sworn pacifists," Mathgen pointed out. "They have no will, means, or skills to fight. The way I've planned to take control, a hundred men will be enough. Once we control, of course, the barriers can be dropped. Your whole force can come in if you wish it."

"It seems very risky to me," said Balor.

"Nevertheless, it is the only way. Or none."

Again the giant nodded. "I agree. Captain Tarbh-chu himself will lead. He is one of our best men."

Mathgen gave the officer a swift appraisal and nodded. "Good enough. But we must move quickly for my plan to work."

"Preparations will begin immediately. Guards, show this man back to the quay."

"Beg pardon, my Commander," Cuthach said. "I'm going too."

"You, old man?" said the giant. "But you've done your work already. Stay here. Rest. Enjoy the laurels you have earned."

"I'd as soon stay with Mathgen, if it's the same to you, sir," Cuthach said. "He and I started this thing. I'd like to see it through."

"Commendable," boomed Balor. "Then, when you return, it will be to a celebration of you as the Hero of the People, the greatest man we've ever known."

"Really?" the old man said, beaming. "I'm most honored, sir."

"It's only a part of what you deserve. Guards, take them

both down. The captain will come in a moment. He and I
must decide on our best ship for this enterprise."

The guards led Mathgen and Cuthach back toward the
lifting room. Balor waited until they had passed well out of
sight. Then he addressed Captain Tarbh-chu in low tones:
"I have no trust in that cunning one, Captain. Ready three
ships. Fill them all with the best men and weapons we still
have. Take one for yourself and him. Have the other two
follow, keeping you just in sight. The fool will lead them
through these hazards as well."

"Understood, Commander," the man said.

He lifted a hand in smart salute, then began to turn.

"Oh, and Captain," Balor added.

The man turned back. "Yes, Commander?"

"When the isle is secured and the barriers down, we'll
have no more use for him. See that he's killed."

Lir thumped hard on the invisible barrier with his sword.
The blade rebounded as if striking an elastic but quite solid
surface.

"Very clever," he said, *"and* very strong! Shows the sly
one's got to be hiding something in there."

"And that he's got some very impressive power," put in
Diancecht, looking out toward Mathgen's tower on its
rocky point. "This shield cuts off the entire promontory.
Even the queen's druids would be hard-pressed to create
something like it."

"How do we get through?" asked Morrigan. "I might fly
over, but you . . ."

"There has to be another way in," said Lir. "When
Dagda and I visited here before, Mathgen and his chariot
somehow sprang into being from nowhere. I wondered how
at the time. It was right around here . . ."

He began to search among the rocks along the cliff line.
The other two joined him. They examined every stone and
every stretch of ground. Finally, at a large rock outcrop-
ping, Diancecht made a discovery.

"There is a fissure in the face of the stone here that
forms a wide, high arch," he said, tracing it around. He put

a palm over a section of it. "I can feel air being drawn through the crack."

Morrigan moved up beside him and put her nose to the spot. "I scent a mustiness within, and the smell of animals too. Something's in there."

"If it's a door, then there must be a way to open it," Lir said, looking over the section and the surrounding rock.

He noted a particularly knob-shaped protuberance and pushed it experimentally.

The section swung inward, revealing a tunnel.

"A promising start," said Lir. "Shall we go in?"

"Certainly," said Diancecht. "But we must be careful. If Mathgen is involved in some deceit, he won't like visitors. We have to be ready for anything."

"Right," said Lir.

He looked over the others. Diancecht was unarmed. Morrigan, having shape-shifted out of her flying mode, was garbed in only her leather shift and also weaponless.

Lir drew his own sword. "I'd better go first."

They moved cautiously into the tunnel. The darkness, insects, and rats did not faze them. But the huge shadow that reared up suddenly before Lir did give him quite a start.

He looked up at the enormous rodent form with its sharp, bared teeth and glinting red eyes and drew back his sword to strike.

"Wait," said Morrigan, moving past him to confront the beast unarmed. She squeaked out something. It squeaked in reply. There was a brief further exchange of the shrill noises, and then the rodent dropped to all fours and scuttled away into a small side passage.

"Well, I'm certainly glad you happened along," Lir remarked to her.

"We don't have to worry about Mathgen," she said. "He's gone. The tower is empty."

"How do you know that?" asked Diancecht.

"The rat told me," she answered simply. "Come on." They went on, meeting no more obstacles. But as they reached the opening to the interior of the tower, Diancecht stumbled over something on the floor.

The three looked down. A few well-gnawed bones were

scattered about, along with shreds of cloth. Lir picked up a shred, examining its silvery material.

"The cloth of a druid's gown," he said grimly. "Looks like we've found our missing Oigear, poor lad."

They went on into the tower room. As the rodent had reported, it was empty.

They searched carefully, seeking any clue as to what Mathgen was about. It told them very little.

"Finding that poor dead lad certainly proves Mathgen's purpose is a most terrible one," said Diancecht.

"I'd say he has designs on the druid's power," said Lir. "He can't really control their magic without the energy of the lines . . ."

". . . which is why he built his tower here," the healer finished.

"Yes. He's got to be the one draining off the energy. But he can't use it unless he accumulates it somehow, and channels it into a sphere. Or"—his eye fell on the pool—"something of the like."

He went to the edge and peered into the black depths. Morrigan and Diancecht joined him.

"You think it could be here?" the healer asked.

"A 'stream' of energy?" said Lir. "Accumulated in a 'pool'? I know it sounds like a bad joke, but it might be quite efficient."

"Yes, and well hidden too," added the healer. He took hold of the twine and suspended the hazelwood ball out over the water at arm's length. It instantly began a violent swinging back and forth, tugging at his hand.

"Incredible!" said Diancecht, pulling the dowser back. "There must be an immensely strong energy source down there."

"Something's happening," said Morrigan. "In the water."

They peered down at the pool. The surface was shimmering, coming alive with a white glow. Streamers of color appeared, writhing within the white, twining and curling and forming into a definite shape.

In moments the startled three were gazing on the image of Mathgen himself, grinning up at them.

"Hello," he said affably. "So, someone has found a way

in here, discovered this pool, and disturbed its energy. I left this message behind just in case someone did. I certainly hope it's Lir. He's the only one whose interference I've really worried about. None of those other fools were capable of discovering what I was doing, except perhaps that meddling healer, Diancecht."

The two men exchanged a glance.

"By the time you're seeing this image," he went on, "I'll likely be well under way. I'm planning to bring back a force and seize all of Danu's power. I'm going to the glass tower for my help, Lir. I believe you know very well who they are. They certainly were interested in you back in the Blessed Isle. Oh, the reason I'm telling you this is so that you'll know exactly what I did to you. You see, you won't be there to witness it. I've no more use for my isolated little tower. So you're going to be sealed up where you are. Forever!"

At the last word, the tunnel opening rumbled and snapped shut like a closing jaw.

The metal ship plowed through the water at high speed, leaving a broad, foaming wake. It was visible for only a short distance behind, vanishing into the dense, enveloping bank of fog.

Mathgen stood at the rail on the second level of the ship's pyramidal superstructure, Cuthach beside him. Behind them, through the open hatchway, a seaman could be seen at the large steering wheel. Nearby stood the ship's captain, his concerned gaze moving from a bank of instruments to the boiling fog outside.

On the main deck forward of the pyramid, several dozens of the tower's fighting men ignored the thick, damp atmosphere to inspect and clean their weapons. All the men were equipped with one of the jewel-tipped power rods as well as shortsword and dagger. They were dark, thick, solid-bodied men, their faces hard and cruel. They tended the lethal tools of their trade with practiced efficiency.

"They look a hearty and ruthless lot," Mathgen said with satisfaction. "They should do the job quite well."

He noted an especially thick patch of the fog off the ship's port bow. He brightened at the sight.

"Ah, that's just fine," he said, and turned to call back into the wheelhouse. "Oh, Captain, turn a bit more to the left here, please. Just over that way." He pointed off toward the thick cloud.

The captain directed his helmsman to adjust the course. The wheel turned slightly and the bow came smartly around to point into the patch.

"Very good," Mathgen said softly to his henchman as the heavy fog blanketed the ship. Even a view of the deck below was obscured now. "That should help insure their becoming lost."

"Lost?" said a confused Cuthach. "Us, Cap'n?"

"No. Those who follow. A few turns and twists through the most blinding spots will make it impossible for anyone to keep us in sight. We'll get through the barrier safely, leaving them to wander hopelessly inside."

"Who, Cap'n?"

"The ships that Balor sent to follow us," Mathgen replied easily. "My little conference with our large metal friend was enough to tell me how he thinks. He is as devious as I. And I wouldn't miss such a chance. But there'll be no more of his ships or warriors involved in this than what *I've* decided."

"Aren't you afraid of ourselves being lost?" the old man asked him.

"Oh, no." He reached into his cloak and pulled his glass rod out. It glowed very faintly in the gloom.

Lifting the cloak to shield his movements from the captain, he swept the rod out before him, back and forth. At one spot its tip flared with a stronger light.

"See there," he declared. "It points the way. I've attuned it to Danu's sphere of power. It'll keep bringing us back on the right course toward Tir-na-nog."

He slipped the rod out of sight.

"I don't quite feel right about it, though," Cuthach said uncomfortably. "Letting my mates become lost like that. Left to die."

"They may find a way out," Mathgen said. "Feel your sorrow for these, if any." He waved a hand over the troops below. "They'll certainly have to be destroyed."

Cuthach looked to him in shock. "What?"

"Well, knowing Balor so well now, as I said, I assume he'll have ordered them to deal with me, once the isle's secured. They don't realize that once I have the power, they won't be able to do anything." He shrugged dismissively. "It doesn't matter. I never intended to let them survive anyway. This conquest is for us alone."

"I was to be rewarded back home," the old man said with chagrin. "I was to be made Hero of the People."

"Don't be a fool," Mathgen said harshly. "You'd have some worthless praise, and nothing else. Balor and his officers would take all the power. They're no better than Danu and her chief druids. If you want real reward, if you want your youth, you'll stay with me and accept everything I do."

"You're right, Cap'n. Of course," Cuthach agreed. But his hand moved, unseen by Mathgen, to reassuringly caress the hilt of a dagger he'd concealed beneath his tunic.

Chapter 25

Escape

"Two days of this!" groused Lir, kicking at one of the tower's stone walls, then wincing at the pain.

"I would advise that you save your energy," Diancecht said calmly. "Otherwise you'll only starve to death the sooner."

"We'll die anyway, sooner or later," Lir shot back, "unless we find some way out of here." He probed into a crack between two stones with his sword tip.

"You've gone over every section of the wall and floor a hundred times," the healer pointed out. "Mathgen's sure to have sealed them tight. No exit that way."

"Curse the walls and curse Mathgen to a bloody end," Lir said angrily. He turned to look at Diancecht. "And just what is it that *you're* doing?"

The healer was strolling slowly around the pond, carrying a lighted taper in his hands. He was closely contemplating its flame.

"I'm just assessing something," he said vaguely. "Nothing to speak of now."

"Well, you look as if you've gone mad," Lir told him. He looked around the room. "And where's Morrigan got to?"

There was a sharp, triumphant caw. The gaunt figure

rose up from where it had been crouched behind a table near the wall. She held a small, struggling object in one hand.

"What's that?" said Lir.

"A rat," she said. She lifted it and snapped out with her sharp teeth. They clamped over the rat's neck. There was a crunching sound. The rat went limp.

Lir grimaced in disgust. "I thought you didn't believe in killing poor creatures."

"I kill for my revenge, for self-defense, and for food," she rasped tersely in reply. "This is food. Would you want some?" She held it out toward him.

"Be my guest," he told her.

She shrugged and turned from him, her mouth dropping to her kill. Lir looked quickly away.

"I have it!" said Diancecht excitedly.

"You haven't caught a rat too?" Lir asked.

"What?" said the healer, clearly unaware of what had just transpired. "No, no. Look here. See the candle flame?"

Lir examined it. It flickered toward one side, causing the taper to gutter.

"So?" Lir said.

"I've noted a faint movement of the air," Diancecht explained. "A breeze was moving down the tunnel quite noticeably when we came in. I've been using the candle to check. Something is pulling the air in from all around the room. Pulling it right up there." He pointed toward the ceiling high above.

"Up there?" said Lir.

"See that round spot, like a patch, in the center?" the healer asked. "I think it's a ventilation hole of some sort. Without something of the kind, the atmosphere in here would soon become unbreathable."

"But you said Mathgen would have sealed the walls and floor tight," reasoned Lir. "Why leave the ceiling?"

"Because it's one place he would assume we couldn't reach. However, perhaps we can."

Both men looked toward Morrigan, still hunched over her meal, slurping noisily.

"Uh, Morrigan," Lir said a bit hesitantly, "may we disturb your, um, dining?"

She cast the now drained and gutted carcass aside and

turned to them, drawing an arm across her mouth to wipe clean her bloodstained lips.

"What do you want?"

"There may be an opening of some kind up there," said Diancecht, pointing to the ceiling. "It's the only place we haven't checked. Could you fly up and see?"

She nodded and immediately began the metamorphosis. In moments the great black bird was flapping toward the ceiling, confined by the narrow space to a tight upward spiral.

She glided in a circle just below the ceiling, examining the copper plate that formed it with a sharp eye. Then, by dint of much furious wing work, she hovered for a brief time at the spot in the center. Finally she turned and glided back to them, perching on a tabletop.

"A round hole, like a smoke hole," she cawed in a barely intelligible voice. "A cover over it, but there's a space. I might squeeze through."

"You have to, Morrigan," said Diancecht. "It's our only chance. Get help."

"And get warning to Danu," Lir added as the bird began to flap upward again. "We may not have much time!"

The raven-woman reached the ceiling, once more hovering by the hole. She grasped its edge in her strong claws, wings beating hard to keep her suspended there as she began to work her head through a gap between the hole and a rain-shield of copper fixed over it on metal posts.

The head slipped through, and then the neck, stretching out and quivering with strain as she fought mightily to pull the body through. Sleek though it was, it seemed too large to make it. For long moments it seemed jammed in the opening, wriggling and thrashing futilely while the two anxious men watched from below.

Then, abruptly, it popped free, although leaving a number of its feathers behind. The last that a relieved Lir and Diancecht saw was the long tail being drawn from sight.

On the roof the raven-woman recovered quickly, giving her wings a quick shake and preening to get them back in proper line. Then she lifted, soaring away, heading toward the north.

"Nuada!" a familiar voice called urgently.

He looked up from the fire into which he'd been staring broodingly to see Dagda, Angus, and the boy named Cian entering his house. Behind them entered the raven-woman, once more in human form.

"What's this?" he asked, rising quickly as he saw their troubled looks.

"Morrigan came to us on the practice field, and we came straight to you," said Dagda. "There's great danger for Tir-na-nog."

"It's Mathgen," she explained. "He's bringing a force from outside to invade the isle."

"From that glass tower," said Dagda. "He left some days ago. Lir and Diancecht discovered it with Morrigan. That scheming wolf trapped them in his tower."

"Wait, wait! This is too fast," Nuada said in bewilderment. "It's too incredible!"

"Believe it," Dagda urged. "Mathgen intends to take over Danu's power. Morrigan managed to escape his trap and bring the news to us. We've got to move quickly. There's no telling how much time we've got to act, if any."

"Mathgen," Nuada spat out bitterly. "We've grown so full of complacency we've even trusted him. And he's betrayed us. We have to warn Danu!"

"That's not enough," said Dagda. "We'll have to make her listen to us, and believe. Then we'll have to get her to act somehow to stop him, if there's anything she can do. That will take time. We've got to be certain she's protected first. We'll need every fighting man."

"The village is nearly deserted," said Nuada. "They've all gone to the ceremony. It's at noon today."

"Get everyone you can find," the big champion told him. "Everyone left who's still able to fight. Morrigan and Angus can help you."

"Me?" Nuada said. "Why not you?"

"Someone's got to get Lir and Diancecht out," Dagda replied. "But we can't spare any more men than we have to. I've the best chance of rescuing them alone. Nuada, it's up to you."

"I . . . can't," he said in anguish. "To risk people's lives again . . ."

"You'd rather see everyone enslaved?" Dagda argued. "You'd stand by and watch them die without a fight? Who knows what Mathgen might do if he gains power?" He put a big hand on Nuada's shoulder. "My old friend, there's no man who can deal with this better than you. You have to take the lead."

Nuada met the big man's fierce gaze a moment. Then a light of renewed determination entered his own eyes.

"All right," he said. "Go swiftly. Bring them back. We'll meet you at the temple of the sphere."

Dagda grinned. *"There's* the man I fought beside." He gave Nuada a hearty slap on the shoulder, nearly staggering him, then wheeled and charged out of the house. Nuada looked to the others.

"Angus, Morrigan, go house-to-house," he ordered briskly. "Find every loyal warrior, man or woman. Get all of the First Ones you can find."

He stepped to a sheathed sword hanging on a peg. He drew the weapon out, seeing the red-brown streaks of long disuse along the once-bright blade.

"Find Goibniu and get his best swords and spears and shields," he added, slamming the blade back.

"What about me?" said Cian, stepping forward. "I want to join you."

Nuada looked him over doubtfully. "You're very young."

"Not too young, sir," he said stoutly. "I can fight."

"He's a good warrior already," Angus endorsed. "One of the best."

"All ready for a hero's death," Nuada said grimly. "Then get your weapons, lad."

The storm thrashed angrily about the metal ship. Its waves thrust up in high cliffs to roll thundering down. But all its power and savagery was futile against the craft.

Mathgen stood at the rail of the bridge, holding up his magic rod. It blazed with intensity now, projecting a silver ray of light far ahead of the bow. The ray acted like a sword thrust into softest gauze, slicing a way through the tempest. Before the ship an avenue of smooth sea opened up. Storm clouds and waves piled up on either side as if striking a glass wall.

"Are you certain you can keep this up?" the captain in the wheelhouse asked Mathgen, shouting to be heard over the shrieking gale winds.

"I won't have to for much longer," Mathgen shouted back. "Be ready." And to Cuthach beside him he said: "Keep a watch out for first sight of land. This will be the tricky bit."

Both men watched keenly as the ship slid ahead. Soon, down the opened corridor through the storm, a stretch of rock-strewn coastline became visible.

"There!" proclaimed Mathgen. "There it is! All right, Captain," he shouted back into the wheelhouse. "Slow your ship now. Slow it!"

Tarbh-chu fiddled with his knobs, levers, and instruments. The vessel's forward motion decreased.

"There's a good spot to starboard," Cuthach said, pointing out a narrow section of the shore off the right bow. "No big rocks, clear beach. We can run in there."

"A bit right, Captain," Mathgen ordered. "Now a bit more. Slower yet. Slower. Good. Good. Now straight in."

Barely more than drifting now, the ship crept toward the spot Cuthach had indicated. They approached the shore. There came a faint scraping of the bottom against the keel.

"Stop!" cried Mathgen.

Tarbh-chu yanked a lever. The vibration of the ship's powering mechanisms ceased. The craft glided lightly in, softly scraping to a stop in the shallows, neatly beached.

The storm, seeming to recognize that it had been defeated by their successful landing, began to fade at once. In moments the winds were no more than a stiff breeze, the white-capped waves reduced to gentle swells.

"Now, get your men off, Captain," Mathgen said.

At Tarbh-chu's command, nets were cast over the bulwarks to hang at the ship's sides. The soldiers swarmed down and waded in the last stretch to the shore. They lined up there, waiting at attention as the captain, Mathgen, and Cuthach waded in.

"We're here, then," the captain said, gazing around. "Now what?"

"Aye, Cap'n," Cuthach said to Mathgen somewhat apprehensively as he looked along the desolate beach. "Where're the little men?"

"Have a bit of patience," Mathgen coolly replied. "I have full confidence."

"Captain, look up there!" said one of the tower soldiers, pointing.

They looked up to the top of the high cliff behind the beach. A small human figure was visible peering down. It was Onairaich.

Mathgen waved. The Pooka waved in answer and vanished from sight. In moments the first of the winged steeds came into view, lifting from the clifftop and soaring down toward them. It was swiftly followed by a flock of others.

The tower men stared in openmouthed amazement.

"By the burning eye of Balor!" Tarbh-chu exclaimed. "What manner of creatures are those?"

"No manner at all, Captain," Mathgen said lightly. "They are men, but ones with a special skill. And they will use it to transport ourselves to the magic island."

"What? We're to ride on them?" the captain said with some obvious dismay.

"Can you be afraid of heights, Captain?" Mathgen teased, "after living in your high glass tower?"

"I'm afraid of nothing," he replied indignantly, drawing himself up. "Neither are my men."

The flying horses settled onto the shore. There were over three score of them. One, a white stallion with golden wings, quickly metamorphosized back into the chief Pooka's human form.

"We are here as agreed, Mathgen," he announced. "Nearly my whole clan. And this is your army?"

"These are our *friends,* our *allies,*" Mathgen emphasized for the captain's benefit. "They will share equally in the results of our joint enterprise."

"Share?" said Onairaich, sounding confused. "But you said we . . ."

"It will be handled most fairly," Mathgen said quickly, stepping forward to put an assuring hand on the little man's shoulder. "When it is through, they will receive all that they deserve." Out of sight of the captain he added a broad, meaningful wink.

"Oh," said Onairaich, nodding in understanding. "Well, I've no argument about that." And he winked in return.

"Well, *I've* an argument," came another, new voice, "about being allies with the likes of these!"

They turned to see that another of the winged steeds had transformed back to a man. He was small, wizened, and completely bald, his pointed chin fringed with grizzled beard. He stepped forward, his manner belligerent and bold.

"You told us that it would be an outside host that would help us gain freedom," he gruffly barked at his chieftain. "You didn't say it would be them. It was they who persecuted us in the old life, before we came to the isle. They're a worse lot than Danu's folk by far!"

"You only think you remember that, Blonag," Onairaich replied. "You're old now. That was many centuries ago. Anyway, it doesn't matter what might have happened then. The important thing is what's happening now! These men will help liberate us. We will have beauty and power. For that I don't care who they are."

"Well, I do," Blonag said. "I hate our treatment by Danu's people too, but not as much as I hate these evil ones. I will not help them." He looked to the other Pookas. "And any of you who do are desecrating the memories of our ancestors who suffered at their hands!"

Several of the Pookas exchanged looks at this. Even as horses, their looks of uncertainty were clear.

"This is not good," Mathgen murmured to their chief. "He's swaying them. Stop him."

Onairaich nodded and stalked up before the rebellious one. "No one challenges me in this," he said threateningly. "I am your leader. I have given our word."

"We also gave word to the queen never to threaten the safety of the isle," Blonag pointed out. "Your father, my dear old friend, gave you the name of 'Honor.' Where is your honor now?"

"I am doing what is best for all of us," the chieftain argued. "I am gaining us a new life."

"At what price?" The old Pooka shook his head. "I can't let you do it. I have to tell Danu."

The glowing aura began instantly to rise about him as he began a transformation.

Onairaich, enraged, acted swiftly and desperately. He grabbed up a fist-sized stone from the rough beach. He cocked back his arm and hurled the jagged missile at the head of Blonag, now only a vague shadow fully encased in its shimmering cocoon.

The stone shot through the case of light, striking the head. The effect was startling. There was a sharp cry from within the glow, and the form began to convulse wildly. It stretched, wriggled, portions jerked violently this way and that.

"What's happening?" asked Mathgen, aghast.

"Interfering with the shifting process is most dangerous," Onairaich answered tersely.

Within the pod of light the form's spasms were ending. Like something gone liquid it sank down upon the ground. The aura faded. The watchers looked upon a grotesque shape.

Caught in mid-metamorphosis, the dead Blonag was now a bizarre conglomerate. Part—head and torso—was still identifiable as the man, and part—feathers, claws, and beak—the unknown bird into which he'd begun to change. Both were mingled in a convoluted mass as if they had been two wax beings melted together in a flame.

Mathgen and the tower men stared in revulsion. The Pookas reacted with shock. Onairaich acted quickly.

"He would have betrayed us," he said forcefully. "He would have ruined it all. Is there one among you who doesn't want what we've been promised?"

There was no reply.

"Is there anyone else who would challenge me?"

Again, no response. All remained as flying horses.

"Well done," Mathgen congratulated, patting the man's shoulder. "But I suggest we act quickly to fly out of here before any more of them have a chance to change their minds—or anything else."

Onairaich agreed. He took command, briskly ordering his people to line up and take the tower men upon their backs. Captain Tarbh-chu directed his troops to respective steeds and commanded the men—some of whom were a bit reluctant—to mount. With some of the Pookas carrying double, there were easily enough for the whole force.

Last of all, Onairaich changed back to the white stallion's form to carry Cuthach and Mathgen.

With everyone prepared, the Pooka leader gave the word to depart. The flying horses and their riders lifted up from the shore and winged away across the sea.

They left behind the one tiny figure crumpled on the stony beach, alone.

Chapter 26

Rescue

Queen Danu, in her feathered, emerald-hued robes of state, marched solemnly, slowly, grandly through the respectfully silent and attentive throng to the outer ring of monoliths.

The many thousands of her own people and of the outsiders filled the area about the circular temple that housed the great sphere. Bobd Derg, resplendent in fine robes of checked green and white, awaited her at the main opening through the ring in the company of the queen's white-feathered druids.

She stopped just before this group, raising a bejeweled, silver scepter of state to point out the young man.

"Do you come willingly to Us to pledge your full allegiance to Our rule?" she asked him.

Bobd Derg gave a little bow of acknowledgment. "I do, my Queen."

She turned, sweeping her scepter around to take in the crowd of outsiders. "And are you all prepared to freely accept the name of Tuatha de Dannan—Children of Queen Danu?"

As from a single voice the reply thundered back: "We are."

"Then We will pass into the inner sanctuary now," she

proclaimed. "To solemnize your choice by ceremony. And when We return to you, you will be thereafter full, equal citizens of Our realm."

She turned back toward the temple. The group of druids parted, opening a way to the entrance between the copper-clad stones. She started forward, but stopped as a commotion arose suddenly in one section of the crowd.

All looked about to see something surging upward through the densely packed people. As the disturbance neared the temple, its source could be identified. A group of people riding on carts, wagons, chariots, and individual horses was forcing a passageway.

The group burst out of the throng into the cleared space before the temple's entrance. In a chariot at its head rode Nuada, Morrigan at his side. In vehicles behind them could be seen Luchtine, Goibniu, Angus, Cian, and some two score of others, all armed with spears, swords, and shields.

"What are you doing?" Danu demanded angrily. "How dare you bring weapons into the sacred precincts?"

"Is this some desperate ploy to stop the ceremony by force?" asked the chief druid Urias in alarm. "Nuada, we thought much better of you."

"These weapons aren't to threaten the queen, but to protect her," said Nuada, leaping down from his chariot. "She's in great danger. We all are." He approached Danu, making appeal urgently to her. "Queen, you must call upon your powers. Call up a defense of some kind for the isle."

"A defense?" she said in bewilderment. "Great danger? Why?"

"We are to be invaded," he said quickly. "It may already have happened."

"Nonsense," said chief druid Arias.

"Mathgen is doing it," said Morrigan, joining Nuada. "I've seen the proof. I know he has the power."

"No one but a druid of the highest order could have such power as that," said chief druid Senias. "How could he get the secret skills?"

"By stealing them from you," Nuada said with growing exasperation. "Please, just believe us. You must act quickly."

Now Bobd Derg spoke up. "This is all a fantasy, my

Queen," he said with force. "Don't you see? It's some kind of plot to make you think our people have wicked designs on you. They mean to make you withdraw your favor from us. Don't listen to them."

"You keep out of this," said Angus Og, leaping from a cart and advancing on his brother. "Your foolishness could bring disaster on us all."

"Where is Lir?" the queen asked, clearly most befuddled by these cross-arguments. "Perhaps he could make this clear to Us."

"Lir is trapped, Queen," said Nuada, "along with Diancecht. Mathgen did that too."

"More likely you've done something to him yourselves, because he wouldn't go along with your scheme," Bobd Derg accused.

Enraged, Angus stepped closer, bringing up his spear threateningly. The crowd gasped in horror at the violent display.

"Is it come to this, brother?" Bobd challenged. "Will you strike me down now?"

Angus caught himself, lowered his weapon, and stepped back.

"You want Our help, and yet you show such savagery?" Danu said in shock.

"There's no time for arguing," Nuada said. "A force of people is coming from the glass tower."

"The tower?" This evoked a new, greater look of consternation from the queen.

"Yes. Mathgen has a scheme to bring them here somehow. Queen Danu, you have to do something!"

"Perhaps We *could* consult the sphere about this," she said, struggling in the face of things to keep a certain decorum. She looked around to her chief druids. "Arias, Urias, Fin . . ."

"Look there!" someone cried, pointing upward.

They looked up. Winged horses, each carrying one or two riders, were sweeping down upon them from all sides. The riders all wore grey uniforms and brandished long rods with glowing tips.

Nuada recognized the weapons at once.

"Too late!" he said. "Come on!" he shouted to his friends. "Get the queen inside!"

Some of the flying horses were already settling to the ground. Their riders swept the rods out at the crowd around them as they did. The tips drew crackling curves of light that caught some of those in the crowd, sending offshoots of the energy flickering over their bodies. There were screams of pain. People began crumpling to the ground. The others in the crowd panicked.

"By Danu," cried Bobd Derg in disbelief, "they're killing our people!"

As the terrified throng surged back, Nuada's companions pushed forward to join him. The warriors moved in around the stunned queen and most unceremoniously began to hustle her and her flock of terrified druids toward the temple.

Still overhead, Mathgen aboard Onairaich saw the group surround Danu. He saw the glint of their weapons and he recognized Morrigan and Nuada.

"Curse it!" he cried angrily. "How did they know?"

He waved to the men on the winged steeds in the air about him, pointing out Danu and shouting: "Look there! The queen! Stop her! Don't let her get inside!"

Several of the Pookas obeyed, diving at the warriors. Their riders held the power rods out like lances, the jewel-like points thrust forward past the horses' heads.

Below, Angus, Morrigan, and some others had held back to cover the retreat. Bobd Derg had also stayed, frozen by the sight of the savage, unprovoked attack. He stood stiffly upright, defenseless, and a perfect target for the first of the steeds that swept in at him.

Angus saw his brother was in jeopardy. He leaped before Bobd Derg, drew back his spear, and launched it with all his power.

It struck square on the flying horse's broad chest. The spearpoint—one of Goibniu's new, most lethal ones—shot through the steed's body, bursting out its spine. The stricken Pooka lost control, sailing past with the soldier on its back to slam head-on into one of the monoliths.

The power rod's point was smashed against the copper-sheathed stone. There was an instant, brilliant blooming of released energy, consuming man and winged horse at once and totally.

As the flare of destroying light faded, the rest of the diving Pookas banked sharply away and up, breaking off the attack and rising to escape the other threatening spear points.

"No, no!" Mathgen screamed at them. "Cowards. Cowards! Attack!"

"We didn't agree to this," Onairaich told him. Then the Pooka chieftain called to his clansmen: "Land everyone. Set them all down. Set them down at a safe distance!"

Leading the way, he settled down in the yard well away from the temple. The other flying horses still aloft swiftly followed him in.

Meantime, Nuada and his comrades had managed to herd Danu and her druids through the temple's first ring and were moving toward the second. When those holding the rear saw this, they began to back away after them, weapons still ready. Angus drew his sword and started backing too, but stopped when he saw Bobd Derg still just standing there, stunned to complete helplessness by the events. He sighed and simply scooped his brother up, carrying him along.

With the Pookas down, all the soldiers dismounted, forming up quickly to surround the temple with a ring of power rods. They looked to their captain.

Their captain looked to Mathgen.

"What now?" Tarbh-chu demanded. "They've moved a fair-sized force inside."

"We could have stopped them," Mathgen said, looking accusingly to Onairaich, "if your people hadn't pulled away."

"Why should they risk themselves?" the Pooka chief countered. "You said it would be easy. You said it would be safe."

"Somehow they got warning," Mathgen said angrily.

"And now Danu will use the power against us," the Pooka said in despair.

Mathgen looked at the temple, then around at the many hundreds of the crowd still scrambling to get away. His lips curled in a cunning smile.

"No," he said. "She won't."

Inside the temple, Nuada's group had reached the central domed ring housing the sphere.

"Cover the openings," Nuada ordered his people.

Several moved to block each of the narrow spaces beneath the dozen high, thin monoliths. Angus dumped his brother on the floor and joined them. Nuada faced Danu.

"Now, Queen, you must listen to me," he told her. "We may be able to keep them out of here, but only for a while. You must call up the magic of that sphere, and quickly. You must get help."

"I . . . I'm not sure," she said, still badly shaken. "You mean, do something to harm them?"

"If you don't, they'll certainly harm you," he said uncompromisingly.

She looked to her druids. "Is he right? Should we do something? *Is* there something we can do?"

"Danu!" came a shout from outside. "Don't use that sphere!"

"It's Mathgen," said Morrigan, turning toward the shout. "What does he mean?"

"Better look here," said Angus, pointing out between the stones.

Nuada joined him and peered out. Through the openings he could see into the yard. Not far from the outer ring several scores of helpless and frightened people—both Danu's and his own—stood surrounded by tower men. And Mathgen stood before them.

"Do you see these hostages?" Mathgen called to those inside. "If I even suspect that you're trying to use the sphere's magic power against us, they are all going to die."

The giant rodent snuffled around the floor of the tunnel, seeking some scent of food. It had gone unfed for days now and it was hungry.

It nosed at the scattered bones, now reduced to well-cleaned fragments. It peered curiously at the blank wall of stone that had not long before been the opening into Mathgen's tower. No longer any possibilities there.

A sound got its attention. It sat up, whiskers vibrating

with anticipation, tiny red eyes staring up the tunnel toward the outer end. Something was definitely moving there, and coming closer. It was the sound of footsteps.

The rodent bared its pointed teeth, slavering in anticipation. A chance for food!

It waited, tensed to strike. The footsteps grew nearer, louder. They were very determined footsteps, and very heavy ones. The beast saw a figure come into view out of the gloom. It was tall, massive, and gripped a thick, long something in its hands. The end of the something glinted with many points of light.

The rodent was still puzzling over this when the figure charged forward suddenly, giving forth a great bellowing sound. This descending juggernaut was too much for the beast. It fled in terror, scampering away to safety up its side tunnel as the shouting figure thundered past.

Inside the sealed-up tower Lir and Diancecht were dozing from boredom when the rising sound aroused them. They sat up and stared toward where the shout was coming from—beyond the wall where the tunnel's mouth had been.

"It sounds like a wounded elk," said Lir.

"No. Better," said the healer. "That's Dagda's battle cry!"

A long object of glinting end slammed through the wall, cracking the thick stone. It was followed almost instantly by a much larger form that crashed into the wall, pulverizing the cracked stone, punching out a much larger hole as it drove through in an explosion of flying debris.

Having made his dramatic and successful entrance, Dagda staggered forward a few steps into the room, stumbled, and toppled to the floor.

The two men ran to him.

"Dagda!" said the healer, kneeling by the champion. "Are you all right?"

"Of course I am," he said indignantly, sitting up. "And why wouldn't I be?" He clambered to his feet, brushing the dust from his clothes.

"How did you get through the wall?" asked Lir, examining the hole.

"With this." Dagda picked the long object up from the debris. It was a bundle of some fifty spears strapped tightly together with leather thongs, the fifty spear tips forming a single bristling head.

"Goibniu made them," he told them. "He said one of them could cut through the strongest shield. I thought: If one could do that . . . then many . . ."

"A most clever idea," said the healer. "And most effective."

"What's been happening out there?" asked Lir. "I assume Morrigan got word to you. Any sign of Mathgen?"

"Yes, Morrigan told us what you'd found," said Dagda. "There was no sign of Mathgen. But I really don't know what's happened since I left this morning. Nuada was going to gather all the help he could and go to Danu. She and almost everyone were preparing for the noon ceremony at the temple. Likely it's started by now."

"We have to hurry," said Lir. "Mathgen might well have been intending the ceremony as his time to strike. Dagda, is my chariot still outside the tunnel?"

"Close by it, the horses nibbling grass. That's how I found the opening."

"Good. We'll all take it. At the team's full speed it'll carry us back like lightning. Come on! Our friends could already need our help."

They started at a run for the open tunnel. As they entered it, Lir added: "Oh, you didn't happen to bring some food along, did you? Anything at all. Except for rat."

"This tactic of yours isn't getting us anywhere," said Captain Tarbh-chu impatiently.

"It's keeping us from being swallowed by the earth, or devoured by monsters, or something more unpleasant," Mathgen shot back.

"We don't know if she can do any of that," said the tower man, "or if she would, given the chance."

"He has a good point there," said Onairaich. "She hates violence of any kind, even in self-defense. They all do. You might simply walk in there and take the sphere."

"But we can't be certain she won't act from desperation or panic if we go rushing in there," said Mathgen. "Can we take that risk? Besides, there are Nuada and his lot to deal with."

"That rabble, armed with only swords and spears?" Tarbh-chu gave a dismissing wave. "A swift foray by my trained fighting men and they'll be wiped out."

"It wouldn't be so easy as you think," Mathgen replied. "I've seen them fight before. Nuada and that raven-woman alone could cause considerable damage to your men. Do you want that?"

"All right," the captain barked, "then just what other course would you suggest? We can't sit here forever."

"Look, why don't I go in?" Mathgen suggested. "I might reason with the queen. Perhaps I could convince her that it's better to surrender, that she can save everyone that way."

"You might find that difficult," Tarbh-chu said. "But why not? It could work." He gave a little smile. "And if you don't come back, we still have our own methods to try."

"I'll come back," Mathgen promised. "You just keep a good watch on those hostages."

He started toward the temple. Cuthach immediately fell in beside him.

"I'm going with you, Cap'n," he said firmly.

"That's not really necessary, my friend."

"Oh, yes it is," the old man replied. "I don't know what kinds of schemes are going through your cunning mind, but I'm not letting you out of my sight!"

Mathgen grinned. "Cuthach, you are much more clever than I ever guessed."

The two men approached the outer ring. Mathgen called to those inside.

"Hello, in there. Take no alarm. Do nothing rash. I only wish to talk."

"Why should we talk to you?" Nuada's voice came back from inside.

"Because there's really no other choice if you wish to keep everyone quite safe."

There was a moment of silence within. Then Nuada's voice came again. "Pass inside. But bring no weapons and make no unusual moves."

The two passed through the outer rings, entering the

central enclosure. A dozen spears were lifted, ready to strike at each of them.

"What do you want?" Nuada demanded.

"I wish to make a very simple deal," said Mathgen. He looked to the queen. "Surrender to us, Danu, come out of here, and none of your people will be harmed. We'll all talk as friends."

Queen Danu had recovered much of her control by this time. She drew herself up and addressed him sternly: "Friends? How can you say that when our oldest enemies threaten our people?"

"They wish to do no harm," Mathgen reasoned smoothly. "They only took your people hostage to protect themselves. They come to be friends with you, to gain the help your magic could give them—the help they say you denied them by running away."

"Running away?" Danu said indignantly. "We were *forced* away. Forced by their cruelty. Their great wonders of machinery and science had turned the world out there to a ravaged place. Their greed and stupidity were destroying everything. You saw the illusion We created for you on the giants' isle. Its awful details were nothing We invented. It was a model of the way things had become outside—dying trees, burning rains, rivers filled with poisonous muck, skies blackened by choking fog. And when the creators of those wastelands discovered that the earth powers we had developed might mend things for them, they tried to enslave us, force us into giving them the secrets. But we escaped. We left their world and came to this spot, hidden and protected from them and their contamination."

"It wasn't these people," Mathgen assured her. "It was their ancestors, centuries ago. They've changed. They are most contrite now. They only wish to survive, like you. Please, come talk to them. Make peace."

"Is that truly possible?" said Danu, consideringly now. "Should We deal with them?"

"No, my Queen," a voice spoke up stridently. "You can't surrender to the likes of them."

This came, most unexpectedly, from Bobd Derg, who had listened silently, gravely to all this.

"Brother!" said a surprised Angus Og. "That's the first sensible thing you've ever said."

"These people haven't changed," the poet went on with force. "They aren't your friends. Haven't I just watched them attack and harm your people and my own? Defenseless people who wish only peace? One nearly killed me! Queen Danu, these are evil men. You must act against them."

"You speak so harshly," she said with surprise. "Are you asking for revenge?"

"I'm asking you to stop them from taking control. Such men want no fair deals. If you give them anything, you'll have to give it all. You have to fight."

"How can We do that?" she said. "It would only cause more people to be harmed."

"There must be something you could do," he insisted.

"You wish Us to risk Our people's lives?" she said, sounding most astounded now.

"Is it worth risking a few lives to stop something so monstrous?" he asked her.

"That is a most savage, most ruthless thing to say," she told him scoldingly. "Now you sound like your father."

"Perhaps I am more of my father's blood than I believed," he boldly returned. "Witnessing the brutality of those men caused a change in me. I feel as if I've been wakened from a dream by a hard slap. I see reality now. I see that it can't be ignored."

"You really don't understand us, do you?" she said in disappointment, shaking her head. "You claimed to be like us, but in your heart you aren't. The will to do harm doesn't exist in us. It never has. It's why we left the outside instead of fighting back, why we came to found Tir-na-nog and gave up the old life."

"Then perhaps you gave up too much, Danu," Bobd told her.

"Are you so certain they're really still evil?" she said in anguish. "Is there still a need to fear?" Distraught, she looked around her desperately. "Lir! He could tell Us. He would know the truth. Our Lir. Where is he now?"

Chapter 27

Decisions

Lir was at that moment just beyond the outer wall that encircled the temple and its surrounding yard.

He, Dagda, and Diancecht had arrived by means of the speeding chariot not long before. They had questioned some of the thousands huddled fearfully outside the wall about the situation. They had peered through the entrance into the temple grounds in time to see Mathgen going inside.

Now the three were speaking strongly, appealing to the bewildered people in a desperate attempt to bring them to act.

"The ones inside the temple cannot hold out against those men," Lir said. "They must have help."

"There are only a hundred of the enemy," Dagda added. "We are thousands. They can be overwhelmed."

"At what loss?" said one trembling man. "I saw what one of those glowing sticks did to a friend. It fried him like an egg. Burned off his hair. Made his eyes . . ."

"That's enough," Lir quickly interrupted. "Look here, all of you, it's Queen Danu in there. It's the great sphere. Your friends are held hostage. Your island, your *lives* are in jeopardy!"

"It's no use, Lir," one of Danu's people told him. "There's no spirit for it in us."

"I hadn't realized how useless, how past all hope you'd become," he said bitterly. "I'm ashamed to be one of you. Our greatest enemies invade our home and threaten us, and still we can't fight them. Then we truly are beaten. And we deserve to be."

"You're too harsh," another one told him. "We are a people pledged to love and peace. Can you condemn us because we're willing to sacrifice ourselves for our belief?"

"Yes, if it means sacrificing the whole world as well," he fired back. "Don't you realize what will happen if they succeed? Uncountable people may well be destroyed, whole territories laid waste. The world was nearly free of their kind of insanity. You'll make it a slave again."

"We will not fight, Lir," another said, unmoved. "We are Danu's people. It is how Danu would wish it."

"I'll fight them," said one man. "I'm not one of Danu's people yet."

Dagda looked to him. "You're Tuirbe, aren't you? A son to Goibniu?"

"I am," he said. "I'll not pretend to you I don't have fear. But it's my own father in that place, and I won't turn away and let him die for my own cowardice."

"I'll join in too," said another man, and then others of Dagda's and Diancecht's people began to speak up as well.

"I say there aren't any children of the First Ones who can refuse to fight," someone else said. "For it's all our fathers and grandfathers and other kin who are there."

"It's the true heart of my people you're giving voice to now," said Dagda proudly, hearing the undertone of agreement that followed this.

And the undertone grew louder, rising to a rumble, to a roar as the word spread. Now, for all the superficial sameness in manner and dress to Danu's people, the difference in the outsiders could be seen. Their reawakened spirit for battle glowed in their faces as they came forward, separating from the folk of Danu with whom they had mingled, gathering around the three men. Soon they were a host of many hundreds.

"I applaud your courage," Lir said. "But understand: it won't be easy. You'll have to attack unarmed."

"Not completely," said Dagda.

Quickly he fetched the bundle of spears from Lir's chariot. He cut the thongs and passed out the fifty weapons.

"That will be some help," said Lir. "It will still be very dangerous. We have surprise on our side, and numbers as well. We can win. But there will likely be many hurt."

The son of Goibniu looked around him at the others. There were nods and voices of assent from everyone.

"We understand," he said. "We're ready to fight."

Dagda drew his sword and grinned.

"I never thought to hear those words again," he said. "Follow me!"

Inside the temple of the sphere, meantime, the arguments had continued between Danu's people and Nuada's about what should be done.

Mathgen, still under guard, had stood by listening through this, and the light of a new scheme had begun to glow in his cunning eyes.

"Look here," he put in, "I can understand your quandary. It's possible you are quite right about these people of the glass tower. I've had some doubts about them myself. They are dangerous men."

"What are you meaning?" Nuada asked suspiciously.

"Only that perhaps I can resolve the problem in a way agreeable to everyone. Everyone *here,* that is."

"Don't listen to him, Queen," Morrigan advised. "Don't trust in anything he says."

"No, let him speak," she said. "I must consider everything."

"It's quite simple," he told her. "If it's these tower men you fear, I can deal with them for you. I've certainly no love for them. Turn the power of the sphere over to me. I'll see the hostages released. And then I'll use the power to rid us all of these enemies. You, good Queen, need not compromise your own strong principles."

"You've betrayed us," said Nuada. "Now you're ready to betray your own allies. And we should trust you?"

"Why not? I've no wish to share any power with them. Listen, Nuada, my success here can even work for you. You wish your people to go back to your Blessed Land? I couldn't agree more. So I'll deny them citizenship. I'll force them to leave with you."

"Just go off and leave Tir-na-nog in your hands," said Nuada. "And once you've mastered the power, it'll be you seeking to control the outside world, not those tower men."

"You malign me," said Mathgen, sounding greatly hurt. "I wouldn't think of interfering with you. Look here, you know me. You know I don't mean harm. I never have. I only want to restore the wealth and authority my family once had, and perhaps punish those who so cruelly stripped them from us. You can have your Blessed Land. That's your own dream. And Danu and her people can live on just as they are now, in their benign, blissful state. Only with myself as ruler here."

"It seems a reasonable enough thing," Danu said. "The only sacrifice is mine. A small thing to save my people."

"If he is so sincere in this," challenged Morrigan, "let him have the hostages released first. Then surrender power to him."

"Now, that would be foolish," Mathgen said. "I've no more trust in you than you've in me. Besides, our friends out there quite likely won't agree without Danu surrendering first. They're not total fools."

"There seems no other course to insure no harm being done," Danu said with finality. She looked to her chief druids. "What do you say, Our friends?"

The four men exchanged a look, then nodded agreement.

"Very well," she said to Mathgen, "We agree to your terms."

"You can't!" protested Nuada. "We can't let you."

"You have no choice," she told him. "It is still Our realm and Our power. If you interfere, you will only be causing innocent people to die. You don't want that."

"No," he said despairingly. "If you refuse to use your magic, we're helpless."

"Put down the weapons then," Mathgen advised.

"There's still the matter of trust," Nuada told him. "I

think we'll keep them until we know you've kept your word."

He shrugged and smiled. "It's of no matter anyway."

"Come forward then," Danu told him. "My druids and I will activate the sphere. You will be attuned to its energy and know the secret to using its powers."

She and the four men formed a pentagram around the iridescent ball. They linked hands and raised them high. They bowed heads. In unison they uttered a softly muttered chant.

In response, the surface began to turn more brilliantly opalescent, flickering with the play of the varicolored streamers.

The five raised heads. Danu released the hand of Arias beside her, opening the ring.

"Step through," she invited. "Stand directly beneath the sphere. At Our command, its light will flood upon you and you will be bathed in its energy. The power of the sphere will enter you, enlightening your soul. In that moment you will be initiated into all its secrets."

As Nuada and his comrades stood watching in frustration, Mathgen hastened to obey, taking position beneath the sphere. He stood head back, the shifting lights shining on his face. He spread his arms, ready for the deluge. He grinned.

Danu reclosed the ring. She and the four druids bowed heads again.

The final chant began. The softly muttered words grew louder, sharper. The play of lights grew steadily more intense within the sphere. Its brightness began to focus at the base.

Mathgen stared upward into the light, almost trembling with anticipation.

"Now!" he murmured gloatingly. "Now it will all be mine!"

Loud shouts arose suddenly from outside. Then came crackling sounds and cries of pain.

Startled, the five dropped hands and turned to look, breaking their contact. Instantly the sphere's colors faded, the focus of light died.

"No!" the thwarted Mathgen cried.

"It's the people," Angus Og said, peering out. "Hundreds of them. They're attacking."

"Then let's help them!" said an elated Nuada, leading his comrades out in a rush.

Danu and her druids moved to the openings to look out after them. A wild melee was certainly under way outside.

"Come back," Mathgen implored, still underneath the sphere. "Finish the spell. Give me the power."

"It seems that wouldn't help save Our people anymore," Danu told him. "The choice has been taken from Our hands."

Reluctantly he moved up behind them and looked out. The soldiers of the tower were wielding their power rods with brutal efficiency, but the carnage they were inflicting was not daunting the attacking host. Roused to full battle fury now, the outsiders swarmed in, armed or not, overwhelming their foes.

The entrance of Nuada and his armed ones into the fray began tipping the balance even more rapidly. The powerful strokes of Angus and Dagda simply slashed through the enemy power rods, releasing the energy to sizzle across and electrocute their own users. Morrigan deftly sidestepped all assaults, striking in around the weapons to cut opponents down. Nuada finished one foe with a skillful parry and lunge, then found himself confronting the burly Captain Tarbh-chu.

In a first, furious interchange, Nuada managed to knock the power rod from the captain's grasp. The tower man drew his sword, and the two engaged again.

It was becoming swiftly clear that the battle would be decided in moments more. Mathgen saw a panicked Onairaich exorting his people to escape before it was too late. Some had already transformed back to flying horses and were lifting away. Here lay his only clear means of escape.

In the confusion, he crept from the temple, scooping up a power rod from a fallen tower man and running across to the Pooka chieftain. By now the little man was shape-shifting himself.

As Onairaich came out of the chrysalis of light once more a winged steed, Mathgen was upon him, leaping astride his back, bringing the rod's glowing jewel point up close to his startled eye.

"Take me out of here, and fast," Mathgen ordered. "Don't balk or I'll use this." He shook the rod. "I've nothing more to lose."

The Pooka nodded and began at once to flap his great wings, hooves lifting from the ground.

But Cuthach, having followed his erstwhile partner out, was not about to be left behind. He ran up as the horse began to lift, trying to climb aboard.

"Sorry. Only room for one this time," Mathgen said, lifting a foot and kicking the old man back.

Cuthach staggered away. But determinedly he ran in again, jumping up to grab Mathgen's leg just before it was lifted beyond reach.

He gripped Mathgen's knee, his sudden weight nearly jerking Mathgen from his seat. Forced to grasp the horse's flowing mane to keep from being pulled off, Mathgen brought the rod around with one hand and awkwardly slammed at Cuthach with its butt.

Battered about the head, the old man started slipping back. In moments he dangled by one hand, the age-weakened fingers slowly losing their grip as the winged steed lifted ever higher.

In despair and anger, he fumbled the hidden knife from his belt with his free hand.

"If I don't escape, then neither will you," he snarled through gritted teeth. And pooling his last strength, he swung his arm upward and plunged the blade into the horse's side.

Onairaich jerked from the pain. Cuthach was shaken loose and fell back to earth, plummeting a good distance to smash hard against the ground.

The broken old man looked up to the departing winged horse and its rider as the last sight faded from his eyes.

"I only . . . wanted . . . to be young," he rasped out with his final breath.

"Mathgen! He's getting away!" shouted Lir, pointing after the flying pair.

Hearing this, Nuada was distracted, glancing around.

The tower officer used the opening to thrust in, but another weapon parried the blade away.

The startled officer looked around to see Angus, Dagda, and Morrigan facing him. Beyond them the last of his own men was being driven to the ground.

"You're all that's left," Dagda told him.

"Then I surrender," he answered, throwing down his sword.

"No," said Morrigan. "You don't." And the vengeful raven-woman cold-bloodedly struck out, her blade's point driving right to the man's heart.

He toppled, dead before he struck the ground.

Across the yard, Lir was already running for the outer wall's gateway and his chariot parked outside.

"Lir's going after Mathgen," Nuada said, starting after him. "I'm going too."

"Not without me," Dagda said, following his friend. "Make certain they're all dead," he shouted back to the others.

"My pleasure," Morrigan said, dark eyes glinting. Lir was already in the chariot and shaking the reins when the two warriors leaped in behind him. They grabbed for handholds as the vehicle shot forward behind a team that went instantly to racing speed.

The flying horse and rider were in sight, heading toward the east.

"He must be making for the sea," said Lir. "I'm surprised that Pooka's not going any faster. We can keep up with them."

The Pooka's speed was being affected by the deep wound venting a pulsing stream of blood. The wings pumped with increasing effort but decreasing results, and the course of flight grew steadily more erratic.

"That stab hurt me more than I first thought," Onairaich told Mathgen. "I'm losing strength."

"Just keep going," Mathgen urged. "We've got to make the ship. I'll see to you there."

They reached the coast, sailing out over the water, the winged horse climbing with tremendous strain to clear the isle's invisible barrier. Much of its strength was drained away by that. It kept on, gliding more than flying now, covering distance but always slipping down closer to the sea.

Below and behind, the chariot had continued its pursuit, unslowed when it reached the shore, the team galloping out over waves, the car rolling behind.

Dagda looked down at water spraying up around the wheels somewhat apprehensively. "You're certain this is all right?"

"You've got other concerns," Lir said. "If Mathgen gets away, he could bring more of the tower men back here."

"Where's he heading?" Nuada asked.

"By the direction, I'd say for the giants' isle, if he makes it that far. What's wrong with that Pooka?"

The flying horse was nearly skimming the waves ahead. But the isle's coast was visible now, and the waiting ship.

As Onairaich approached the craft, a last effort brought flying steed and rider up just high enough to clear the side. Then the exhausted Pooka collapsed upon the deck, throwing Mathgen off.

"Help . . . me!" Onairaich weakly implored an unhurt Mathgen who got quickly to his feet.

"No time for that," said Mathgen callously, stepping around the winged horse's sprawled form.

The shimmering aura of transformation rose about the dying Pooka as Mathgen ran to the base of the ship's bridge. He shouted up to the lone seaman in the wheelhouse who was staring down in surprise: "Get us out of here! All the rest are dead. We're in danger. We've got to get away!"

The seaman didn't argue. He leaped to the banks of operating levers. A few moves started a deep rumbling within the ship as its propulsion system came to life. The seaman leaped to the wheel as the craft began to back out, steering it away from large rocks as it cleared the shore. Once into deep enough water, he spun the wheel. The craft began a turn.

Still some distance away, the three in the chariot watched the craft swinging around.

"If that thing gets up to its full speed, we might not catch it," Lir said. He snapped the reins. "Come on my lads. I need all you have now."

The animals' muscled bodies pumped yet harder, their

sleek necks stretched out farther as the loyal team put its utmost effort into the run. The metal ship had finished its turn and was just beginning to glide forward when the chariot pulled alongside.

Lir looked up at the sheer metal ship rising above them with intense dislike. "Why am I always having to get aboard these things?" he said. "And no ropes to climb this time."

He looked to the big warrior. "Dagda, are you strong enough to . . . well, *throw* me up there?"

Dagda gauged the distance with a practiced eye, flexed a bulging arm muscle, then nodded. "Of course I can."

"Not you," Nuada told Lir. "Mathgen's one of mine. I'll see to him."

Lir nodded and moved aside to let Nuada and Dagda prepare. He skillfully kept the horses and chariot steered in near to the side—no mean feat with the ship's wake trying to push them out. Slipping his shield off, Nuada climbed to Dagda's shoulders. He stood upright, stretching arms upward, bracing himself against the ship's hull. The deck rail was still out of reach by half his height.

"All right," he told his massive friend. "Give me a toss."

Dagda slipped his hands under Nuada's feet, tensed, and heaved upward.

It was almost too much. Nuada went completely over the rail headfirst, somersaulting onto the stern deck. But the agile man arose unhurt. He waved down to the others. Dagda tossed up his shield. He slipped it on, drew his sword, and crept forward, around the base of the superstructure.

The deck before him was empty, save for the sprawled figure of a little man. Nuada moved to him. It was Onairaich, his human form restored to him, lying in a vast, already coagulating pool of his own blood. Nuada knelt by him and checked the body. The Pooka was dead.

A faint noise from behind him brought the warrior up and around just as Mathgen charged in, thrusting out with the power rod.

Nuada sidestepped the rush, wheeling as Mathgen went past to slap the man hard across the back with his shield. Propelled by the blow, Mathgen stumbled on, slamming into the deck rail. He doubled forward over the waist-high rail, teetered there a moment, then began to slide forward, pulled by the weight of the power rod. He released the weapon, flailing out for a hold. Finding none, he slid on inexorably toward the sea.

A hand grabbed his cloak, hauling him in. He came back over the rail to safety, his feet thudding to the deck. He turned to face his savior—Nuada.

"You did the same for me once," Nuada reminded him.

"Nuada, Nuada," Mathgen said, shaking his head. "You just never have been quite ruthless enough."

He moved suddenly, his glass rod appearing in his hand. Light flared at its tip, and instantly Nuada's sword and shield burst into roaring flame.

The shocked warrior instinctively released them, stepping back from the blazing weapons as they clattered to the deck.

With a laugh of triumph, Mathgen stooped and grabbed up the flaming sword. Its fire died at once, as did that of the shield.

"You fool," he said to Nuada. "It was just illusion. No heat at all. I made your own mind betray you. Now, step to the rail." He made a sharp gesture with the sword.

"What are you going to do?" asked Nuada.

"First, it's your turn to go over the side. Knowing your friends, I'm certain they'll stop to pick you up, giving me the time to get away."

"And then?"

"Then I return to the glass tower. I'll fetch their whole force this time. You won't stop me again."

"You won't get back through the barriers," said Nuada.

Mathgen brandished the glass rod. "The power still in this will see I do. Now move!"

Nuada moved. He leaped straight at Mathgen, grabbing the glass rod.

Mathgen struck out with the sword, driving its point deep into Nuada's side. The warrior jerked back, pulling free of the blade, at the same time yanking the rod from Mathgen's hand.

"Curse you!" Mathgen snarled, lifting the sword to swing a savage cut at the wounded man.

Nuada rolled sideways over the rail, dropping into the sea.

"No!" Mathgen howled, looking over the side.

The ship was swiftly carrying him away from the splashing man and his precious rod. Lir and Dagda had seen Nuada and were already pulling up to get him, as Mathgen had supposed.

As Dagda reached out to grab Nuada, Lir looked after the ship gliding so speedily away, and at the man looking back to them, shaking fists and shouting curses in his rage.

"Mathgen's still alive?" Lir asked Nuada as Dagda drew him into the car.

"Yes, but without this," Nuada said, showing the rod. Then he grimaced in pain.

"He's badly hurt," Dagda told Lir as he examined the wound. "Not deadly, but we've got to get him back to Diancecht."

"We're not finished yet," said Lir. "Mathgen's still too dangerous."

He looked up to the sky, face tightening with concentration, voice coming slowly, clearly, urgently: "Danu, hear me now. You have to act."

He waited. Nothing happened.

"What are you trying to do?" asked Dagda.

Lir waved the man to silence and tried again. "Danu, you must hear me. I need your help. Don't fail me now."

A faint haze, like a wispy cloud, came into view above. It formed a vague but still recognizable image of Danu's face. Her voice came faintly. "I hear you, Lir. What is it?"

"You must use the sphere now. Raise up the storm barrier with a force like it has never had. Attack the metal ship with winds and seas so massive that it can't survive."

"Purposely destroy a ship?" she said.

"I know your feeling, but there is no other choice," he told her. "If you want to be certain Tir-na-nog stays safe, please, Danu, raise that storm!"

There was no reply. The face faded away. The ship continued to speed toward the horizon, shrinking rapidly away.

"Do you think it worked?" asked Nuada.

"Look there," said Lir, pointing.

As if rising from the sea, a black wall suddenly loomed

up before the ship. It swept in, assaulting the craft with towering waves, gale winds, lightning and torrents of rain. For brief moments the three men could see the ship being battered, twisted, smashed from side to side. Then the clouds and seas swallowed it completely.

"Now we can go home," Lir declared.

Epilogue

"And for your betrayal of Our trust, We will now mete out fit punishment to you," came the stern, ringing voice of Queen Danu.

The people of Tir-na-nog were once again gathered before the central temple. This time the queen's own people, clad in their bright hues, stood at one side. The people of Nuada, now all returned to wearing the plainer, more practical garb of their traditions, stood at the other. Between them, huddled in a forlorn group right before the queen and her druids, were those of the Pooka clan.

"You sought to become men like all others," she told the beings, "a thing even Our magic could never give to you. But for the promise of that reward, you betrayed Us. For this most terrible act, you will be banished forever from the enchanted isles. More, though you will be left your shape-shifting power, We have deemed it a most fitting punishment for your crime that you never be able to wear *any* human form again."

She waved her ceremonial scepter over the huddled group. Immediately the aura of shape-shifting light enveloped the whole clan. When it faded, a flock of white gulls rose up where the small people had been and winged slowly, sadly away into the eastern sky.

"They weren't evil people," Morrigan said, looking after them. "I pity them."

Diancecht, beside her, gave her a curious look at that.

"Now for you," said the queen, looking toward the massed outsiders. "We understand that you have chosen your destiny. You will be leaving Us after all."

"We have discovered that we truly do not belong here," Bobd Derg said, speaking for the rest. "It would be wrong for us and for you if we were to stay. I see that my father and the other First Ones are right. We must have our own place, fulfill our own dreams, create our own paradise."

Dagda grinned widely at that. He put an arm around Boand who stood beside him with the baby, giving her an affectionate hug. She smiled proudly in return.

"But we owe a great debt and feel a great affection for you and your people," Nuada put in. "Because of that, we have also chosen to carry a new name with us into the outer world. From this day we will proudly call ourselves Tuatha de Dannan—The Children of Danu."

"We are most gratified," she told him, allowing herself a small, regal smile. "We know now that you will do great things in your own mortal realm."

"And we'll be able to see that those tower men won't be bothering you or anyone again," Dagda added.

"The need for that cannot be denied," she admitted. "Though We still cannot condone the use of violence."

"You can keep to your belief," said Nuada, "so long as you stay safely here. But we did note a bit of contradiction in your actions, Queen. You would have let Mathgen do your violence for you."

"To protect our people, perhaps so," she admitted. "And that is why We are so much unsuited for the harsh world you will go to. We hope you will not face too great a hardship there."

"We don't intend to go until we've made some preparations," said Nuada.

"Yes, there're a few of us who'll need to learn some fighting skills first," said Angus, eying his brother.

"And how to do some good, hard, honest toil," put in Goibniu.

"I mean to go along and look after them for a time," said Lir, who stood with Nuada and his comrades. "That is, if it's all right with you."

"We give Our leave for you to go and stay with them as long as you wish," Danu told him. "We are sorry We ever doubted your great value to Us. And you know that such an admission is not easy for Us to make."

"I know," he said most seriously, giving a little bow. "Thank you, my Queen."

"Then We will make Our formal good-bye to you now," she said, lifting the scepter to wave over them. "Our blessing be upon you and our affection go with you. And, henceforth, may our realm be inviolate and most separate from your own."

Beyond the outer rim of the barrier fog, an armada of sleek metal ships prowled.

On the deck of the largest, in a vast metal chair, sat the black, armored giant called Balor. He and his fleet of ships, all crowded with men, had cruised there for days in anticipation of the barrier dropping, allowing them to invade the enchanted isles in force. But the coils of fog had remained unchangingly thick and forbidding.

Now a cry from the bow of one ship brought the vast metal head around.

"What is it?" clanged the voice.

"Something there, Commander," came the reply. "Just off the starboard bow. Drifting out of the fog."

The head moved again, bringing the visored front around toward the spot. A dim form was visible there within the grey, becoming clearer as it drifted forward.

Soon it was clearly visible: the battered hulk of a metal ship like theirs, superstructure smashed away, hull cracked and badly listing, deck nearly awash. And tangled in the twisted remains of railing at the base of the ruined bridge, a single human form.

Balor's ship ran alongside. Seamen leaped onto the wreck and moved to examine the figure.

"He's badly broken up, Commander," one man announced. "I can't tell if he's even still alive."

"Let's get him out of this," another man said.

Gently they untangled the bent metal from around the man's form, then lifted him up. As they did, he gave a groan of agony and his head slowly lifted.

Through the screen of dark hair matted across the battered face, the eyes of Mathgen could be seen.

They blazed brightly with the fire of hate.

AN247 -- 6/91